MURDER IN THE MEADOW

Rosemary Grey Cozy Mysteries, Book 1

TRACY DONLEY

Summer Prescott Books Publishing

**This book is a work of fiction. Any similarities to persons, living or dead, places of business, or situations past or present, is completely unintentional.

For my family.

I love you more than I can say.

I

"Hold on there a second, Dr. Grey. Are you saying there's really a Sleepy Hollow?"

Rosemary waited for the students' excited chatter to die down. These guest lectures at small colleges were her favorite—where she could actually look into the audience and see the sparks in the eyes of the undergraduates, could almost hear their chairs scraping the floor just a little bit as they sat up straighter upon realizing that this particular lecture would not be the dull, compulsory torture they'd expected.

"That's right—what's your name, please?"

"Roger," the young man called from the middle of the small auditorium.

"That's right, Roger. And this is one of those wonderful instances when history and literature collide. There really is a Sleepy Hollow, in upstate New York. But back in Washington Irving's time, remember, it was known by another name."

And here, Rosemary affected her soft, ever-so-slightly-spooky storytelling voice.

"Irving spoke of a little place, about three miles from Tarrytown, New York, 'in a little valley, or rather lap of land among high hills, which is one of the quietest places in the whole world.'" She almost whispered these last words.

The students were silent now—a miracle in Rosemary's estimation.

She clicked the small remote in her hand to display a photo of a beautiful, picture-postcard New England village on the screen behind her.

"Most likely, Irving spoke of the village of North Tarrytown," she said, gesturing toward the photo. "And named it Sleepy Hollow in his writing. And get this: It's only a few hours away from here. I encourage you to visit there sometime—but be sure to stay overnight, so you can look out for the horseman."

There was a mix of giggling and quiet conversation among the students.

"So today we've learned that studying literature from a historical perspective gives the great stories so much more depth and helps us to appreciate them in entirely new ways. We've learned that there really is a Sleepy Hollow. We've learned that there truly was an Ichabod Crane—but that it was another man entirely who *actually* inspired the lanky, awkward character we all know and love. And the headless horseman himself? We've uncovered his probable identity."

Rosemary clicked through more slides, ending with one of an old, covered bridge.

"Did a ghostly headless horseman really gallop up to this bridge and disappear in a 'flash of fire and brimstone'? Probably not. Probably the Dutch settlers in the area were just great storytellers. But as you leave here today and go out into the world, I would encourage you to remember that there is some bit of truth to be found in every legend."

There was an enthusiastic round of applause as Rosemary thanked the university for hosting her. Then she gathered her papers, shoved them into her worn leather messenger bag, shook a few hands, and was off.

Out in the parking lot, Rosemary encouraged her rickety convertible to start. It was a 1979 Volkswagen Beetle in the original Alpine White, and it refused to put up with nonsense of any kind, including inclement weather, obnoxious passengers, and low-quality engine oils. "Come on, baby. It's seventy-two degrees and the humidity's low. Your favorite weather conditions!" She cranked the key again and the engine finally thrummed to life. "Yes! I knew you could do it!"

She'd even been able to wrestle the top down—a complicated procedure in the case of this particular Bug, involving snaps, Velcro, folding, tucking, and a lot of elbow grease. Top-down meant messy hair, but it didn't matter. Not where Rosemary was headed. She hurriedly slipped a rubber band around her auburn curls to keep them out of her face and put the car in gear.

It was a glorious Connecticut afternoon, and as Rosemary ambled along winding roads past charming towns and villages, she smiled at the memory of buying the old convertible all those years ago. Sure, it was finicky, and only started with a bit of coaxing and the occasional threat, but on days like this, when the top came down, the car seemed like the highest luxury in the world. Was there anything better than a crisp fall day under a blue sky?

And best of all, Rosemary was on her way to visit her favorite person in the world: her best friend, Jack Stone. She and Jack had met in college and had instantly clicked. She'd been working on her undergrad in history; he, on his in literature. Their paths crossed as often as their various humanities intertwined at their university, and they had remained fast friends all the way through grad school and beyond.

Jack and his new husband Charlie had bought an old New England farmhouse, complete with a large pond, woods, an ancient, crumbling barn, and a small orchard. They'd wrapped up most of the renovations to the house about six months ago, but Rosemary had yet to see the place—or meet Charlie in person. However, since Jack's taste was impeccable, both in décor and in people, Rosemary had no doubt she'd love both the house and Charlie.

She'd been away lecturing in England when he and Jack had married, and even though she'd seen photos and visited with Charlie on the phone a few times, her European tour had kept her from meeting him face to face. She knew he was tall, dark, and handsome, and was a bestselling novelist and an excellent cook to boot. And if Jack loved him, then so would she.

Paperwick, the village where Jack and Charlie lived, was proving to be harder to find than Rosemary had anticipated. It wasn't on her area map—it was apparently too tiny to be taken seriously by most map makers—and so Jack had given her very precise instructions. Unfortunately, he had absolutely no innate sense of direction, which had gotten them both lost countless times before, so after an hour of driving in circles, trying to locate "a stream right next to a large maple tree with a cute little swing hanging from one branch," Rosemary was relieved to see a farm stand and picnic area beside the road just ahead.

She'd been seeing signs for miles: *Potter Farm 10 miles ahead!* A few miles later: *Apple Picking at Potter Farm!* A few miles after that: *Don't forget to stop in at Potter Farm today! We've got pie!!* The perfect place to pull over, stretch her legs, have a snack, and buy a small gift to take to the guys. Plus, she could try again to decipher Jack's directions and ask for help from the farm stand attendant.

She walked up to the little wooden structure and peeked around. It seemed to be empty—that is, there was no attendant on duty. But the shelves were packed with jams and jellies, pies, bags of cookies and maple sugar candy, and stacks and stacks of empty baskets, presumably for gathering apples. Just as Rosemary's stomach let out an audible growl, a round little lady came hurrying along a cobbled path that ran between the stand and a beautiful old red barn whose roof was topped with a weathervane in the shape of what looked like a large cheese. A generous, triangular wedge of Swiss, to be exact.

"Hello, hello, hello!" the woman sang when she spotted Rosemary. "Hope I didn't keep you waiting long. Busy day!"

Rosemary gave her a big smile but couldn't help letting her eyes wander over the peaceful quiet of the scene and wondering exactly what 'busy' meant to this woman.

"I am Mrs. Potter," she continued. "Welcome to Potter Farm, home of Potter's Perfect Pumpkin: village festival champs for nine years running."

“Wow,” said Rosemary. “Nine years running!” Village life—full of pumpkins and apples (and apparently, cheese), and devoid of stress and pollution and hurry. Rosemary felt her tensed shoulders relaxing at the very thought of it all.

“And we’re about to make it an even ten at this year’s festival,” Mrs. Potter continued. “But that’s neither here nor there. What can I get for you today? You look like you could use a freshly picked apple. Or how about a hot apple cider donut? I have a batch just about to come out—look! There’s my Abbey now with the basket.”

A teenaged girl walked up and set a steaming basket of donuts on the counter. She gave Rosemary a shy smile.

“Those smell amazing,” said Rosemary, her stomach growling again as if on cue.

Mrs. Potter immediately wrapped a warm donut in a napkin and handed it over.

“On the house,” she said gleefully, and waited expectantly for Rosemary to take a bite.

In fact, both Mrs. Potter and her daughter were watching in anticipation of Rosemary’s verdict, and Rosemary, who was more than happy to oblige them, blew on the donut to cool it, then took a big bite. She closed her eyes, blissfully tasting the warm sugary dough tinged with sweet apples and cinnamon.

"Is that nutmeg?" Rosemary asked. "This is honestly the best cider donut I've ever had!"

"Yes, that *is* nutmeg! The secret is that we press our own cider here at Potter Farm, from our own special apples which we grow specifically *for* our donuts. Can you believe it? Come on, I'll show you!" Mrs. Potter merrily trotted off with a quick glance back at her daughter. "Abbey, man the shop!"

Rosemary had to jog to keep up with Mrs. Potter. The woman couldn't have been five feet tall, but she was speedy.

A few short minutes later, Rosemary had to chuckle at her situation. She was standing in a corner of the Potters' apple orchard, holding a basket up over her head as Mrs. Potter—who, as it turned out, was more agile than one would think she'd be—balanced on a ramshackle ladder and expertly pulled down a dozen apples, which she then set gently into the basket that Rosemary held.

"So, what kind of apples are these, Mrs. Potter?" Rosemary asked, glad that Jack wasn't expecting her for another hour. She wished he was here right now. He would love this place—and besides, everything was more fun when Jack was around. When the two of them were together, they always ended up laughing. They'd laugh until they had tears running down their cheeks—about silly things, about nothing at all. *Everyone*, Rosemary thought, should have a friend like that. She only wished that she and Jack could spend more time together.

But, Rosemary, who had always dreamed of travelling the world, had her lecture circuit. And Jack, who had always craved the comforts of home, was married and settled. Rosemary had a condo in New York that she rarely saw. Jack had a husband. And a town he loved. And, according to his latest email, a flock of egg-laying chickens, several pygmy goats, and a couple of pigs.

For the next two weeks, Rosemary was determined to simply relax and enjoy her time with Jack and Charlie on their farm. She wouldn't think about work or the future, she wouldn't count a single calorie or worry about hitting a gym. She might just wear her most comfortable sweats the whole time. That is, if she could ever *find* Paperwick, which seemed to be lost somewhere in the state of Connecticut.

Jack, happily employed as an English Lit professor at the small university that lay in the heart of Paperwick, was also a history buff in his spare time. In fact, a borderline-nerdy love of history was one of the things he and Rosemary had bonded over early on in their friendship. So, he'd gladly taken on the role of President of the Paperwick Historical Society when it fell vacant. He had summoned Rosemary to help him with a very special project for the annual Paperwick Founders Day Festival—a project that called for a historian who specialized in 17th century American history. One who knew a lot about the New England witch trials that had happened in these parts—

lesser known than the Massachusetts trials, but significant, nonetheless.

This year at the festival, Jack had hatched a plan to help raise money and boost interest in local history: The society would host a tour of the historic cemetery and the adjoining meadow —also known as the Witch's Meadow.

Rosemary and Jack would team up to research and script the cemetery tour so that as people wandered through, they could meet the spirits of a few of those buried there and learn a little something about the history of the town along the way. The other members of the society had gladly volunteered to act as the "ghosts." The big finale would come as participants wandered into the Witch's Meadow, where Hortence Gallow —a woman who had been accused of witchcraft in 1668—was said to haunt the shadows to this day.

And it was Rosemary and Jack's job to bring the whole thing to life—Rosemary, with her knowledge of history and solid research, and Jack, with his creative spirit and style, along with their mutual glee over anything spooky.

Rosemary was lost in thought about the festival—wondering if it might possibly be the same one which featured Potter's Perfect Pumpkin—or if that was some other festival in some other village. After all, Rosemary had no idea where she was now. And the whole area was dotted with quaint villages and charming towns, most of which, Rosemary suspected, hosted autumn festivals in late October, when the tourists flooded New England to see the fall foliage. She'd been swept up in Mrs. Potter's enthusiasm over the apple crop and hadn't gotten around to asking for directions just yet.

Mrs. Potter nimbly descended the ladder, cheeks flushed and with a leafy twig sticking out of the bun she'd gathered on top of her head. Rosemary lowered the basket and peered inside at the nice pile of small, red-and-yellow-speckled apples.

"They smell good," she said, reaching into the basket and picking up an apple. "And they're so pretty."

"We cultivated this variety many years ago. We call it *Maggie's Pride*. We grafted and re-grafted until we arrived at the *perfect* cider apple. We mix these in with a couple of our other sweet apples and our Fall Pippin, which is a bit tart, to create the ideal balance. But Maggie's Pride is definitely in the forefront of the flavor. She's the star. Unfortunately, these hybrid trees are finicky. They require special attention, so they only grow in this small section of the orchard."

"Sounds like my car," mumbled Rosemary.

Mrs. Potter looked wistfully at the trees that surrounded them and sighed with a contented smile. "Generations of Potters have looked after these trees. Maggie's Pride is named for Mr. Potter's great-great-great—oh, I forget how many times great-grandmother. Her father came over from England to claim this very land—well, that, and the religious freedom that came with it. He was something of a horticulturalist, always trying new things. I can just imagine him out there in the fields, harvesting those first pumpkins, rye, squash, beans, and corn." She smiled proudly. "Anyway, we make a limited amount of our own special cider from our apples every fall—and of course, use it in the donuts. People rave about our apples all over these parts. And I'm very proud of every variety we grow. But we keep *this* little grove just for our own use."

"And what are all of these other trees?" Rosemary asked, motioning toward the rest of the orchard, which stretched far out and away from where they stood.

"Oh, you know. McIntosh. Courtland. We have a group of Chestnut Crabs over that way."

With each apple name, Mrs. Potter pointed toward clusters of trees, smiling over them as if they were her children. But if they were all her children, it was clear that she favored and spoiled Maggie's Pride.

"I'd love to take some apples to my friends' house. Of course, I know it probably can't be these. But maybe one of the other varieties? And some of the donuts, too," said Rosemary.

"Going to a friend's house, are you?" Mrs. Potter nodded, a hint of curiosity in her voice. "Well, I have a knack about knowing people, and I have a good feeling about you." She gave a little wink. "If you'll keep it between us, I'll let you take a few of Maggie's Pride."

"Really? Thank you!" said Rosemary. "Maybe you can help me figure out where I'm going. I'm a little lost."

"I don't really believe we ever get lost," said Mrs. Potter matter-of-factly. "You're where you're meant to be, my dear. But where is it you think you're going?"

"To a village called Paperwick. My friend Jack lives there."

Mrs. Potter smiled broadly. "Well, that's convenient."

"Really? Why?"

"Because you're here, my darling girl. This is the edge of the village. You must be Jack's friend Rosemary. In that case, I'm sending one of my caramel apple pies along with you, too. The boys love them."

"The boys? Jack and Charlie, you mean? So, you know them?"

"Everyone knows everybody in Paperwick. And we Potters have been here for so long, we know everybody *and* their uncle!"

Mrs. Potter laughed heartily as she hurried along the path back toward the little roadside market stand. Rosemary was surprised to find she was getting out of breath trying to keep up. As they moved through the trees, Mrs. Potter gathered apples, choosing different varieties and muttering to herself—or maybe she was talking to the trees, for that matter. She gingerly placed about a dozen apples into a cloth sack, then nested them into a cardboard box alongside a brown paper bag filled with warm donuts and a pie which she'd carefully chosen from one of the shelves.

When Rosemary tried to pay for everything, Mrs. Potter waved her away.

"Nope. I will not accept your money. Just come see us during your stay in Paperwick. And be sure to find us at the Founders Day Festival this weekend. We'll be the ones with the prizewinning pumpkin—that is, of course, if Mayor Wright decides we have another winner. Oh! And come out to the farm, and bring the boys. We're doing our annual corn maze and there will be hayrides and marshmallow toasting all weekend."

"Wouldn't miss it. And how handy, that the town's mayor is also a good judge of pumpkins."

Mrs. Potter laughed. "Samuel Wright is a good judge of just about everything. He's one of the reasons our town is so great. I'm sure you'll meet him."

"Really? I'll look forward to that."

"He's always out and about. A fine man. Active in every community organization and a member of almost every club. A friend to all," she sang cheerily. "His family's history goes back almost as far as ours. In fact, just between you and me

—" At this, Mrs. Potter glanced around as if she was about to divulge some great secret. "The Potters and the mayor's family haven't always gotten along as famously as we do nowadays. But that's all water under the bridge, of course."

"Really?" asked Rosemary, intrigued. "A family feud, was it?"

"Many generations ago," Mrs. Potter said, nodding.

"I'd love to hear more about it while I'm here. History is my bag," said Rosemary with a smile.

"Well, I should hope so," said Mrs. Potter. "You being a history professor and an author and all."

"Wow. Jack told you all that?"

"Yep. He's been bragging on you—and it's well he should be. Come back when you have time to chat. Our family has a long-standing tradition: We never throw anything away! I can show you old birth certificates, land deeds, photographs. You name it!"

"I would love that. I'll definitely be back."

Mrs. Potter proceeded to give Rosemary clear instructions on how to get into the village and find her way to the university. Just as she was hefting her box of goodies to take to her car, another car pulled up and a family got out, stretching their legs. Rosemary smiled as a man, a woman who was clearly expecting a baby, and a toddler came ambling in the direction of the stand—probably there to pick apples. Rosemary felt a familiar little pang, looking at the way the little boy was holding onto his mother's hand—a strange mix of happiness and hope that she'd been noticing she was experiencing more and more these days.

"I'd better be on my way," Rosemary said, and was surprised when Mrs. Potter gave her a quick hug.

"Give Jack and Charlie my best and don't be a stranger," she said, before cheerily turning and walking toward the family. "We'll see you and the boys at the festival!"

"Good luck with your pumpkin!" Rosemary called. Mrs. Potter smiled and held up crossed fingers, and Rosemary gave her an enthusiastic thumbs-up, then headed to her car, arms loaded with good food, enveloped in the smell of apples.

2

Rosemary bit into a second warm donut as she headed down the road, confident she'd find the university using Mrs. Potter's excellent instructions.

"Let's see . . ." she said, looking to the right of the road. "Yep. That's got to be Little Mill Creek. Hello again," she said, giving a nod to the babbling brook, which could be seen weaving through the thickening trees that grew along the roadside, glinting here and there in the sunlight. She'd been here several times already today.

Ahead, a three-pronged fork in the road led off in different directions. Rosemary's confusion on her other attempts to find the tiny village of Paperwick was rooted in Jack's directive to go to the right of a tree with "a large rock next to it that looks like a possum." There were lots of trees and plenty of rocks around, but the tree with the possum rock was definitely on the left side of the left-most fork prong . . . which meant that all three roads were technically to its right. Rosemary had assumed that Jack meant the road that ran closest to the possum.

But now, she took the gentle rightmost curve, which ambled along into the trees. The road took her to a covered bridge that crossed the creek—and sure enough, just before the bridge was the aforementioned huge maple tree with a swing hanging from one of its branches.

Rosemary felt as though she'd entered another world as she exited the bridge on the other side of the creek. Shaded lanes crisscrossed the road, and peering down them, she could see cozy New England cottages set in among the trees. Further along the main road, she came to the village green, which was shaped like an odd, slightly lopsided rectangle, around which shops and leaf-strewn brick sidewalks were neatly arranged. The green in the center looked like a park with a little pond, where a couple of mothers sat on a bench chatting and watching their children throwing bits of bread to the ducks. Rosemary peered at Mrs. Potter's hand-drawn map, took the first left next to the bandstand on the green, went down past a row of shops, turned right at the village market, and found herself entering the grounds of Paperwick University, which was, according to the sign, home of the oddest school mascot Rosemary had ever heard of, the Fighting Trout.

The grounds of the school were intimate and beautiful, generously sprinkled with trees in the height of their fall finery, old brick buildings, and black lampposts festooned with swags of orange, gold, and brown. Students hurried about, backpacks slung over shoulders, cell phones in hand, some of them proudly sporting t-shirts or sweatshirts that featured an angry-looking trout on the front.

Rosemary texted Jack, letting him know she was on campus, and then found her way to Langner Hall, where Jack's office was located. She pushed open a large wooden door that creaked on its hinges, stepped inside, and breathed in the smells of books, pencil shavings, and chalk dust, and let her gaze travel up the great, wide staircase to a balcony that overlooked the lower floor. She could already hear her best friend's voice. And there he was, just arriving at the top of the stairs, enthusiastically debating something with a very tall and handsome man who had to be his husband, Charlie.

The three of them had made plans to stroll around the campus a bit, and then have "linner"—which was Jack and Rosemary's silly word for late lunch/early dinner—together before going over to Jack and Charlie's farm.

As the old oak door groaned shut behind Rosemary, it creaked loudly again, and Jack glanced down and spied her.

"Well, would you look at what the cat dragged in!" he called with a big grin.

"Hey!" Rosemary called back, in a mock-offended voice.

The two men came down the stairs and Jack caught her up in a big bear hug before she could say another word. He attempted to twirl her around a little, too, but as Rosemary was almost the same size as Jack, the twirl didn't go far.

"You're finally here, you gorgeous thing!" He stood back to look at here. "Glad you found the village."

"No thanks to your directions," Rosemary teased. "Mrs. Potter *alone* is responsible for my finding this place. The possum rock threw me off. Big time." She rolled her eyes and caught Charlie chuckling and nodding in agreement as if he understood completely.

"Ooh, you met Mrs. Potter. Charlie and I adore her," said Jack.

"She sent a pie," Rosemary said.

Jack clapped gleefully. "Her caramel apple pie? Did she show you the special apples?"

"She did," Rosemary nodded.

"That means you're in. Mrs. Potter's approval is everything in Paperwick."

"What a relief!" Rosemary laughed. She turned to Charlie. "It's wonderful to finally meet you in person, Charlie. And wow—you're even more handsome than you look in pictures." She held out her hand, and he took it warmly.

"Thanks. Do you really think so?"

She did think so. In photos from the wedding, Charlie had, of course, been wearing a suit and his hair was neatly combed to one side, and he wasn't wearing glasses. Today, his dark hair was slightly messy, and he was wearing a pair of wire spectacles. He had deep green eyes and a smile that was both charming and lopsided, which made Rosemary trust him instantly.

"He's quite the hottie, isn't he?" Jack agreed.

"Well, Jack, I'd expect nothing less. And it's good to see you so happily matched," said Rosemary, smiling at her friend, still holding Charlie's hand.

Except that he turned out not to be Charlie.

"Oh, by the way, this is my friend and colleague, Dr. Seth McGuire. Anthropology," said Jack with a snort. "He does look a bit like Charlie, now that you mention it."

Rosemary's jaw dropped just a little bit, and even as she regained her composure, she felt her cheeks burning. *Betrayed by those confounded cheeks again!* She had learned over the years to affect a polished and professional demeanor when she needed to. But she could never figure out how to keep herself from blushing.

"Jack's right about Mrs. Potter, by the way," said Dr. McGuire. "It took me months to get on her good side. I'm amazed you're already approved."

"She seemed pretty friendly to me," said Rosemary, who was feeling a giddy mix of embarrassment and amusement at the moment. "Wonder where you went wrong."

"I made the mistake of turning down a donut on account of them being deep-fried," said Dr. McGuire, shaking his head dolefully.

"No wonder!" said Rosemary. "And I inhaled a donut immediately upon meeting her, and then got a dozen more. So that must've been what tipped her off that I'm okay."

It was at that moment that Rosemary and Dr. McGuire simultaneously noticed they were still shaking hands and quickly let go.

"Well," Jack said, clapping Dr. McGuire on the back, "See you later, Seth. We're off." Jack took Rosemary's arm and pulled her along with him.

She cleared her throat and looked back at the man who still stood at the foot of the stairs.

"It was nice meeting you, Dr. McGuire," she called over her shoulder. "Sorry about the mix up."

"It's Seth," he called back. "Nice meeting you, too!"

Once outside, Rosemary shot a deadly glance at Jack, who was smiling cheerfully.

"What?" he asked, all innocence.

"You know what," said Rosemary. "You said you and Charlie were meeting me here. And that guy wasn't Charlie."

"Well, Charlie had to work. He's meeting us for linner," said Jack. "And you know, I really do see the resemblance, now that you've mixed them up. Seth and Charlie are both tall and dark-haired and good looking." He leaned in and admitted, "But even if I were available, Seth is not my type."

"I'm mortified," groaned Rosemary, as they walked along the brick sidewalk that wove its way through the campus.

"Why? Just because you mistook Seth for Charlie?"

"No. Because I gushed on about how handsome he was. Is. And then turned as red as a beet, like I'm thirteen years old." She slapped Jack's arm. "*Why* didn't you introduce us right away?"

"Trust me, Rosie. No man takes offense when a beauty such as yourself calls him handsome. Or pretty much when anyone calls him handsome. He's probably still smiling."

“Maybe I’ll get lucky and never see him again,” said Rosemary.

“Not likely. Everyone knows everybody in Paperwick.”

“So I hear,” said Rosemary with a roll of her eyes.

“And besides, Charlie and I invited Seth over for dinner tomorrow night.”

3

"And in answer to your question: Yes," said Jack in his smug know-it-all voice, as he unlocked his small, butter yellow car —which Rosemary had affectionately dubbed "Holly Golightly" years ago, because being an electric car, it made very little noise.

"Yes, what?" asked Rosemary, climbing in and buckling her seatbelt, trying to look clueless (all the while cringing inwardly, because Jack always knew what she was thinking, which was maddening). Oh yes, he knew *exactly* what she was thinking. And worse, he knew that she knew that he knew—and that she was only pretending not to know. So it was perfectly reasonable, at that particular moment, for him to give her a look that said, *Please. You know exactly what I'm talking about.* Which, of course, she did.

"Ugh. Okay. So Dr. McGuire—Seth—the same Seth who is coming over for dinner tomorrow night, is…single, then?" Rosemary asked. But before Jack could answer, she added, "But it doesn't matter whether he is or not because I'm not in the market for a relationship, and you know it."

"Rosie, we're not even *contemplating* a relationship. A date, though. That might be nice. What's wrong with a date? You remember those, don't you? I know you haven't had one in years, but long ago, you used to enjoy them. And yes, Seth is single. Never married. Dated a woman fairly steadily before he took the job at the university and moved to Paperwick. They didn't care to make it work long distance, so it couldn't have been that serious. That was almost a year ago. Which means he's ripe for the picking."

"You're making him sound like one of Mrs. Potter's apples! And I'm only here for two weeks, and I want to spend all of that time with you and Charlie. Besides, we've got work to do."

"Three things. First, I call 'em like I see 'em, so no apologies for the apple comparison thing. Second, thank you. I love you, too. And third, I can't wait to show you around the cemetery tomorrow," said Jack. Rosemary was relieved they were transitioning to another subject. "You're going to think you've died and gone to historian heaven."

"Heaven in a cemetery? Is that what you English professors would call irony?"

"As the case may be," sang Jack. "It's going to be the best Paperwick Founders Day Festival ever—and we'll raise loads of money for the Historical Society."

"Raising money while we 'raise' the dead?" Rosemary said with a giggle. "I can't wait to *dig* further into the history."

"Madam, you are the queen of puns today," said Jack as they exited the university campus and headed toward the village green.

"I've done a lot of work already on New England in the 17th century, but let me tell you, it isn't easy to find much on Paperwick itself. I've got some preliminary research on the list of names you sent. It's astounding that so many of the founders' families are still living around these parts."

"Isn't it, though? Charlie and I are among the few who don't have a Connecticut pedigree. But he did once spend a summer in Mystic when he was a kid, and I've driven through Hartford, so that scored us a few points. I know Paperwick is a bit of a no-show in the history books. But something happened here in 1668. And it's significant." Jack paused for dramatic affect. "There is the history itself." He leaned a little closer to Rosemary and lowered his voice, "And then there is the *legend*."

"The legend? Tell me more."

"Not until later, when we can make ourselves comfortable and I can tell you the whole story," said Jack, wiggling his eyebrows at Rosemary.

"And there it is. The eyebrow wiggle. I know what that means."

"That I'm being mysterious?"

"That you have something juicy you're not willing to part with quite yet, and no amount of nagging will get it out of you."

Jack pulled into a parking spot along the green, next to a charming row of shops and restaurants. "You do know me so well," he said with a sigh.

"Out with it!" Rosemary said. "At least give me a hint."

"Oh good, there's Charlie's car," said Jack, completely evading the subject. "He'll have gotten us a table."

"You're evil," said Rosemary, shaking her head and following Jack along the sidewalk until they came to a cluster of small, umbrella-capped tables sprinkled with patrons who were sipping from oversized, steaming mugs.

"Okay. One little hint. *The Witch's Meadow*. It has to do with that."

“The Witch’s Meadow. Over by the cemetery?”

“Not another word until later,” Jack insisted.

Rosemary looked at the café sign, surprised. “Potter’s Café? Is this the same Potters who own the farm at the edge of town? As in, Mrs. Potter with the apple orchard?”

“The very same,” said Jack. “Don’t let their humble outward appearance fool you. The Potters are a very prominent family in Paperwick, with a *very* long history here. They own half the countryside. But you won’t meet any of their family members in the graveyard. They have their own ancestral burial plot out at their farm.” He followed this statement up with another eyebrow wiggle.

“So that’s why they weren’t on my list of names,” said Rosemary.

“But Mrs. Potter is a fount of information when it comes to village history,” said Jack. “She can definitely fill you in on the triumphs, trials, and tribulations hereabouts.”

Just then the door swung open, and a tall and handsome dark-haired man greeted them.

“Please tell me that’s Charlie,” said Rosemary under her breath.

“That’s the actual Charlie,” said Jack, smiling at his husband.

"Rosemary, we're so glad you finally agreed to come and stay a while," said Charlie. "Jack, you're right. She's gorgeous!" he said, giving her a warm hug. "I feel like I know you already."

"Me, too," said Rosemary, returning his hug.

"Cold front on the way," said Charlie, eyeing the blue sky. "I got us a table inside."

"Did I mention he's a closet meteorologist?" said Jack, following Charlie through the door.

"No. Is he any good?"

"He's never wrong. If he says a front is coming, button up your overcoat."

Inside the café, they were seated at a sunny table near the front windows that overlooked the sidewalk diners and the village green. The front facade of Potter's Café was made of what looked like very old, weathered brick, and inside, worn wooden tables and comfortable chairs were arranged around a cozy little fireplace that crackled away cheerfully on the back wall, which also housed a swinging door that led back to the kitchen.

"This building used to be a blacksmith shop, way back in the 1600s," said Charlie.

"That explains the ever-so-slight whiff of coal I always smell on entering," said Jack.

"Are you a history buff, too?" Rosemary asked Charlie.

"Definitely. In fact, the book I'm working on now is a mystery set in seventeenth century New England."

"Really? My favorite time and place! And there's nothing I love more than a good mystery. Is it possible you're my soulmate?"

"Well, he's *my* soulmate, but he can be your spirit animal," said Jack. "He loves history and mysteries and spooky movies and candles and anything to do with stationary and good fountain pens."

"Just like us!" said Rosemary, giving Jack's arm a squeeze. "Oh, Jack, you did good."

"My heart is all warm and fuzzy at this moment," said Jack. "My two favorite people in the same room at last. We're all cut from the same cloth, you know."

"The good stuff," agreed Rosemary.

"That's why Jack and I have decided it's time for you to settle down in these parts," said Charlie, and Rosemary caught him exchanging a brief conspiratorial glance with Jack.

"Ah-ha. So, you've been planning my life for me, have you?" Rosemary looked from one to the other of them. "I *just* got here!"

"We'll talk about all that later," said Jack. "I'm starved. Let's order."

As if on cue, a young waitress, who looked very familiar, brought out a basket of warm brown bread with fresh butter, and three mugs of hot apple cider. When Rosemary smelled the fresh apple and cinnamon aroma of the cider, she realized why the girl seemed familiar. She was Mrs. Potter's daughter Abbey, who Rosemary had met at the farm stand. Rosemary gave her a little wave, but the girl didn't seem to remember her.

"I hope you don't mind that I took the liberty of having Gabby bring us a round of their special recipe cider," said Charlie.

"Oh, my heart!" said Jack, smiling at Charlie across the table. "Just what we needed!"

"Perfect for a day that's turning chilly," said Rosemary, wrapping her hands around her mug. "Thank you, Charlie." She looked up at the waitress, who was passing out menus. "Wait. *Gabby*? I thought your name was Abbey. We met earlier, at your farm?"

Gabby smiled. "We fooled you," she said. "Everyone always mixes up me and Abbey."

"Well, yeah," said Jack. "Because you're identical twins, and you always insist on dressing alike."

"That might have something to do with it," Gabby admitted with a wink, and left them to look over their menus.

The lunch special that day was the "Almost-Thanksgiving" sandwich: thick sourdough bread, toasted and topped with mounds of shaved turkey, cranberry sauce, sharp, melting cheddar, and herbed cornbread stuffing, smothered in gravy and served open-faced with homemade potato chips and a cup of smoky butternut squash soup. They ordered three specials and sat back, sipping cider and watching the people walking by on the sidewalk outside.

"Look, there's Mayor Wright," said Charlie.

"The mayor? Wow, this really is a small town. Isn't he also your local celebrated pumpkin contest judge?" said Rosemary, chuckling at the memory of Mrs. Potter and her champion pumpkins. "I wonder if he'll..." Rosemary's words slowed and came to a complete stop when she laid eyes on the mayor, who came bustling into the café, giving a little wave to young Gabby, who pointed him to an empty table set for two in the corner near the fireplace.

As he made his way in that direction, he stopped to shake a few hands and glancing around, caught sight of Jack and Charlie. A broad smile spread across his face.

"Hello, my friends," he said, coming to stand at their table, where he shook hands with the guys. Then his gaze wandered over to Rosemary. "Who is your lovely guest here?"

Rosemary had imagined that the mayor-slash-pumpkin aficionado would be a little old man with patches on the elbows of his corduroy blazer, and probably smoking a pipe. *This* man looked to be in his mid-thirties, was boyishly charming, handsome, well-dressed, well-mannered, and had an easiness about him that made him instantly likable. The perfect set of qualities for someone in politics. His smile was so genuine that Rosemary didn't take it as a flirtation, but more as a sign that he was truly interested to meet a newcomer to his town.

"Mayor Wright," Jack said with a smile, "this is my dearest friend, Rosemary Grey. She's come to Paperwick to visit, and is, in fact, considering relocating here permanently. She's a professor of history, an author, and a fabulous public speaker."

Rosemary felt the heat rising to her cheeks for the second time in one afternoon.

"I'm here for a *visit*, and to help Jack at the town festival," she said. "It's very nice to meet you, Mayor Wright."

"Oh, enough with all this 'mayor' business," he answered, slapping Jack playfully on the back even as his eyes stayed on Rosemary. He extended a hand across the table to her. "I'm Samuel. Or usually just plain Sam. And if I'm honest, I think Jack here is onto something," he said with a wink. "You *should* move here. We need more citizens like you in Paperwick."

"See?" said Jack. "Now it's official. Even the mayor thinks you should come and stay."

"Well, he just met me," said Rosemary through a slightly embarrassed smile. "He might change his mind."

"Oh, I doubt that. I have a knack about these things," Samuel assured her.

You and Mrs. Potter, thought Rosemary.

"Give us a few days. Paperwick'll grow on you." And there was that smile again. Genuine and charming at once.

"We'll see," Rosemary said, ready to change the subject to something other than herself. "From what I can see, Paperwick does seem like a wonderful town."

"Join us for lunch, Sam?" said Charlie, motioning toward the empty chair across from Rosemary.

"I can't tell you how much I wish I could. But I have a meeting in…" Sam looked at his watch, "about three minutes."

"Duty calls," said Jack, giving him a little salute. "Maybe next time."

"Definitely," the mayor answered, smiling once more at Rosemary before turning to go to his own table. "Oh, and welcome home, Rosemary," he added, briefly looking back.

"You're too much," said Rosemary, turning to Jack after the mayor had moved off. "How long have you been after me to settle down and live in one place?"

"Oh, let's see," said Jack, pretending to calculate on his fingers.

"Forever," said Rosemary, giving him a playful shove. "How about this: I promise I'll let you know when I'm ready."

"Fair enough," agreed Jack.

"Wow. So that's the mayor," said Rosemary, hoping her cheeks had gone back to their normal shade of pink. "He doesn't seem all that . . . mayoral. Or he does, but he isn't what I'd expected."

"Yep, he's a cutie," said Jack, reading Rosemary's thoughts once again. "But he's also a good leader. Hometown boy. Already finishing up his second term, with no end in sight."

"He's up for re-election later this month," added Charlie. "But no one is running against him, of course, so it's a done deal."

"Mrs. Potter said his is another one of the old Paperwick families," said Rosemary.

"Oh yes," said Jack. "They've been around here since the early days. Sam gave a talk at the Historical Society. He said the first Wright moved here just after the turn of the 18th century."

"So early 1700s, then. Wow. So, I take it the Elias Wright on your list for the festival is Sam's relative?" said Rosemary.

"Yep. Born in 1705. And the best part is, the mayor himself is going to bring him to life. A local celebrity in our little production!"

"We're hitting the big time," said Rosemary with a laugh.

Just then, a beautiful woman with gleaming blond hair entered the café and went to sit down with the mayor in the corner. Every head in the place turned—and with good reason, Rosemary thought. The two of them made a striking couple. The mayor, so handsome and charming, and his companion, dressed in the perfect New England fall outfit—long skirt, rust-colored shirt cinched at the waist with a wide leather belt, a soft, flowy cardigan sweater overtop, and leather boots peeking out at the hem of the skirt.

"Wow," whispered Rosemary. "Who's she?"

"No idea," said Jack, glancing at Charlie, who shrugged.

"I thought everyone knew everybody in Paperwick," said Rosemary.

"She's not from around here," said Charlie.

"Maybe she and the mayor are an item. She has *First Lady* written all over her, don't you think?" said Rosemary.

"They do make an arresting couple," observed Charlie.

"Magazine-cover beautiful," agreed Jack.

Their attention was brought back to their own table when Gabby approached with a large tray heaped with sandwiches and soup. She unloaded everything, refilled their cider mugs from an oversized teapot, and left them to enjoy a wonderful meal, eating and talking about history and blacksmithing and life in small-town Connecticut.

"Let's go home for coffee," said Jack with a yawn about an hour later. "This food has made me sleepy."

"Good idea," agreed Charlie, giving Gabby a wave for the check. "And we need to get you all unpacked and settled in," he said to Rosemary.

"You know what goes perfectly with coffee? Donuts and pie," suggested Rosemary, remembering the box full of homemade goodies in her car back at the university.

"Perfection," said Jack. "And since we're already carb-loading, might as well finish on a high note." He turned to Charlie. "Rosemary and I will take Holly Golightly and zip by school on the way. I can collect my things and we'll get her car, and we'll meet you at home."

Gabby arrived with the check and a little plate with a selection of cheeses.

"Did I mention the Potters are also known for their award-winning cheeses?" asked Jack, popping a piece into his mouth.

"They make these right on their farm. Did Mrs. Potter show you the special cows?"

"We never made it to the cows," said Rosemary with a chuckle. "Guess I still have a ways to go before Mrs. Potter likes me *that* much."

They gave Gabby a wave, left her a generous tip, and headed out into the late afternoon that seemed to be getting chillier by the minute, just as Charlie had predicted it would. Clouds were rolling in, and evening was already coming on. It had been a busy day and to Rosemary, it seemed ages since her morning Sleepy Hollow lecture.

She smiled at the thought of getting to finally see Jack and Charlie's restored farmhouse. She'd seen photos from back before they'd started the renovations, and in them, the place looked pretty dilapidated. A drafty old house and a fallen-down barn. Even for a someone with Jack's interior design know-how, this was quite a project, and Rosemary had prepared herself that it might still be a work in progress. Jack hadn't sent her any photos since the beginning, though, because he wanted to keep the house as a surprise. She couldn't wait to see what they'd done with the place.

As she waited for Jack to unlock Holly Golightly's door, a sudden chill breeze blew Rosemary's hair into an auburn swirl around her face and she shivered, happily looking forward to a cozy blanket and a piece of pie. This was shaping up to be the most relaxing, peaceful two weeks ever.

⸙ 4 ⸙

Jack and Charlie's house was neither dilapidated nor drafty anymore.

On the contrary, it was decidedly one of the coziest places Rosemary had ever encountered. In the dusky light, she'd just been able to make out the trees along the little lane that led to the house. She could see the outline of what must have been the barn (*and what appeared to be a silo next to it*?) just to the side. The rest of the land had pretty well faded into the shadows of the brewing storm, but the house itself was glowing warmly, inviting a weary traveler to come and stay awhile.

A sturdy windowed door—painted a toasty shade of burnt orange and sporting a fresh, green, boxwood wreath—opened into a sweet little entryway room, where there were hooks for hanging coats and caps, and a long wooden bench for sitting down to take off muddy shoes. There was a basket containing Jack and Charlie's slippers, another laden with umbrellas and snow scrapers, and a third was full of dog toys.

"What's this?" asked Rosemary, gesturing to the dog toys in surprise. "Has there been an addition to the family that I'm not aware of?"

"As a matter of fact, there has," said Jack proudly, as he hung his jacket on a hook, slipped into his warm, fuzzy slippers, and handed Rosemary a brand-new pair of her own. "A very recent addition," he smiled, then called "Izzy! Come here, sweet girl!"

The fleece-lined slippers felt like heaven on Rosemary's cold feet. Jack, true to his typical style, was definitely bent on spoiling her rotten during her stay in Paperwick. He led her through the wide opening, its French doors standing ajar, that connected the entryway to the main living area. Rosemary had to stop to take it all in.

"Jack, it's perfect. It's—wow."

A huge stone fireplace with a rustic wooden mantle stood on the opposite wall. Charlie was already home and stoking a crackling fire, and he'd lit candles which flickered warmly here and there around the room. On either side of the stone chimney, which climbed all the way up to the high ceiling, there were double glass doors that overlooked what was either a huge pond or a tiny lake, the rippling water glistening in the last little bit of deep amber sunset that was able to push its way through the cracks in a growing wall of storm clouds. Rosemary could just make out the woods beyond the pond, as the dancing silhouettes of trees were barely visible in the background.

"It *is* wow, isn't it?" said a beaming Jack. "Normally at this time of day, we're out back, watching the sun set over the pond. You'll love it."

"It'll be a clear day tomorrow. But colder," Charlie piped in.

Just to the left of where Rosemary stood at the room's entrance, a long wood farm table was tucked into the corner, surrounded by an eclectic collection of chairs that somehow made perfect sense together. Beyond that, on the wall to the left, was another large, cased opening, through which Rosemary glimpsed a cheerful farmhouse kitchen, glowing gold with the flickering light of a smaller fireplace. In front of the living room fireplace was a couch that looked like the kind you sink deeply down into when you sit, and on either side of the hearth were soft, comfortable chairs. Lamps gave the whole room a golden glow, and baskets brimming with rolled-up quilts and books scattered here and there made it easy for Rosemary to picture Jack and Charlie, sitting here by the fire in the evenings, reading or watching the television that was probably tucked away inside the old, burnished oak wardrobe cabinet that stood off to one side of the fireplace.

There were huge windows on the wall to the right, along with another cased opening that led off to the bedrooms. And there was yet another reading nook with bookshelves in the corner to the right of where Rosemary still stood, shaking her head in amazement.

"You guys have done an incredible job. I can't believe this is the place from the photos you sent. Amazing!"

"We *did* do an incredible job, didn't we?" agreed Jack.

"Wait until you see the rest of the place," said Charlie, grabbing Rosemary's suitcase and heading down the hall to the right.

"Later," Jack called after him. "Rosemary and I are going to make the coffee."

Just then, they heard the pitter-patter of little paws trotting up, and a small, very scruffy terrier sporting a tiny plaid scarf in fall colors, came sleepily over to stand at Jack's feet.

"There's our girl," said Jack, scooping up the little creature. "Were you napping in the study again? Rosemary, meet Isabelle. Izzy, here is your Aunty Rosemary. She's the one I've been telling you all about."

Rosemary reached out to stroke Izzy's soft hair. "Hello, sweet Izzy. I like your scarf," she said. "She's adorable." Rosemary looked at Jack and felt the hint of a couple of tears stinging her eyes. “You’ve done well for yourself here, my friend,” she said softly.

“I’m home,” Jack said with a happy sigh. “Now. These are the original hardwood floors, that’s the original fireplace—can you believe that stone had been plastered over? It was hideous! And the beams that run along the ceiling—a couple hundred years old,” said Jack, setting Izzy down, and leading Rosemary into the kitchen.

Rosemary headed straight for the coffee pot while Jack unloaded Mrs. Potter’s pie and donuts and slid them into the oven to warm. A few minutes later, they went back into the living room where Charlie joined them and they all sat by the fire, chatting and enjoying hot coffee and the apple treats.

Charlie groaned happily. “I never tire of Mrs. Potter’s caramel apple pie. It’s amazing. Too bad she refuses to share the recipe.”

“I’m so stuffed,” said Jack. “Think I’ll just sleep here by the fire tonight so I don’t have to get up.”

“Me too,” said Rosemary with a yawn. “Is it tacky if I unbutton the top button of my pants?”

“You’re among family now, so no,” said Charlie. “Wish I could stay, but I have a deadline fast approaching, so I’m off to my study to get some writing done. I’ll be back to check on you two later.”

There was a low rumble of distant thunder outside.

"Luckily he has a short commute to the office," Jack said, pointing at the cased opening that led to the bedrooms. For the first time, Rosemary glimpsed the wide hallway, lined with loaded bookshelves that framed doors leading off to the left and right, which must've been the bedrooms. Double French doors stood open at the end of the hall, lit from within. The perfect writer's alcove.

"You two have fun," said Charlie, turning to go.

He headed off to his study, Izzy at his heels, and Rosemary and Jack, who were lazily snuggled up on the couch under a thick knitted blanket, both said at once, "Movie night!"

"Let's watch something spooky," said Rosemary.

"Something eerie and haunting," agreed Jack.

"But first, tell me all about the Witch's Meadow."

5

"Yes! Okay." Jack cackled a little bit in his excitement, and turned to face Rosemary on the couch. "But before you learn about the legend, you need to know the history. But trust me, in this case, the truth is stranger than fiction. Ready for this?"

Rosemary sat up straighter and nodded enthusiastically.

"As you know, there were witch trials here in Connecticut before the whole *Salem* thing ever happened." He made air quotes around the word "Salem" and gave a little snort.

Rosemary nodded. "Right. Mostly in the 1600s."

"Very good, professor. Between 1647 and 1697, to be exact. Massachusetts didn't really catch the bug until 1692. By then, witch trials were old hat here."

"I know there were two major Connecticut panics: Hartford in 1662 and Fairfield thirty years later."

"Right again," said Jack.

"And here in Connecticut, Governor John Winthrop, Jr. made a lot of progress by requiring more evidence be presented in order to prove someone was a witch," said Rosemary. "There were no more executions after 1662."

Jack nodded slowly. "Except for one."

"What?"

"Winthrop did change the rules, thank goodness," Jack agreed. "But there was one tiny village that didn't get the memo."

There was a long pause. The fire popped and crackled, and the rain started to pour in earnest outside.

"Paperwick?" Rosemary's eyes widened.

"Paperwick," Jack confirmed.

"So, there was another witch trial right here?"

"There was an accusation. There was a death. But there was no trial."

"*Get out*!" Rosemary shoved Jack back into the pillows of the couch. "But how have my history books overlooked this?"

"That's just it. Someone needs to write a new book." Jack raised an eyebrow at Rosemary. "Wouldn't you agree?"

"If this is true, then yes, I emphatically agree."

"As president of the Paperwick Historical Society, I can offer various documents and artifacts tomorrow for your perusal when we go into town. But here's the gist of it: There was a woman accused of witchcraft. And there was an execution of sorts—or that's what folks around here have called it all these years."

"I don't follow. What should it be called?" asked Rosemary.

"Murder, perhaps?" said Jack.

Thunder rumbled outside, sending a shiver down Rosemary's spine, and Izzy came scampering in and hurled herself at the couch. Jack reached down, picked her up, and nestled her into the folds of the blanket.

"Poor baby," said Rosemary, petting Izzy. "She doesn't like the thunder."

"But apparently she does like you," said Jack, surprised as Izzy got to her tiny feet and curled up in a ball next to Rosemary. "She usually takes a while to warm to people."

"Well, that's just the effect I have on animals."

"On professors as well, as we have seen this very day with the stodgy Dr. McGuire."

"Stodgy? That guy? He seemed pretty friendly to me."

"Oh yes, my dear. You clearly charmed him. I thought he'd never let go of your hand."

"Charmed him? Surely not!"

"I know the man, and trust me, he was charmed."

Rosemary's cheeks began to burn. Time to change the subject.

"Don't get off track. I want to hear about the Paperwick witch."

"Make that *witches*. There were technically two of them, or so the story goes. And get ready to get seriously spooked. Because it all started right here."

"Right here in Paperwick," Rosemary nodded.

"Right here *on this farm*."

"Wait. *What?* Are you *kidding* me? You and Charlie bought the witches' house?" Rosemary looked around with a shiver.

"Well, no. The house is old but not that old. But our land was part of the original Gallow farm. Travel back in time with me, if you will. The year was 1668. Hortence Clark Gallow lived on this land with her husband Jonathan Gallow. Her sister, Mercy Clark Brown, who had been widowed at the ripe old age of 19, was living with the couple at the time. The Clark sisters grew up on this land. Hortence was the village midwife, and in fact, there are descendants of babies she delivered who still live here to this day."

"Seriously? Over three hundred years later?"

"Yep. The old families of Paperwick stuck around like glue. Think about it. You've already met a few. The Potters. Mayor Wright. And by the way," Jack said as an aside, "it's not easy to crack the social code here, but Charlie and I have done it. The town loves us. We're as good as natives."

"How could they resist your modest charm?" said Rosemary with a laugh. "So back up. This woman—this Hortence Clark—married a man with the last name of 'Gallow'? How unfortunate."

"It was as if fate had struck the blow in advance, giving her that name," agreed Jack with a nod. "*Hortence Gallow*. Pretty great, right? Anyway, our Hortence was a midwife, like her mother before her, but she also practiced a sort of rudimentary medicine, using herbs and roots and things like that to treat everything from dysentery to warts. Her sister Mercy assisted her and kept surprisingly detailed records. They made house calls all over this area."

"So, Mercy was the second witch," said Rosemary.

"Correct. The nearest doctor was a few villages away, and even on horseback, it would've taken a while to get to Paperwick. So, the sisters stayed pretty busy, by what I can gather."

"But let me guess: Their kind of medicine ended up getting them into trouble."

"Exactly. Especially Hortence. She was a sort of wild beauty. It was easy enough for a few jealous housewives or snubbed suitors to decide that because she messed around with roots and herbs, because she practiced a very old kind of medicine that had been passed down to her by her mother and grandmother—that there was something disconcerting or even dangerous about her."

"People are always afraid of what they don't understand," said Rosemary.

"Or can't control," agreed Jack. "Other people, of course, were just happy there was someone around who knew how to deliver a baby."

"I bet that was the more commonly held sentiment."

"But one well-poisoner can kill a whole village, and someone had it in for our Ms. Gallow—or the *Widow* Gallow, as she was known by the time the trouble really started in the fall of that year. You see, Jonathan Gallow had died quite suddenly during the summer under mysterious circumstances. There were rumors—one that he'd been killed in a duel or a fight, another that Hortence had killed him herself. Frankly, most folks wouldn't have been surprised either way, because Jonathan Gallow was by all accounts an awful person.

"Anyway, Jonathan was dead, but after a while, the rumors about his demise died down some, and people got on with their lives. Hortence had allies in the village and with her sister Mercy's help, she was able to keep food on the table and hold onto the farm by way of her midwifery and dispensing her remedies around the village when people needed them. But there were always those rumors, bubbling just beneath the surface, waiting for any reason to flare up again.

"There were stories that Hortence and Mercy were prone to disappearing at night, and were seen walking in the moonlight."

"They would've *had* to be out and about at night, though, if they were visiting sick people and delivering babies," said Rosemary.

"Sure, but then there were other rumors. For example, there is a surviving letter from that period that says Hortence was seen dancing. Without a partner. And without music. '*As though she were charmed by some unseen phantom.*' I'll show you the letter tomorrow. It's in the museum."

"Well, that was . . . odd behavior . . . I mean, if it was true," admitted Rosemary.

"So, you see, the stage was all set: Two widowed sisters. Rumors flying about moonlit shenanigans and witchy medicine. There was talk of Hortence being seen with a baby—but then the baby would disappear. So, we had a figurative pile of dry kindling, just waiting to catch fire. And then, in November of 1668, the match was struck: A child died."

"One of Hortence's patients?"

"Yes—one she'd been treating for fever. And then a mother passed away during delivery, and yet another mother delivered a stillborn baby. All within about ten days' time."

"Oh no."

"And the common link between all of these deaths?"

"Hortence Gallow," said Rosemary.

"Exactly. The village fell into a panic, and what was probably really something like an influenza epidemic was laid on the shoulders of the local eccentric widow."

"They needed someone to blame," Rosemary nodded. "But why not blame Mercy, too?"

"Oh, she was on thin ice herself. But while Mercy was described as a plain, shy girl, Hortence, remember, had a sort of dark, dangerous beauty about her that the local women didn't trust, and the men weren't quite comfortable with. Mercy tended to blend into the woodwork. Hortence stood out. She was bold. She was known to speak her mind—a rarity for a woman in that place and time. She didn't care what people thought. And to top it all off, not only did she have an unusual cat companion, but she bore…get this: *the witch's mark.*"

"A cat, you say?" Rosemary shuddered. "Um. Unusual in what way?" She shifted nervously in her seat, causing Izzy to open one bleary eye before nodding off again.

Jack gave a deep sigh and shook his head.

"I'll never understand how you can study the history of witches in early America so thoroughly and be deathly afraid of cats," he said. "Yes, the cat was a fluffy tortoise shell with bright green eyes. Unusually intelligent, or so the story goes. But didn't you hear the part where I said, *she bore the witch's mark*?"

"Sorry. Tell me more about this witch's mark," said Rosemary.

"In Hortence's case, it was a birthmark in the shape of a goat's horn. On her back, somewhere around her right shoulder blade."

"And everyone back then thought the devil could sometimes take on the form of a goat," said Rosemary, nodding. "That sure could've sealed her fate in the eyes of the good people of Paperwick."

"Of course, no one would have ever known about the birthmark, except that on drunken nights at the tavern, Jonathan Gallow—before his untimely death—liked to talk. And one of the things he talked about was his wife. And how she bore that mark, and apparently, he said it wouldn't bleed—which, of course, confirmed her witchy status."

"How did he know it wouldn't bleed? And what was a Puritan doing drinking at a tavern?"

"Who knows? He was probably just spouting off. And presumably, the tavern was more of an inn that served ale, and Jonathan was known to indulge a bit too much. He wasn't well liked by the time he died. But when he first moved to the area, he'd managed to charm Hortence's parents and win her hand —and get *his* hands on the family farm. But even with all of these strikes against her, the case against Hortence might've blown over if it weren't for the fact that people started getting sick just as the rumors were beginning to rise. That much we know for sure."

"Historians agree now that incidents of this nature—deaths happening in groups like this—were probably caused by something like the flu spreading through the population, like you mentioned. The culprit also might've simply been a fungus running rampant on grain grown in the area at the time," said Rosemary.

"But back then, it was a dark mystery. And the villagers were horrified and desperate for a solution, and it must've seemed all too easy to 'fix' the problem if the cause could just be strung up from the nearest tree and wiped out forever."

"So, they killed Hortence?"

"That's where the story gets even stranger," said Jack. "She was formally accused of witchcraft, taken to jail, and set to go to trial. We have the judge's journal. He was quite clear about the details of the accusation. One, Hortence bore the witch's mark. Two, disappearing baby. Three, visited by an imp—the cat. Four, her patients were dying. Five, eyewitness accounts of dancing and walking around at night. It didn't help that the judge himself was Matthew Graves, who lived on the farm next door to the Gallows. He'd observed the sisters' strange comings and goings firsthand. But get this: The morning of the trial, when the constable came at sunrise to escort Hortence to the judge, he found her cell still locked up tight. But Hortence was nowhere to be found. A search party was sent out, and they soon hit pay dirt. They found Hortence in the Witch's Meadow—the very same Witch's Meadow that you'll visit tomorrow over by the churchyard."

"So that's why they call it the Witch's Meadow? Because she was found there?"

"Well, even before that night, village folk had told tales about that meadow being a meeting place for witches. Anyway, that's probably why the search party headed straight there to look for Hortence—and they found her there, strangled and lying face down at the foot of a maple tree, a signed confession in her hand and her dress torn, exposing her right shoulder."

"Revealing the witch's mark."

"Yep. Confirming all the rumors. The judge said the confession included Hortence's admission that she was, indeed, a witch, and based on that, he also surmised that she had killed her husband, Johnathan Gallow. And since no one wanted to be the one to move her body, they buried her right there, under the maple tree. Naturally, she couldn't join her husband in the respectable graveyard next door—even though by most accounts, she was by far the better person of the two."

"So, she's buried there, in the meadow—still?"

"Her grave is marked now, but she's still there."

"Didn't her descendants want her moved to the family plot? And what ever became of her sister, Mercy?"

"Seems she escaped in the night, taking one small piece of top secret, precious cargo with her."

"What was it?"

"A baby. Hortence had a baby—a daughter. She'd been pregnant when the horrible Jonathan Gallow died. The child's name was Lilly. Apparently, the sisters had kept the baby a secret for those first few months of her life."

"The disappearing baby," said Rosemary, sighing deeply.

"We know about Lilly, because of Mercy's impeccable records. She'd delivered her niece herself—a healthy baby girl."

"But why hide the baby? And how on earth have you obtained all of this information?" asked Rosemary, amazed. "I've researched this whole area, and I knew about the region's history with witches. But never have I heard of Hortence or Mercy or Jonathan Gallow or any of this."

"Local evidence and stories passed down through generations, mostly," said Jack. "We have letters and Mercy's medical notes at the museum. Thank heaven someone from every generation was smart enough to preserve them. In fact, it was the women of Paperwick who held onto them in the first place, presumably because they wanted a record of babies born. And remember the judge, Matthew Graves from the farm next door? His wife, Elizabeth, took over as midwife after Hortence and Mercy were gone. Oddly enough, even though the good judge apparently had issues with Hortence, Elizabeth is known to have been a friend to the sisters, and I would bet they'd showed her the ropes. She would've been the first to use the notes the sisters left behind. She would've needed to study them."

"Of course. The women of Paperwick protected Mercy's records. They wanted to be able to refer to those notes to take care of their families and each other."

"But I also have another very special primary source. And it's a bit of a riddle that I hope you can help me solve." A grin spread across Jack's face.

"A primary source? Jack… What have you found?"

"I can't believe I've been able to keep this from you until now, but I wanted to show you in person," said Jack excitedly. He went and opened a cabinet beneath a bookshelf, took out a small box, and brought it back to the couch. "We found this when we started to explore the old barn here on our land," he said, opening the box to reveal another, smaller box which looked to be made of rusted tin of some kind.

"Whoa," Rosemary breathed. "What's inside that?"

"Open it," said Jack, barely able to contain his excitement.

Outside, there was a bright flash of lightening, followed within seconds by a huge clap of thunder. The lights flickered and went out.

"Oh my gosh! No! Not now!" said Rosemary, who had just been reaching for the lid of the little box.

They moved closer to the fire, and between its light and that of the candles, Rosemary could see again. She gingerly opened the lid to reveal a small square of yellowed parchment—a letter, written in careful, scrolling script. Rosemary lifted the parchment out of the box, revealing a tiny key that lay beneath it.

"What does the key go to?"

“No idea,” said Jack. “Probably something that’s long since gone. But read the note.”

Rosemary’s eyes scanned the short missive to the signature at the bottom.

“Are you kidding me?” she said, breathless. “Mercy wrote this? Hortence’s sister actually wrote this?”

“It would appear so. She signed it,” said Jack, pointing to the small but beautiful curling signature. “Like I said, we’ve got Mercy’s old records at the museum. The handwriting is a match. Of course, I’ve alerted the Historical Society about this find, and as soon as I turn it over to the town, it’ll go straight into the museum. But I wanted to show it to you first. The early American script is a bit hard to read, of course, but not too challenging for an expert such as yourself.”

“Or yourself, either,” said Rosemary with a smile. “Isn’t it handy that we’re both academics?” She refocused on the letter. “It’s pretty badly faded, but it’s amazing that it’s in this condition—and even that it survived at all. It was in your old barn?”

“In a cache under the floorboards.”

“But how—"

“Seems our Mercy was one smart cookie,” said Jack. “This metal box was sealed with wax.”

"Seriously? She had the forethought to seal it in the midst of all of that craziness? Brilliant."

Rosemary leaned closer to examine the scrap of paper. She slowly read the words aloud, deciphering the old English and swirling handwriting as she went:

I pray now for my poor sister's soul. I had gone to her cell to keep vigil and pray for her through the night. Not arrived in time. Only to see her ruined, running away. I gather our beautiful flower now, the only good to come from it. Proof that flowers can grow up through the mud. We leave tonight. Forced to leave our home. I pray God we return someday to our family lands, to this land which we love so much. Faith the truth will out. I conceal this missive in hope, even now in hope of revelation. The day will come when God will lead some honest soul to find these words of mine. If thou that reads this is that soul, please seek true justice for my dearest. Justice held the only key. Truth and justice no more intertwined. Now set my sister's restless soul at peace."

"What do you make of it?" asked Jack.

"The flower she's gathering is the baby—Hortence's baby."

"Lilly. Yes, that's my conclusion, too."

"She says that Lilly is the only good to come from it. From Hortence's marriage to the awful Jonathan Gallow?"

"Presumably that's the 'mud' she speaks of," said Jack.

"And Mercy was rightfully afraid. She was trying to say something without saying it. I think she knew who'd had it in for her sister, but was too afraid to come out with it. The answer is in these words somewhere. I believe she's trying to tell us who murdered Hortence."

6

"I can't believe you found this. And I can't believe you've kept it a secret for two months."

The lights had flickered back on as if on cue, and Jack, Rosemary, and Izzy were snuggled back into the couch, Mercy's letter carefully laid out on the coffee table in front of them.

"I know! Right?"

"What are the odds that you would move to Paperwick and buy a farm that once belonged to an accused witch, and then decide to renovate the barn and happen upon this treasure?"

"Ah, but if you really think about it, the odds were tipped in my favor," said Jack. "Number one: I'm in love with early American literature and history and married a man who has the same passion for those things, along with anything spooky or witchy or mysterious—that's what drew us both to this area in the first place. Number two: We wanted to live in a college town with an excellent liberal arts department—but that town also had to be steeped in early American history to inspire Charlie's writing. Number three: We heard this farm was up for sale, and once we read about its history—that it had been home to an accused witch—we knew it was the place for us. We saw that old barn and knew it was a relic. We're here precisely *because* we wanted to tap into the history of this place. And when we started digging…"

"You hit pay dirt," said Rosemary.

"Right under our very noses. See, this place was known as Gallow Farm only because Hortence, the eldest of the Clark girls, married a Gallow and her property passed into his hands."

"So, the farm didn't originally belong to Jonathan Gallow. It belonged to Hortence and Mercy."

"To their father, yes. They grew up here. That's why they didn't leave the farm when Jonathan died. They wanted to stay on their family land."

"I get it," said Rosemary. "That's why in spite of everything, Mercy was hoping to come back someday. This was her home."

"Exactly. The only home she'd ever known. But with Hortence dead and Mercy gone, the family next door—the Graves—eventually absorbed this farm into theirs."

"But didn't you say that Matthew Graves was the judge who was ready to condemn Hortence? What if he just wanted her land and executing her was his sick way of grabbing it?"

"But remember, he didn't ever get the chance to execute her. She escaped from the jail the night before her trial."

"Oh. Right."

"As the years went by, the farm passed through various hands, and was divided into smaller parcels of land. Our old barn was fortified, and then improved, but then left to fall to ruins. A couple of months ago, when I wanted to get the goats and the chickens, we decided to renovate it, and in the process of removing what was left of the old, rotting floors, we unearthed this little beauty." Jack took a deep breath.

"Oh, this is good, Jack. This is the best thing ever. It's a great find on its historical merits alone. But do you realize? If we can solve Mercy's riddle, we can tell the true story of what happened to Hortence Gallow."

"*Now set my sister's restless soul at peace*," said Jack, quoting Mercy. "There's a book in there somewhere, and I think you should write it."

"What do you say we collaborate?" asked Rosemary with a smile. "We haven't done that since our senior thesis: *When Words—and Worlds—Collide: History and Literature, Two Sides of the Same Coin.*"

"And it was brilliant," said Jack. "Especially that title. Let's do it!"

Charlie came into the room. "Still coming down like cats and dogs out there," he said. "Oh—sorry, Rosemary. Just dogs. Not cats. Never cats."

"Thank you," said Rosemary, who had the willies from just thinking about cats falling from the sky in great numbers.

"Did Jack show you his prize?" asked Charlie.

"He did," said Rosemary. "We're already planning our bestseller."

"Excellent!" said Charlie. "I'll be the first one standing in line to buy an autographed copy. I'm going to make popcorn." He headed into the kitchen and Rosemary turned back to Jack.

"And as far as your research goes, did Mercy and the baby just disappear? They never came back?"

"Oh, but they *did* come back," said Jack. "Well, Mercy never came back, but Lilly would grow up and have a daughter of her own: Mary. And Mary came back with her family. They lived on the other side of town, though. Not on this farm. But believe it or not, there is still a descendent right here in town —a strange and colorful descendent."

"Seriously? This is amazing! I can meet this descendent?"

"Oh yeah. You're going to meet her."

"I know that those accused of witchcraft were posthumously pardoned by the state of Connecticut in 2006. I bet Hortence's family appreciated that, even if it was hundreds of years too late."

"Pardoned. Yes, they were," said Jack, pouring each of them a fresh cup of coffee. "But not Hortence Gallow."

"But why not?"

"Because remember, Hortence never made it to trial. She was never formally sentenced. Or *officially* executed, either. And even though the records from her case do exist, they're over three hundred years old, and shoddy at best. The point being, Hortence didn't make the list of those who were pardoned. And this descendent—this great-great-great-whatever granddaughter who lives here in Paperwick now—is none too happy about it. In fact, she's mad about a lot of things. And also, she's a nut."

A sudden crash of thunder rattled the windows and both Jack and Rosemary jumped. It was pitch black dark outside now, although every time the lighting flashed, Rosemary could see the silvery trees thrashing wildly in the wind.

Jack got up and added some wood to the fire.

"That's the *history* part of the story as far as I can tell it," he said, sitting down again. "And tomorrow, while I'm at school, you can poke around the Witch's Meadow, where you'll meet someone who can tell you all about the *legend*. And the curse."

"Whoa. The curse?"

"Hortence's curse."

"She cursed the village? Ooh. Did she curse the judge?"

"I'll say no more," said Jack, primly shaking his head. "The rest can wait until your date at the cemetery tomorrow."

"Hold it. Date?"

"Well…research-date-appointment."

Before Rosemary could press the matter, Izzy's ears perked up, and Charlie came back into the room with a huge bowl of buttered popcorn.

"What's the movie tonight?" he asked, plunking down between Jack and Rosemary and giving Izzy a scratch behind the ears.

"I'm going to gain twenty pounds before I leave here," groaned Rosemary, but she took a big handful of popcorn anyway. "But you know what? I don't seem to care. Let's get this party started."

☙ 7 ❧

They'd stayed up so late that Rosemary hadn't even gotten a good look at her bedroom in the old farmhouse before falling into a deep carb-induced sleep. When she opened her eyes the next morning, she didn't know where she was for a moment.

Birds were singing in the trees outside. Light was filtering in through sheer linen curtains. The four-poster bed, which she'd literally sunken into, was covered in a white, fluffy, feathery comforter, tossed with numerous luxurious pillows. The walls were painted a peaceful color that was a cross between sage green, tiffany blue, and an eggshell gray, depending on how the light was hitting it.

Against the far wall was a petite fireplace, trimmed in tiny, colorful mosaic tiles—a surprising splash of color against the neutral paint. A generous basket of fatwood sat next to it.

There was a desk, stocked with a cup of pens and a fresh pad of paper. Jack knew her well.

Rosemary stood, her feet landing on a fluffy faux fur rug that had been tossed over the old hardwood floors. She slid into her slippers and shrugged on the thick, cozy robe that hung from a hook beside a door that led into an equally well-appointed guest bathroom. She splashed a little cool water on her face, made the bed, and then opened the curtains and looked out at a beautiful, sunny day. The rain had left cold, clean air behind. The trees and damp grass sparkled in the sunlight.

Rosemary followed the smell of freshly brewed coffee down the hall and through the living room, into the kitchen, where Jack sat at the table, sipping from a steaming mug and reading the newspaper.

“Good morning, Sunshine,” he said. “Sleep well?”

“Like a rock,” said Rosemary, pouring herself a cup of coffee and taking the chair beside Jack. “Where’s Charlie?”

“Out for a run,” said Jack, shaking his head. “Can you believe I’m married to a person who actually enjoys exercise and gets out and sweats almost every day? By *choice*?”

Rosemary laughed. “Well, they do say opposites attract.”

“Indeed, they do,” said Jack, standing. “I’m making omelets. How many eggs for you?”

"Two. What time's your first class?"

"Not until eleven. I thought I'd drop you at the churchyard while I'm in class, and then at twelve-thirty, we can meet for lunch, and I'll take you to the museum."

"Sounds great. I can't wait to get a look at those headstones. There's so much history in this part of the country."

A few minutes later, as they enjoyed Jack's cheesy mushroom and leek omelets and the caffeine finally kicked in, Rosemary could feel her energy returning.

"So, about this curse . . ."

"Nope. I'm not cracking. You're going to have to wait until we get to the church. I've got an expert ready and waiting."

--

Energized by breakfast and with extra time before she and Jack were to head into town, Rosemary decided to take a brisk turn around the farm, which included a few minutes spent sitting in an Adirondack chair on the dock at the edge of the large pond/small lake that lay just down from the house. The water was shimmering in the morning light, and surrounding its grassy banks were woods that made the whole place feel beautifully secluded. The only other house in view was a snug little cottage which sat about a quarter of the way around the circle of the pond from Jack and Charlie's house. An old red truck was parked outside, and Rosemary wondered who the neighbor was, but the thought slipped from her mind when she heard the honking of a flock of wild geese flying overhead. This place was breathtaking. In the cool air, Rosemary could smell wood smoke and fallen leaves and a hint of pine. She couldn't remember the last time she'd felt so peaceful or content.

She showered and dressed, and she and Jack made the short drive into town.

Jack dropped her near the old graveyard, not far from the town square, alongside a historic church which ironically, was resplendent in its simplicity. A square saltbox of a structure, its facade had large, arched, clear glass windows on either side of a neatly trimmed wooden door. The graveyard itself formed a rough rectangle, stretching out away from the little church, with trees on three sides, the church on the fourth.

The church bore a historic marker that read "First Church: 1628" and went on to describe the Puritan congregation that had founded the parish, with a small note beneath it announcing that services were still held in the church every Sunday morning at nine and ten-thirty—with a coffee hour in between—and presided over by a Reverend Robert Smith.

Rosemary smiled up at the simple steeple, which, instead of a cross, was topped by a weathervane in the shape of a trumpeting angel. Then she quietly, reverently made her way into the cemetery, and stood at the edge, looking over the old headstones in amazement.

She walked along the little gravel path that wound between the crooked rows of headstones, stopping to take photos here and there, and planning out the path visitors would take at the festival. Today was Tuesday. Only a few days until the festival opened on Friday. In that time, there were costumes to put together, scripts to write, and final plans to make.

That morning over omelets, Rosemary and Jack had discussed their list of the five historical figures they'd chosen to tell their tales in the graveyard. Hortence Gallow, in the meadow, would be number six, and then visitors could loop back around the outside of the churchyard from the meadow, to the village square, where the rest of the festival would be in full swing.

There were little lights already lining the paths in the graveyard. In addition, they would add luminarias to cast a festive glow, and Jack had obtained twenty-five small lanterns with realistic-looking flickering flames. These they would hang from the trees to bring just the right amount of eerie light to the scene. Groups of visitors would be ushered through the graveyard from one featured character to another. Each ghost would be standing next to his or her own grave, ready to say a little bit about his or her life, and death, in Paperwick.

The graveyard was a haven to a historian. Some of the names were especially wonderful. There was Creedence Willow, wife of John Willow, who passed away in 1667—a mother to nine, grandmother to thirty-three. And Wilbur Smith, who had lived to be ninety—an amazing feat for the 17th century.

"Here lieth buried the body of Felicity Cummings," mumbled Rosemary, as she ran her fingers over the letters of a weathered, cracked headstone.

"Happy name," said a voice from behind her, startling Rosemary.

She turned to see the mayor, Samuel Wright, standing between two old headstones, hands in his pockets, smiling.

"Sorry," he said, picking his way around various plots to come closer. "Didn't mean to spook you."

"That's okay," said Rosemary, standing up and tucking her notebook under her arm so that she could shake his hand. "Thought I'd seen a ghost there for a moment."

"No such luck." He laughed. "How's it going? Jack says you're helping out with the Historical Society's fundraiser."

"Yes," said Rosemary. "He tells me you're all set to play Elias Wright—an early arrival here in the village. He's picked out five other colorful characters to bring to life as well."

"Wonderful idea," said Sam. "Glad to be part of it."

"I think it's especially great that you're going to represent your own family. Can you tell me a bit about the Wright family plot?"

"That's what I'm here for," Sam said with a smile.

So, this was her research-date-appointment? Jack was trying to set her up with the mayor! Admittedly, he was handsome and charming.

"Right this way, my lady," Sam said, leading Rosemary to the furthest corner of the graveyard, which was tucked away toward the tree line, near the entrance to the meadow. "Meet the Wrights." He swept an arm out over the corner and made a little bow. "And here lies old Elias, born in 1705, whose name I actually bear as my middle name. Elias was the first son born here in Paperwick."

"Have you done a lot of research into your family tree, then?" asked Rosemary.

"Would you still respect me if I told you no?" Sam answered with a boyish grin. "Around here, it's practically blasphemy—not knowing your whole history—so please don't tell on me. My secretary is always after me to sign up for one of those ancestry things. She's into the whole genealogy bit. I've just never gotten around to really digging deep. Too busy in the land of the living, I guess. I do know we Wrights showed up here in the early 1700s and have been here ever since."

“Then your family missed the whole witch drama?” asked Rosemary, raising an eyebrow.

Sam laughed heartily. “Has the president of the Paperwick Historical Society been bringing you up to speed on that story?”

Rosemary smiled. “He knows I’m as big a nerd as he is when it comes to history.”

“Yes, sadly, my family missed out on that drama,” Sam said. “But better late than never.”

He stepped a little closer and locked eyes with Rosemary, and she felt a wave of heat coming to her cheeks.

“I, um, like your shirt,” Rosemary said, gesturing to the bright orange, gold, and green plaid, then inwardly chiding herself for not being able to think of a more clever thing to say.

Sam glanced down at his shirt and then smiled at her. “It’s nice, huh? I’m trying to match the trees.”

“Very appropriate for the mayor of Paperwick,” Rosemary said with a smile.

“And you look very nice today, too,” said Sam, taking in Rosemary’s casual jeans and cardigan. “Your hair is even a nice fall color.”

Rosemary put a hand to her hair, which she'd twisted into a loose bun using the tiny mirror in Holly Golightly on the way into town.

"Thank you. This place is a real treasure," she said, looking across the whole scene, taking in the church and the maze of headstones—and hoping the mayor wouldn't notice her turning as red as one of Mrs. Potter's apples.

"It is indeed," he agreed. "Believe it or not, that's why I'm here. I have a meeting in a few minutes to address protecting this treasure."

"Oh? Then you're not—I mean, a meeting here in the churchyard?"

Maybe Samuel Wright wasn't Rosemary's research date after all. She must've misunderstood him. And if she was honest, she felt relieved that Jack didn't have Sam in mind for her. She couldn't deny he was attractive . . . But something about him made her uncomfortable. Maybe he was too confident. Too smooth.

"Yep—well, just over there in the meadow," Sam answered, motioning toward a path that ran through the band of trees and into the adjoining meadow. "I want to make some important changes around here—necessary changes, as we attract greater numbers of tourists and put Paperwick on the map. We're in the process of installing monitors, both here in the graveyard and in the meadow. See, I want to be able to welcome people who visit Paperwick to come and see the history here, but I also want to keep it safe."

"I'm glad to hear you're protecting your history," said Rosemary, even though the thought of "putting Paperwick on the map" didn't sit well with her. She hated the idea of this peaceful village swarming with tourists. "So where are the monitors? Are we on camera right now?" Rosemary looked around and saw no sign of any modern contraption.

"Oh, they're all around. In the trees, mainly. They're installed, I should say. But the kinks haven't been worked out yet. That's what the meeting is about. My city manager is in charge of the project. He and I are going to walk the whole place, so he can bring me up to speed and we can figure out what's going wrong."

Rosemary nodded.

Sam smiled and looked at Rosemary's notebook. "So how does it all work, anyway? How did you and Jack decide who to..." He waved a hand across the graveyard. "Who to re-animate, as it were?"

"Well, we've both been doing preliminary research on the village—and especially on the founders and earliest inhabitants. Guests will enter by way of the church, over there. And the first spirit they'll come across is Josias King, right over here." Rosemary pointed to an old crumbly marker, half covered in moss. "He was pastor for forty-seven years at the First Church. A very interesting man."

"To say the least," said Sam, nodding. "In fact, if you ever want some juicy reading, you've got to check out Old Josias's church logs. The original books are in a museum in Washington, D.C., but around eight years back, after my first successful election, the Historical Society did a reproduction and gave it to me as a gift. Josias kept records of the usual stuff—births, deaths, members of the parish. But—get this—he also recorded the confessions he heard and kept track of the advice he gave. He used this record to create extensive prayer lists, reminding himself how to pray for his parishioners. Fascinating stuff!"

"Wow! I bet no one would've told him anything if they'd known he was recording their confessions for posterity."

"No kidding. He kept the books hidden away and locked up tight, because of course, he was thinking that would protect them from prying eyes, and in his time, it did. And he tried to protect them even after his death by requesting that they be burned. He'd asked his wife to do the deed, but when it came down to it, she just couldn't bring herself to destroy all that was left of the love of her life. So, she kept them under lock and key, probably always thinking that one day she'd work up the gumption to toss her husband's writings into the fire. But she never did."

"Amazing. And you have a copy?"

"Yep. The only copy, actually—I mean, aside from the real thing. The Society had them typeset and bound into one thick volume, just for me. They jokingly titled it *Paperwick: The Original Sins, A Cautionary Tale*. I'll lend it to you if you'd like."

"I'd love to read it. Absolutely."

"Great. Keep this on the down-low, but I haven't really even read it yet myself, aside from flipping through it a couple times."

"I'll be glad to give you a full report once I've read it," said Rosemary.

"I was thinking maybe we could read it together. I've got it at my house—well, in my backyard, technically. I have a cozy little woodshed that I converted into a home office. I'd love to show it to you. Stop by anytime," said Sam, and something in the tenor of his voice made Rosemary hope he wasn't flirting with her. This defied the usual logic, since Sam seemed like a great guy—the kind of guy whose attention most women would enjoy. But then why did Rosemary have the feeling that she might be only one of many women whom Sam had invited to his "home office" for one reason or another? She would go there and borrow the book, all right. But not without Jack in tow.

"So, who else, other than the esteemed Reverend Josias King is on your list of ghosts?" he asked.

"Well, aside from him and your own excellent Elias Wright, we've got Joseph Filbert, Phillipa Anderson, and Silas Martin. And of course, then folks will move out to the meadow and meet Hortence Gallow."

"The witch herself," said Sam. "The grand finale. Perfect. I bet that'll get Ingrid all riled up."

"Ingrid?"

"Ingrid Clark. Great-great-however-many-greats grand-daughter of Hortence."

"Ah, so her name is Ingrid. I haven't met her yet, but I'm looking forward to that."

"Are you?"

"Shouldn't I be?"

A slight shadow passed over Sam's face, but then was gone.

"You're an interesting woman, Rosemary."

Sam walked closer, until he was close enough to smell. And he smelled good, Rosemary noticed. He met her eyes, and for a moment, she said nothing, as she was unable to think about anything other than how blue his were. But then he looked away, a small grin on his face.

"What does this mean?" he asked, going back over to Felicity's marker, squatting down, and running his hand over the winged skull decoration at the top. "I've always wondered."

"Oh," Rosemary knelt down next to him. "That's the winged death's head. First, you have to remember that the Puritans didn't like anything resembling the Catholicism they'd left behind in England. So, no crosses or icons would do for their grave markers. Here, the skull represents death; the wings, resurrection. By the end of the 18th century, this kind of design had all but disappeared."

Rosemary fingered the feathers of the stone wings. "This is really fine workmanship," she said.

"Indeed, it is," he said quietly. But his eyes moved from the stone to Rosemary.

Sam reached up and touched her hand, then looked at her with genuine admiration. "Thank you for coming and doing this for the Historical Society. For the *town*. There's so much history here. It's high time we celebrate all that this place is."

Then he stood and reached out a hand to help Rosemary do the same.

"So, you've lived here all your life?" Rosemary asked, dusting off her pants.

"Oh yes," Sam answered. "Except for a few years away at college, and then grad school. I'm a homebody. Wouldn't want to be anywhere else."

"It's good to feel that about a place," said Rosemary.

He turned to look at her again, a question in his eyes. But before another word was said, Seth walked up.

"Boo!" he said with a smile. "Hope I'm not interrupting."

"Not at all," said Rosemary. "I was just telling the mayor here about these headstones."

"Ah, the winged death's head," said Seth with a knowing nod.

"Hello, Dr. McGuire," said Sam, reaching out to shake hands.

"Please. Call me Seth."

The two men stayed locked in their handshake a beat too long, Rosemary thought—and it wasn't the same kind of long handshake she'd had with Seth the day before.

"And what brings you to the cemetery on this fine day?" asked Sam.

"I have an appointment with Ms. Grey here," answered Seth, nodding at Rosemary.

Now it all made sense. It was definitely more plausible that Jack was trying to set Rosemary up with Seth, rather than the mayor. Rosemary smiled, looking back and forth from one man to the other, thinking about how she was going to exact revenge on Jack for putting her in this awkward situation.

"And you, Mayor Wright?" asked Seth.

"I'm here for a meeting over in the meadow, believe it or not." Sam glanced at his watch. "In fact, I've got some preparations to make beforehand, so I'd better be going."

"Ah, yes—I believe you're considering making it into a park," said Seth.

"A gorgeous park," said Sam, eyeing Rosemary. "Rosemary, it's been a pleasure. Again, thanks for doing this."

"Glad to," said Rosemary.

With that, Sam followed the little path that led past his own forefathers and mothers, through the trees, and into the meadow.

8

"Are you warm enough?" asked Seth, noticing Rosemary give off a little shiver.

"What? Oh—yes. I just felt a chill for some reason."

"You know what they say that means, don't you?"

"No. What do they say that means?" Rosemary couldn't help but warm to this man, with his rumpled sweater, slightly messy hair, and lopsided grin. He was the polar opposite of the charming Sam Wright.

"It means a ghost has just passed through you," said Seth. "And we are, after all, in a graveyard. So, the odds are pretty good."

"I just hope it was one of the nice ones," said Rosemary.

"Oh, I'm sure it was. Most of these folks here are pretty friendly. Except that guy over there, maybe."

Rosemary looked where Seth was pointing and walked there to get a closer look.

"Jonathan Gallow," she read the name. "Died August 1668. Wow. Hortence's husband."

"The very one," said Seth. "A drunk and probably an abusive husband, based on what I can gather from medical records."

"Mercy's records?" asked Rosemary. "So, Mercy even wrote down treatment of her own sister's ailments?"

"Oh, Mercy wrote everything down. She kept impeccable records. That's how we know about the baby."

"Hortence's baby? Lilly?"

"Yep. Glad to hear Jack's brought you up to speed. The story—the history of this place is fascinating. It's one of the reasons I worry about what our esteemed mayor is up to, with his meeting in the meadow," said Seth, looking toward the path that led off through the trees.

"He's turning it into a park?" Rosemary asked. "That doesn't sound so bad."

"He's turning the town into a tourist destination," said Seth, frowning. "The park is going to have a statue of a what is supposed to be Hortence. He's calling it a *tribute*. But the preliminary designs have her dressed to look like a witch—which of course, she wasn't."

"What? You mean, like a pointy hat and all?"

"Not *that* bad. But yes, she does have a broom in one hand and there's a cat at her feet."

Rosemary grimaced. "She was a midwife. A healer."

Seth nodded in agreement. "And he wants to rename some of the streets to capitalize on the history. Worst of all, he's got the town council to agree to offering incentives for developers who want to come and bring in hotels and restaurants and things like that."

"How awful. But the town seems to love him. They keep reelecting him, don't they?"

"He wasn't like this during his earlier terms. He's been a good leader. This business with the development has come up fairly recently. I don't know if someone got to him, maybe made him an offer he couldn't refuse . . . Or maybe his political aspirations have changed. He hasn't put any of these ideas to the voters as of yet, and he's charmed the council into doing whatever he says. I mean, he argues that he's protecting the town, that he wants to share the town with the rest of the world. It all *sounds* good, the way he spins it. But underneath." Seth shook his head. "I hate to say it, but I sort of wish someone would step up and run against him."

"Charlie says he's a shoe-in. Incumbents are always hard to beat," said Rosemary.

"And he's a hometown boy. The old-timers here have watched him grow up—known his family for generations. They trust him to do what's best for the town, and so far, he's done that. I think the only reason I can see any problems with this new agenda is because I've only lived here for a year, so I'm still a bit of an outsider."

"Me too," said Rosemary. "I mean, I know nothing about what's going on in Paperwick—heck, I was barely able to find the place. But even after one day here . . . Well, there's something unspoiled about this place. I wouldn't want anything to change that."

"Me, neither." Seth glanced at her, started to walk on, but then stopped and smiled down at her for a moment.

He didn't say anything and neither did Rosemary. She found herself smiling up at him—not because it was one of those moments when a person is supposed to smile. And not just because he was looking at her that way.

She was smiling because she was happy.

The day was glorious, the leaves were brilliant in shades of autumn and there was a nip in the air. She felt like she was among friends instead of strangers for the first time in a while, and she was surrounded by history. She had a moment, a split second of clarity, that here she was, in an old graveyard on a beautiful day with an interesting man and all that lay ahead that day was time with Jack and Charlie, and learning about the legend of Hortence Gallow, and planning for the festival. And Rosemary had two entire weeks of this ahead of her. She felt like her heart was getting lighter and lighter by the minute.

"So . . . are you ready to hear about the curse?" asked Seth.

"Oh, definitely," said Rosemary.

"Then let's walk this way."

Seth led Rosemary into the tree-shaded path that connected the little churchyard to the Witch's Meadow.

9

The meadow was beautiful. It was a huge clearing framed by trees and sprinkled with fallen leaves and a few late-blooming wildflowers. There was also a scattering of trees growing inside the meadow itself—the most prominent one a gigantic old maple tree, ablaze in its red foliage, that stood right in the center. It was so brightly festooned that Rosemary would've sworn light was coming out of it, beckoning passersby to stop and wonder at its beauty.

"Is that the tree?" asked Rosemary, almost in a whisper, as they stepped into the meadow.

"Where Hortence is buried? Yep," said Seth. "Come on. I'll show you."

Together they approached the tree. How many hundreds of years had it stood here? It was probably just a baby back in

Hortence's time. If only trees could speak, it could identify her killer and finally set the story straight.

Rosemary took a step forward but then stopped in her tracks. There, standing serenely in the shade of the great tree, was a cat. It was a very small cat, nonchalantly licking its paw and then running the paw behind its ear. When a twig cracked under Rosemary's boot, the cat froze and leveled bright green eyes at her.

"Good gosh," whispered Rosemary, suddenly covered in goosebumps. "Go away! Shoo!"

The wind picked up a bit, and Rosemary felt suddenly cold. She cleared her throat and forced herself to take another step closer to the creature. "I mean it, cat. Be on your way."

The cat's green eyes were offset by its long, tortoiseshell hair —a gorgeous creature to one not horrified of cats, Rosemary felt sure.

But while Rosemary was completely discombobulated by the cat, the cat didn't seem to mind Rosemary's presence in the least. It suddenly decided to rub contentedly up against the trunk of the tree, probably making that strange rumbling noise cats make, and then finally sauntered off in the other direction, further out into the meadow, until it slipped just inside the far tree line, where Rosemary was sure it was still watching. She could feel the green eyes.

"I can't believe it. Did you see that?" asked Seth, who'd been completely silent during the whole cat encounter.

"Clearly, I saw it. I told it to go away."

"No, I mean, it looked like her cat—Hortence's cat. Why did you shoo it away?"

"I, uh, don't get along very well with them."

"With cats? Really?"

"I… Well, okay, I'm scared of them."

"Of cats? Really?"

"Stop saying that!"

"What?"

"'Cats' and 'really.'"

"Oh. Sorry. It's just that cats are really so—oops. Sorry. These animals are so gentle and smart. I'd think you'd like them. Bad childhood experience or something?"

"No. I just… Okay, if you must know, those Siamese cats in *Lady and the Tramp* scared me to death, and I've never gotten over it."

"Ah. Well, that was just a kitten. And not evil, like those Siamese cats in the movie."

"But now that you mention it, that cat did fit Jack's description of Hortence's cat—the little imp she supposedly talked to."

"And today of all days for it to be standing in this particular place, when I'm about to tell you about Hortence's curse. It's like magic or fate or . . . *How cool is that*?"

"Oh, yeah. Really cool," said Rosemary, even though she could've done without the furry visitor.

She stopped for a moment and looked up into the branches of the tree, feeling all at once the weight of the truth that a person had actually once died here—a person who had probably done nothing wrong and yet had paid the price for the sorrows and superstitions of a whole village.

"History, even though I've spent my whole adult life and much of my childhood studying it, always takes me by surprise." Rosemary let out a long sigh. "I can read all about the witch trials of Connecticut, for instance, in books, and feel fascinated by the stories, by the facts and the characters. But every time I actually visit a historical site—see the places where the people from the pages actually lived and fought and died . . . Well, I never fail to be astounded."

Rosemary looked over at Seth, who was staring at her with a mix of admiration and understanding.

"You're an anthropologist," said Rosemary. "You totally get that, right?"

"Yes I do. And you've said it perfectly."

A chill breeze rumpled the fallen leaves around the grand old tree as Rosemary caught sight of the stone marker. She knelt beside it to take a better look. Someone had left a small bouquet of rosemary mixed with dried yellow blooms. It was bound with a length of deep wine-colored twine, and it lay alongside the gray stone. She looked up at Seth, who knelt down beside her, picked up the bouquet, and carefully turned it over in his hands.

"Rosemary for remembrance."

"Just like your name," said Seth. "And I wonder what these yellow ones are for."

"I don't recognize them," said Rosemary. "They're beautiful."

She turned her attention back to the stone marker, dusted some dried leaves off its surface, and then read aloud: "Here lies Hortence Gallow, age twenty-five, widow of Jonathan Gallow. Accused of witchcraft, but never tried, Hortence was found here, dead, on November 7, 1668. For many years, her burial place was marked only by this tree and her family's determination to keep her story alive. May humankind learn from its mistakes, lest history repeat itself. ~The Paperwick Historical Society, October 31, 2000."

Rosemary fumbled with excited hands in her bag for her camera.

"Are you kidding me? Did you and Jack plan it this way? Today is November seventh! We're here precisely three hundred fifty-one years after Hortence died? To the day? That must be why someone placed the flowers here. I need to hear about the curse," she said, snapping a few photos of the marker with the bouquet beside it.

"I thought you'd never ask," joked Seth, and they both sat down under the tree. He offered his jacket to Rosemary, who was starting to shiver a little bit as the breeze blew the dried leaves around in gentle swirls.

"As you already know—because I know Jack told you—Hortence was accused of witchcraft and taken to the jail house. There she was left overnight, in the cold, to await her trial the next morning."

"Right. And Mercy was coming to sit and pray with her sister, but the story goes that when she got there, Hortence was not in her cell, but the cell was locked up tight."

"So, you've seen Jack's find from the old barn—the riddle Mercy left behind."

Rosemary nodded.

"The story goes that just after Mercy arrived that night," Seth continued, "another witness had come to offer comfort and friendship to Hortence: the sisters' friend Elizabeth Graves, from the farm next door."

"Elizabeth was the wife of Matthew Graves, the judge who'd accused Hortence."

"Correct. Small towns—am I right? Anyway, Elizabeth would later go on record saying that she'd seen Hortence, outside the jail house, running away from the prison that night. Elizabeth claimed she had gone to the jail, taking some food and a blanket along to offer to the prisoner through the cell's outer window. But when she called out to Hortence and didn't get an answer, she peered into the window, and saw that the cell was empty. She said she heard a wild shriek and turned to see Hortence running through the dark amid thunder and lightning, wearing no shoes, speaking gibberish and calling evil spirits down on the village itself."

"Ooh. Spooky."

"Matthew Graves writes all about this in his journal. He sent Elizabeth home, thinking that Hortence would eventually return to the Clark farm and perhaps Elizabeth could talk some reason into her. He also wrote that 'the witch' had cursed him that night. That he had attempted to speak to her, to pray for her soul, and that she pointed at him and spat out a curse, saying that she knew she was marked for death, but that her death would be avenged many times over."

At this, Seth dug around in his satchel and took out a folder stuffed with papers. He shuffled through them and pulled out a photocopy of what appeared to be a very old document.

"What's this?" asked Rosemary.

"The page from Matthew Graves' journal," said Seth. "Read this passage here."

Rosemary looked at the lines Seth was pointing to.

"The witch hath spoken and in a whisper did sayeth, 'Justice will be served its own death sentence, on a night like this as black as ink, for many ages hence. My spirit will come again and again and destroy the one who ruined me until the truth is revealed. Until that day, his line may never again sit in the judgement seat.'" Rosemary's eyes widened. "So, she was cursing the judge?"

"Yes. And any of his descendants who would sit in judgement, it would appear."

"But did anything happen to him? I mean, I know he got his hands on Hortence and Mercy's farmland."

"He did. And he got to enjoy that land for about a year. But then, Matthew Graves met with an untimely death. He was found dead, right here, at the foot of this tree, the year after Hortence died."

"On a night as black as ink?"

"You guessed it. Judge Graves had started going a bit crazy with worry about the curse by then. He wrote in his journal that he'd seen Hortence's cat a few days before he died."

"Her, um, cat, you say?" Rosemary glanced toward the trees where the green-eyed monster was probably still lurking.

"But wait, there's more. If you read a little further, Hortence had specified that her victims would all bear 'the hateful mark' that had led to her own condemnation."

"The witch's mark? The goat's horn thingy?"

"Yep. It's all in the judge's journal."

"So, when he died, Matthew Graves had the mark?"

"By the time he died, you see, his wife Elizabeth had taken over as village nurse. And so, she had taken up Mercy's record book and she kept it current. In it, she wrote about her husband's death, and she says he bore a mark which she'd never seen before."

"Did Elizabeth blame Hortence for her husband's death, then?"

"Not directly. But Elizabeth Graves was careful with her words. An intelligent woman. She knew what she was writing. She said only that Matthew was cursed, and that his curse had led to his demise."

"*Seriously* spooky." Rosemary pulled the jacket Seth had given her tighter around her shoulders.

"And Matthew wasn't the only Graves to pay the price. He and Elizabeth had five children—all of whom Hortence had delivered, by the way. One of those sons, John, had a son, Thomas, who was also a judge in the later 1700s. Records show that Thomas died at only twenty-five, of a heart attack."

"Did he bear the mark?"

"We're not sure. The medical records say nothing of it, but there were rumors, of course."

"Anyone else?"

"A few generations later, another Graves man was on the town council. He died in a freak carriage accident."

"And the mark?"

"Again, not in the official records, but there were rumors that he was marked."

"These deaths were probably all coincidental."

"And then there was Frederick Graves, an attorney, died 1834 during his run for senator."

"Hmm."

"And DeWitt Graves, died around the turn of the century, 1901, on his way to the courthouse to turn in a convicted thief."

"Wow."

"Of course, we're standing way back and looking at a long period of history—1668 until now—so in hindsight, there aren't all that many deaths that could be attributed to the curse, and of course they could all just be coincidental. Probably are, in fact. But the thought of the curse coming to pass is way more fun. These deaths were all in that family line—all men who had something to do with the business of judging others. And who knows? Maybe Hortence really was more pagan than Puritan at heart. That's why her story is so interesting. In her last moments on this earth, she issued a deadly curse. Was that a sort of admission of guilt? I mean, if she wasn't a witch—"

"Then why level a curse? And how did she know she was about to be murdered—'marked for death'?" Rosemary wondered. "After all, she was very much alive when she said her death would be avenged and laid down this curse. But she was running away, presumably, with the hope of *escaping* death. And *many ages hence?* What does that mean? How many deaths would there need to be for Hortence to call it even?"

"I guess she's on the rampage until the truth comes out about who murdered her," said Seth with a grin. He glanced at his watch. "Oops. It's eleven-twenty. I actually have a class to teach in ten minutes," he said, hurriedly getting up. "Can I give you a lift over to the college?"

"Thanks, but Jack is meeting me here for lunch in an hour. I'll poke around until then."

"Have fun."

"Oh. Don't forget your jacket," Rosemary said, taking the warm fleecy garment off and holding it out.

"Why don't you hold onto that. It's nippy out, and you can return it to me tonight."

"Oh, that's right. You're coming out to the farm for dinner, right?"

"Yep. Looking forward to it." He started off back in the direction they'd come.

"Thank you, Seth. And thanks for telling me about the curse!"

"See you tonight!"

Rosemary watched him disappear into the trees. Then her gaze wandered back to the stone marking Hortence Gallow's final resting place, and she felt a chill run up and down her spine.

"Was that you, Hortence?" she whispered with a smile, and put Seth's jacket back on.

10

It would be exciting to have the actor playing Hortence on the night of the festival act out the curse as part of her presentation. What a perfectly haunting finale for the cemetery crawl!

After jotting down a few notes summarizing her visit with Seth, Rosemary took out her camera again. If she and Jack did decide to write a book—or even a scholarly article—about Hortence Gallow, they'd need plenty of photographs to go along with it.

She decided to photograph the whole meadow, then move back over to the graveyard and take some shots of Jonathan Gallow's grave marker. No one was around, which was ideal, since, in Rosemary's experience, people usually didn't appreciate having their picture taken by a complete stranger.

There were several scenic trails leading off from the meadow into the woods in different directions. Rosemary heard distant voices and caught a glimpse of the mayor and another man, walking through the trees, the mayor pointing this way and that. Rosemary smiled. They must be talking about the security cameras in the trees. Now that she had seen the pristine beauty of this place, she hoped that whatever "improvements" they made would be respectful and unobtrusive.

When they'd disappeared back into the woods, Rosemary decided it would be a good time to take one panoramic shot of the whole Witches' Meadow, and then follow that up with shots of the maple tree and the stone marker. She set her camera on panoramic mode, and then slowly began her scan of the tree-lined grounds.

Suddenly, a flash of movement and bright color caught her eye. She put down her camera and squinted into the distance. Was it a person? Yes, sure enough, there was someone, lurking in the trees, watching in the direction the mayor and his companion had gone. The person was wearing very odd clothing, and appeared to be following the mayor at a safe distance, dodging behind trees and brush.

Rosemary didn't exactly know what to do. Technically, the person wasn't doing anything wrong, but this was certainly suspicious behavior. Should Rosemary call someone? Should she approach the stranger? Call out to the mayor? She moved closer to the trunk of the maple tree and subtly used her camera to zoom in on the lurker for a better look.

It was a woman—a crazy looking woman, with bright, silver hair cut short and sticking out in all directions. She was wearing a billowy purple top over pink and black striped leggings with lime green boots. As Rosemary tried to focus in on the woman's face, her head turned suddenly, as if she had felt she was being watched. She looked right at Rosemary. With a sinking feeling, Rosemary knew she'd been caught red-handed. She felt her cheeks burning as the woman emerged from the trees and stalked across the meadow in her direction.

There was no way to avoid the confrontation, and the woman looked angry, so Rosemary pasted on her most innocent smile.

"What do you think you are doing, young lady?" the woman asked in a sharp tone.

Rosemary chided herself for her own split second of vanity that someone still thought she looked like a *young lady*.

"Oh, hello. Sorry about that," she stuttered, feeling like a kid fessing up to a teacher who'd just caught her cheating. "I was photographing the meadow for a book I'm writing—well, *thinking* of writing. I didn't mean to get you in the shot. It must've appeared that I was taking your picture. But I assure you, I was not." Rosemary cleared her throat and looked at her feet.

"You're writing a book? About what?"

Rosemary was surprised by the woman's response. She looked up and was shocked by the bright green eyes that met hers, clearly examining her with intelligent scrutiny. A ridiculous notion crossed Rosemary's mind, that the cat she had seen earlier had somehow transformed itself into this woman.

"Hortence Gallow," Rosemary said, tilting her head toward the stone marker.

The woman paused for a moment, perking up her ears as the sound of raised voices came from the direction of the woods. Rosemary couldn't tell whose voices they were, but someone was either yelling across a distance, in order to be heard, or else yelling in an angry way.

The strange woman rolled her eyes as though she knew exactly what was going on back in the trees. She seemed to shake off that thought and turned her attention back to Rosemary. "Why would you do that? Why would you write a book about her?" The question sounded grumpy, but no longer angry.

"Because I think Hortence's story is fascinating. And she deserves to have it told. She was a midwife—you probably know that if you're from around here. She took care of people. She didn't deserve to come to such a horrible end."

The woman nodded, still scowling.

"She died right here, you know," said Rosemary. "On this very day—"

"Three hundred fifty-one years ago," the woman finished.

"Exactly," said Rosemary, surprised. "I'm Rosemary Grey, by the way." She extended a hand, which the woman looked at but didn't shake.

"Ingrid Clark," was the curt reply.

"Ingrid Clark? Are you? I mean, you're Hortence's . . ."

"Great, great, great—well, eleven-times great descendent. You get the picture." Ingrid looked back toward the woods, then down at Hortence's stone marker.

"You left the rosemary here, didn't you?" asked Rosemary softly. "Rosemary for remembrance, right?"

This was met with a look of surprise followed by a brief nod of admission.

"And what's this yellow flower?"

"I don't know," said Ingrid. "I do this every year on this day. As did my mother and her mother before her. I was trying to have a quiet moment here, and then that idiot mayor and his imbecile sidekick showed up and started yakking about putting a camera in this tree and that tree, and all their other stupid plans for the meadow. Can you believe they have the audacity to come here and do that today of all days? I'd wager they don't even know what day it is—that's how little they really care. They only care about Hortence as far as they can capitalize on her memory."

"But they want to make it into a park, don't they?"

"Roadside attraction is more like it. Freak show. I can't have that happen to my meadow."

"Is this your land then?"

"The town owns it," Ingrid said, shaking her head. "But that jerk Wright is pulling all the strings. He could tell them all to jump off a cliff and they probably would."

"That's why you were . . . keeping an eye on them, in the woods," said Rosemary.

"Someone's got to. I know for a fact I'm not the only one who's against Mayor Wright's idea of improving this meadow. There are others. Most are too scared to step forward and be named. No one wants the golden boy's bad opinion. But I don't care what he thinks of me, and I'm here to tell you, they'll spoil everything."

Rosemary nodded. "That would be a terrible shame."

Again, Ingrid looked surprised. "You agree with me?"

"I agree that this meadow needs to be protected."

"Maybe the mayor would listen to you. He likes pretty young women."

"Oh, I doubt an out-of-towner like me would have much pull here."

Ingrid came a step closer to Rosemary and peered into her eyes. "No . . ." She seemed to be suddenly lost in some distant thought. "You're not an out-of-towner."

"Oh, I assure you, I am. I'm from New York."

"But not really," said Ingrid, still looking at Rosemary as though she could see right through her.

"What do you mean?"

"I mean you're home."

Rosemary smiled. "What makes you think that?"

"I have a knack about these things."

"Uh-huh. Well, I do *feel* at home here. The truth is, I wander around a lot."

Ingrid gave a little snort. "Nice jacket."

Rosemary looked down at Seth's jacket, confused. "Thanks. It's not mine. It belongs to—"

Ingrid gave another little snort.

"What?"

"Don't fight it, sister. Just let it be."

Ingrid started to walk off.

"Hold on, Ingrid. Um, Ms. Clark. Can I ask you some questions about Hortence? I mean, for the book."

Ingrid stopped and turned back.

"Also, we're putting on a little cemetery crawl—to raise money for the Historical Society, and I thought maybe—"

"What? That dog-and-pony show?" Ingrid gasped. "You're all going to make a mockery of my family! I thought you might be different, but I see I was wrong." She shook her head and turned to go.

"No! Ingrid! I mean, Ms. Clark. I want to set the story straight, don't you see? I want to make them all see how amazing Hortence was."

At this, Ingrid stopped walking but didn't turn around.

"My friend Jack and his husband bought the farm—the farm that used to belong to your family. Jack found a note Mercy wrote before she left Paperwick."

Ingrid slowly turned back and looked at Rosemary in disbelief.

"She said some things in the note that don't make sense. And then there's the curse. I need to know what these things mean.

I want to find out the truth, Ms. Clark. I want to tell Hortence's story—your family's story. Would you please let us interview you, so we can hear your side?"

Ingrid scoffed, then looked back at Rosemary.

"Have you seen her cat?" she asked, finally.

"Um. What?"

"You've seen her cat, haven't you?"

"I saw a cat here this morning."

"Her spirit is on the move again," said Ingrid, looking skyward, her crazy hair catching in a wind that swept in suddenly. "That's what it means."

"*On the move*? What do you mean?"

"It means another death. It means we need to finally set her free. And the only way to do that is to expose her killer."

"Are you serious?" Rosemary pulled Seth's jacket tighter around herself.

"I'll think about it," said Ingrid, and she headed back toward the woods.

"The interview?"

"I'll think about it," she called grumpily over her shoulder before disappearing into the trees.

It took a while for Rosemary's heart to stop pounding. It had only been a couple of short hours since Jack had dropped her off this morning and she'd wandered through the graveyard, but it seemed like an age. It had been quite a productive morning so far. She'd taken notes and photos, reviewed the names for the cemetery crawl and found all of their headstones, learned all about a legend and a curse, and met an actual descendent of a three hundred fifty-one-year-old ghost. And it wasn't even lunchtime yet!

Rosemary's stomach growled, and she glanced at her watch. Noon. Only another half an hour until Jack would be back and they'd be off to lunch.

Deciding to finalize the plans for the walking route of the cemetery crawl, Rosemary headed back in the direction of the tunnel of trees that led into the graveyard. She was just about halfway across the meadow when suddenly, from somewhere in the trees ahead, someone screamed.

✠ 11 ✠

It was not a playful scream or a startled scream. It was a bloodcurdling scream.

Even as Rosemary picked up her pace and moved in the direction it had come from, she felt sick to her stomach. Something was very wrong.

When she heard the second scream, she broke into a run and could just make out, in the woods at the edge of the meadow —just before the trees framed the path back to the old cemetery—a woman. Rosemary had never seen this woman before. She was standing, trembling with sobs, her hands over her mouth, her eyes wide.

“What is it? What’s happened?” Rosemary said, approaching the woman who only kept sobbing, and was starting to shake violently. "I'm here to help you, but I need to know what's wrong. How can I help?"

The woman still didn't speak, but she calmed down enough to meet Rosemary's eyes. Then she pointed shakily at the ground, where the grass was stained with blood.

Rosemary's first thought was that the woman was hurt—that she'd been injured.

"Are you hurt? Can you tell me how to help?"

Rosemary gently touched the woman's hands and pulled them away from her face, looking for the source of the blood. A quick glance over her showed only one injury—a pretty bad cut on the woman's right hand. Definitely nothing that would cause that much bleeding.

"You need to wash that cut. It might need stitches."

"I—I fell," the woman gulped, looking down at her hand. "I hadn't even noticed that I'd cut myself."

Rosemary looked back at the ground, at the blood-soaked grass. This time, she noticed the blood didn't stop at that spot. It led off into the trees toward the cemetery, and the grass along the way was matted, as though a hurt animal or person had been wounded and then crawled away. Or was dragged away.

Rosemary looked back at the woman, who had collapsed into deep, anguished sobs and had turned as white as a ghost.

"I need you to take a deep breath. Calm down. I don't want you to pass out," she said gently, and helped the woman to a nearby bench, where she coaxed her to sit down.

Then Rosemary dug in her bag, found her phone, and with shaking fingers dialed 9-1-1. The dispatcher answered on the first ring.

"Send the police. Right away," Rosemary said as she left the woman on the bench and hurriedly followed the trail of blood through the trees. "Something terrible has happened near the Old Church Cemetery."

When the voice on the other end asked her for details, Rosemary realized she didn't know what to say, because she hadn't yet located the source of the blood.

"There's blood. A lot of it. Someone's been hurt, I just don't know who yet." She walked on until she arrived in the graveyard.

"Oh, no."

She stopped abruptly and dropped the phone on the ground.

She could see where the trail ended, and in a split second, she knew exactly whose blood it was. There, in the very back corner, in the Wright family plot, lay the motionless body of a man, face down, his hair caked with blood, his bright orange, gold, and green plaid shirt torn. Rosemary bent and picked up her phone, and then on shaky legs, walked closer and stopped short of the body of Samuel Wright.

"It's the mayor. Mayor Wright. Send help fast!"

But even as she knelt beside Sam and felt for a pulse, she knew it was too late.

"Oh, Sam," she said, still in a state of disbelief and shock.

Rosemary stood and wiped her eyes. "I *just* saw you. You were . . . you were fine. Who would do such a thing?"

She could hear sirens nearby and was grateful that Paperwick was such a small town. Someone would come and help. Someone would make sense of this madness. She looked once more at Sam.

It was then that she noticed it, where his shirt was torn, on his right shoulder.

The witch's mark.

12

Within minutes, the corner of the graveyard was roped off with yellow police tape, an officer had led Rosemary a few paces away, and a detective and a paramedic were kneeling next to the mayor's body.

"Can I get you anything, ma'am?" the officer asked Rosemary.

"No, I'm calling my friend Jack," said Rosemary, whose hands were still shaking as she tried to focus teary eyes on her cell phone. Just then she remembered the woman from the woods.

"Oh, my gosh. Hurry!" she said, walking in the direction of the path and the bench in the meadow.

"Miss!" the officer called. "We need to get a statement from you. Hold up!"

"You don't understand," Rosemary called back. "There was a woman here. She was here before I was. She's the one who pointed me to the body."

The officer caught up, but when they got to the bench, it was empty. Rosemary looked around, confused.

"I don't understand. She was right here."

"Do you think she had something to do with the murder?"

"Murder?" Rosemary almost couldn't believe her ears. Murder was a thing for the television news. For mystery novels. It was a horrible thing—an unthinkable thing. And it had never touched her life before.

"Well, the death," the officer corrected himself. "You look pale, Miss. Why don't you sit down here?" He motioned toward the bench and looked at her with wide, worried eyes.

Rosemary thought he looked awfully young to be a policeman.

"Thank you, Officer—?"

"Harris," the young man answered.

As Rosemary started to sit, she noticed a smear of blood on the bench.

"Look. See here? The woman's hand was bleeding."

Officer Harris looked down, and his eyes registered a split second of panic before he composed himself again. It occurred to Rosemary that she might not be the only one who had never encountered a dead body before.

"Let's not have you sit here," Officer Harris said, gently taking her arm and leading her back into the churchyard, to another bench. "Why don't you sit here instead, Ma'am? You can call your friend, but please don't leave."

"I won't. But the woman I saw: She was very upset. She was hurt. I'm worried about her safety, Officer Harris."

"I'm going to get Detective Weaser right now. And once he's here with you, I'll go in search of the woman. She's a valuable witness, so we'll need you to describe her. Stay right here."

With that, he went over to where Samuel's body was being loaded onto a stretcher. The detective, in plain clothes, was easy to spot among the other officers who were carefully combing the scene. He was examining the ground where Sam had come to rest, but stood when Officer Harris approached. They had a few words, the detective nodded, and they both walked in Rosemary's direction.

Rosemary had just enough time to send a quick text off to Jack: *Hurry. Come to churchyard.*

"Hello, Miss," said the detective, nodding curtly and then sitting down next to Rosemary while Officer Harris stood by, a little notepad and pencil at the ready. "I'll need your name and where you're from, and then I'll need you to walk me through exactly what happened here today and how you came to find Mayor Wright."

"Of course," said Rosemary, taking a deep breath. "My name is Rosemary Grey. I'm from New York—I'm a historian and teacher based at NYU. I was in the meadow doing research, and I was just packing up and walking this way to come back into the cemetery when I heard a scream. It was coming from the direction of the woods, just over that way." Rosemary pointed, and the detective nodded.

"Go on," he said.

"I started walking toward the sound when I heard a second scream. So, I ran into the trees, and there was a woman, sobbing and shaking. She pointed at the blood on the ground."

"Did it seem to you that the same person had screamed twice? Or two different people?"

"It sounded like the same person screaming twice."

The detective nodded, while Officer Harris scribbled rapidly.

"And where did you say you found the woman—and the blood?"

"I can show you," Rosemary said, standing and taking another deep breath to steady herself.

They walked back down the tree-lined path that connected the churchyard to the meadow and veered into the trees a bit, until Rosemary was able to find the beginning of the trail of blood.

"Harris, get some more officers over here and rope this area off," said Detective Weaser. Then he turned back to Rosemary. "Go on, Miss Grey."

"I tried to calm the woman down, thinking that she'd been hurt—that it was *her* blood on the ground. In hindsight, that makes no sense, because anyone who'd lost that much blood wouldn't be standing there crying. But at the time, I wasn't thinking clearly."

Detective Weaser nodded. "So, she pointed at the blood, you got her to sit down on this bench . . ."

"Yes, she looked faint. I saw that she'd been injured, told her she might need stitches. But then I was confused, because that much blood couldn't have come from a little cut like the one on her hand. Oh—I remember the woman said she'd fallen."

"That's how she cut her hand."

"Right. But then I noticed the trail in the grass. More blood and the grass flattened down, like someone had been dragged. Or maybe . . ." Rosemary felt tears stinging her eyes again.

"Do you think Sam was still alive, and crawled through the grass, trying to get help?"

"Sam? So, you were acquainted with the deceased, then?"

"Barely. I met him yesterday."

"And so, you followed the trail and found the body. You identified the victim to the dispatcher. But he was lying face down, and you say you'd just met Mayor Wright a day ago. May I ask how you were so sure it was him?"

"I'd just seen him about an hour ago. He said he was here for a meeting. Something to do with the security cameras. And his shirt . . ." Rosemary felt sick to her stomach.

"His shirt?"

"I'd commented that I liked his shirt. Bright fall colors. He joked that he was trying to match the leaves."

Detective Weaser looked up at the trees and frowned, then looked back at Rosemary. "And tell me again why you were here in the first place?"

"I'm in Paperwick visiting my friend Jack Stone—Dr. Jack Stone, a professor at Paperwick University. I was in the churchyard and the Witch's Meadow doing research for the upcoming Founders Day Festival."

"Okay."

By this time, Officer Harris and a couple of other uniformed officers had returned and were roping off the blood-stained bench and grass. Officer Harris came running up.

"Sir, we might've found the murder weapon."

"Now hold on, Harris. We haven't ruled it a murder yet. Could still be a freak accident." Weaser looked at Rosemary, who was still standing by. "You stay here, Ma'am," he said, and he and Officer Harris walked into the woods a short distance, where Rosemary could see Harris pointing at something on the ground.

The two men squatted down next to whatever it was, exchanged a few more words, and then Weaser signaled to another officer, who came over with a large, clear plastic bag. The detective pulled on a pair of latex gloves and gingerly picked up something from the ground and dropped it into the bag. When the officer carefully sealed the bag, Rosemary could see what looked like a medium-sized stone, covered in blood.

Detective Weaser peeled off his gloves and walked back over to Rosemary.

"Was Sam hit on the head with that stone?" Rosemary asked.

"Not that it's really your business, Miss Grey, but let's just say it looks like he hit his head. Could be he fell. Maybe it was just an accident."

"Then how could you explain the witch's mark?"

At this, Detective Weaser turned a very serious and suspicious gaze on Rosemary. "What do you know about the witch's mark?" he asked.

"I saw it. On Sam's—on Mayor Wright's shoulder. His shirt was torn."

"And you know about these kinds of marks because?"

"Because I'm a historian, like I said, sir. I've studied the history of this area extensively, and my area of expertise is the early American witch trials. That's why Jack asked me to come and help with the festival. I know about the legend of the witch's mark."

"Tell me more about this woman you say you saw here. Describe her to me," said the detective.

"She was shorter than me. About five and a half feet tall, light brown hair, blue eyes . . . She was wearing a tweed skirt and a pale pink blouse with a bow at the neck. Her hair was a bob. Chin-length."

The detective nodded, looked at the ground with a sigh, and called Harris over.

"Send someone to locate Becky Thatcher," he said.

"Becky Thatcher? Like in *The Adventures of Tom Sawyer*?"

"What?" The detective narrowed his eyes at Rosemary.

"Sorry. I mean, is that who she was?"

Detective Weaser ignored this question and asked, "Did you see anyone else in the area while you were here?"

"I saw the mayor and another man. Hold on," Rosemary frowned and tried to jog her memory. "Mayor Wright said he was meeting with his city manager. That must've been who he was with."

"Harris!" Weaser called again.

Officer Harris, who had just dispatched a uniformed woman to find Becky Thatcher came running over.

"Get me Benedict while you're at it."

"Yes, sir." Harris hurried off.

"Benedict?"

"Benedict Thatcher is our city manager here."

"Thatcher. So, this Becky is his…wife? Sister? Cousin?"

"I'll ask the questions if you don't mind, Ms. Grey." Weaser took out his phone to make a call, but paused and looked back at Rosemary. "Stay here."

He stalked off in another direction. Rosemary backed up and leaned against a tree, feeling like this whole morning might be a bizarre dream.

"Rosie!" Jack came running up, and Rosemary had never been so glad to see another human being in her entire life. "I can't believe this. I just saw George Harris. He said Sam is dead?"

Rosemary nodded, feeling her emotional dam break now that her best friend was here. She fell into Jack's arms and cried.

"I found him," she sobbed. "And the mark, Jack. He had the witch's mark. And that cat was over there." She waved vaguely in the direction of the maple tree.

"What cat?"

"It was lurking, Jack. In the woods. Like it *knew*. And then there was a scream, and that woman, that Becky Thatcher woman, and blood all over the place."

"Becky Thatcher?" Jack pulled back and looked at Rosemary. "She's the mayor's secretary."

"Then maybe she was at the meeting too." Rosemary tried to wipe her eyes.

"Do you mean that Becky Thatcher? Right over there?"

At that point, the woman from the woods was approaching Detective Weaser. She still looked shaken, but was more composed now. She caught sight of Rosemary, and hurried over.

"I owe you an apology," she said, her eyes still red and now swollen from crying. "I shouldn't have run off like that. I was just so upset. So confused."

"I understand. Is your hand okay?"

Becky looked down at her hand, now bandaged. "Yes, thank you. I feel like such an idiot."

By this time, the detective had walked back over, along with Officer Harris, who was still furiously taking notes.

"What brought you to the meadow earlier today, Mrs. Thatcher?" asked Detective Weaser.

"I came to bring a message to my husband," Becky answered. "He and Mayor Wright," her voice cracked when she said his name. She swallowed hard and went on. "They had a meeting here today. Ben had been working with the mayor on the security project. We got a call at the office from the company that installed the monitors. I came out to bring the message, thinking maybe Ben and I could go out for lunch after . . . after he was done talking to—to Mayor Wright." Becky looked decidedly pale again.

"Don't you worry, Mrs. Thatcher," said Officer Harris. "We'll find out who did this."

"I already *know* who did this," said Becky, her pale face turning red with anger, her voice trembling. "I saw her here. Saw her standing over him."

"Hold up, Becky," said Detective Weaser. "Who did you see?"

"That horrible Ingrid Clark!" Becky blew her nose, but to no avail as she started sobbing again. "She did it. I know she did. She hated Mayor Wright! She's a witch, you know. She's all tangled up with that curse!""

"Harris!"

"On it, sir," said Officer Harris, running off, no doubt to collect Ingrid Clark.

"Ms. Grey," Weaser said, turning his gaze back to Rosemary. "Did you happen to see Ingrid Clark here today? An older lady, crazy hair, probably wearing odd clothes . . ."

Rosemary bit her lower lip. In all of the commotion, she had forgotten to tell the detective about Ingrid being in the meadow.

"Yes, actually. I did see Ms. Clark."

"You spoke to her?"

"Yes. We were talking about her relative—about Hortence Gallow. I was asking her questions for our research."

Rosemary glanced at Jack, who was clearly surprised that she'd talked with Ingrid.

"So, you had an appointment here, with Ingrid Clark?"

"No. I had an appointment—a research appointment, that is—with Dr. McGuire, from the university. I talked with him first. Then he left to teach a class. Then after that, I saw the mayor and the man he was meeting with, walking in the woods. Then I saw Ingrid. She was—"

"Yes, Ms. Grey? What was Ms. Clark doing?"

"She was watching them. She was over in the woods, watching the mayor and the city manager."

"Oh, I'll just bet she was," said Detective Weaser under his breath.

Rosemary couldn't help feeling she'd betrayed the old woman, but she knew she had to tell the truth.

"I told you," cried Becky, grabbing Detective Weaser's arm. "Ingrid hated Mayor Wright! You know that as well as I do."

"But then when Ms. Clark saw me taking pictures, she came over and talked to me," Rosemary went on. "Detective, I'm sure Ingrid had nothing to do with—"

"That'll do, thank you, Ms. Grey," Weaser said shortly. "Did Ms. Clark explain why she was watching the mayor?"

"She said someone had to. And that he was going to turn the meadow into a roadside attraction and ruin it. She said—"

"Ingrid is crazy!" Becky cut in. "I knew that. *Everyone* knows that. But I never thought she'd go this far."

Detective Weaser looked at Becky, then back at Rosemary.

"Go on, Ms. Grey. What did Ms. Clark say?"

Rosemary swallowed. "She said 'I can't let that happen to my meadow.'"

13

The energy at the scene began to settle a bit. The ambulance had come and gone—taking Samuel Wright away. Rosemary felt exhausted, and a glance at her watch told her that although it felt like days since she'd been sitting under the maple tree, talking to Seth, it had only been a few hours.

"Let's go to the café," urged Jack, putting an arm around Rosemary. "We'll get you some soup. You need to get away from here and eat something." He took a closer look at her. "And by the looks of you, you could seriously stand to hydrate."

Rosemary nodded and turned to Officer Harris, who was standing right beside them. "May I go now, Officer Harris?"

"I'll ask the detective," he answered.

But the detective's attention was presently fully focused on a man who was rushing up, a concerned look on his reddened face.

"Where is she? Get out of my way, please. Becky!" the man called.

When Becky caught sight of him, she ran into his arms.

"Ben!"

Rosemary recognized him as the man she'd seen walking around the meadow with Mayor Wright earlier. He must be Benedict Thatcher, the city manager. He looked the worse for wear since then, his suit rumpled, his shirt untucked, and a sheen of perspiration glazing his forehead.

"Oh, Ben," Becky sobbed into his shoulder. "It's the curse. I just knew this would happen."

"What are you talking about, Becky?" her husband said in as soothing a voice as he could muster. "There's no such thing as curses. Let's go home and talk about it there. We'll let Detective Weaser and his team do their job."

"But I saw it, Ben. I saw the mark! And that crazy Ingrid—she was standing there. She's one of the Clarks, you know. She killed Sam, Ben!"

"I'm taking you home, Becky," said Benedict.

"Hold on there a moment, Mr. Thatcher," said Weaser. "I don't want to inconvenience you folks any further, but I have just a few quick questions, and then we can all go."

Benedict Thatcher nodded. "Of course. Anything to help."

"So sorry about all this," added Weaser. Rosemary was struck by how polite he sounded. Not at all the short, brusque manner he'd displayed toward her.

As the detective ushered the Thatchers over to a bench, urged them to sit down, and ordered Officer Harris to run get them some water, it occurred to Rosemary to wonder if the sudden outpouring of hospitality had anything to do with the fact that Mr. Thatcher was the city manager—an important person in Paperwick—and the detective knew the value of staying on his good side.

"I understand you had a meeting here earlier with the mayor," he said to Benedict.

"Yes. We were discussing the security system we're having installed here. Samuel wants . . ." He looked quickly at the ground and swallowed. "*Wanted* to get it up and running before any development happens here."

"Ms. Grey," Weaser said, motioning Rosemary over. "Is this the man you saw today with the mayor?"

"Yes," said Rosemary with a nod.

Benedict Thatcher looked at her and frowned. "Do I know you?"

"No. I was in the meadow this morning."

Benedict nodded, still looking a little confused.

"Mr. Thatcher, about what time did you leave after your meeting here with the mayor?" asked Weaser.

Benedict looked at his watch and shook his head nervously. "I don't know, exactly. I guess it had to be around noon. No, it was a little before noon."

"So, the mayor was still here when you left?"

"Yes."

"And where, exactly, was the mayor at that time, Mr. Thatcher?" Weaser continued.

"Please. Call me Ben."

This brought a pleased little smile to Weaser's face.

"We finished up right over there, sizing up those trees," Ben continued.

Rosemary sucked in a breath. Thankfully, she and Jack were standing off to the side, so Jack was the only one who heard.

"What is it?" he whispered.

"He's pointing right to the area where I found Becky," said Rosemary. "That's also where most of the blood is. That had to be where Sam was when he was hurt."

"But he ended up over in the cemetery?"

"Yes. You saw where the police marked off the Wright family plot, didn't you?"

"Yep."

"That's where I found him."

"I still can't believe he's gone. And I mean, what happened to him? And how on earth did he get from over there in the meadow to the cemetery? Did he have an accident and then try to go for help? Did someone else move him there?" Jack shivered a little. "This kind of thing doesn't happen in Paperwick. And did you hear what Becky said about the curse? How bizarre is that?"

"She must've seen the mark," whispered Rosemary. "She must know the legend of the curse and then saw the mark, just like I did. Oh, Jack. It was just as you described it. A sort of curved shape. Black. On his right shoulder. If I hadn't seen it myself, I wouldn't have believed it. I mean, the witch's mark!"

"But think about the legend. Even if it were true, and there really were such things as curses, this makes no sense. Samuel Wright isn't in the Graves family line. And Becky of all people should know that, because she's an amateur genealogist. She's even given talks over at the library about how you can trace your ancestry."

"I kind of knew that, now that you mention it. Sam told me this morning that he knew almost nothing about his own family history, but that his secretary had been after him to look into it." Rosemary studied Becky, who was quietly talking to her husband and the detective. "I bet she knows all about Ingrid Clark's family ties, too. But she doesn't even realize she's contradicting herself with these accusations. First, she said she saw Ingrid here, and that she must be the killer. Then she said it was the curse that did Sam in. It can't be both of those things, can it? I mean, Sam can't have been murdered by Ingrid *and* stricken down by some dark magic."

"To her they might be one and the same," said Jack, shrugging one shoulder. "Ingrid is Hortence's descendant. And Ingrid couldn't stand Mayor Wright and has been very outspoken about that. Becky, on the other hand, is one of his staunchest supporters and closest friend. Maybe Becky sees Ingrid as a bit of a witch-cum-cold-blooded-killer. Magic *and* mortal."

"I met Ingrid Clark this morning, Jack. She seems like a bit of a curmudgeon. She's definitely unusual. But I can't imagine she's violent."

"Oh, but she is. Or has been, anyway. She once got picked up for throwing a rock through the mayor's window."

"You're kidding."

"It's the truth. About a month ago, after the council met and decided to install that security system. She was furious they didn't put it to the taxpayers before moving on it. She'd attached a note to the rock, warning Sam to leave the meadow alone. So that's at least part of the reason Becky is quick to blame Ingrid."

"Well, that and I guess the fact that when she found Sam, Ingrid was standing over him—and then ran away."

"Ouch. That's incriminating."

Rosemary looked back at Becky Thatcher, who seemed to have finally calmed down. "She doesn't look like the kind of person who believes in things like curses. I mean, what well-adjusted, intelligent adult believes in curses these days?"

Officer Harris returned and gave Rosemary the go-ahead to leave. "But don't leave town or anything, okay?" he said.

"Don't worry. I'm not going anywhere," said Rosemary. "Thank you, Officer Harris. You've been very kind."

"You're welcome, Ma'am," he answered.

"Please. It's Rosemary."

"Rosemary, meet George Harris. George, Rosemary Grey," said Jack.

"Nice to meet you, Ma'am—I mean, Rosemary," said George.

"I know you'll get to the bottom of this, George," said Jack, giving a brief sideways glance at Detective Weaser, who was still engrossed in his discussion with the Thatchers. He lowered his voice. "I don't have as much faith in Detective Weaser. He's laying it on pretty thick over there."

The detective was still pandering to the Thatchers, and Rosemary caught a snippet of what he was saying, even though he was speaking under his breath.

"That Clark woman is a nut. You both know it. I know it. She's been after the mayor for some time. My guess is she did it. That, or we have a freak accident here. Don't worry, sir," he said getting up and shaking hands with Benedict Thatcher. "We'll get this cleared away soon so you and I both can get on with the work of taking care of this town."

"George, how did that awful man get to be detective here?" asked Jack.

"He came to the department on the mayor's recommendation," said George, who, Rosemary thought, seemed to be doing a fair job of hiding his own frustration with Weaser's approach.

"Wow. What was Sam thinking?" Jack wondered aloud. He shook his head. "Well, I guess we'll be on our way. Thanks again, George."

George smiled and gave them a wave before returning to the detective's side.

As they walked from the meadow to the churchyard, Rosemary caught sight of a slight movement in the side of her eye, near the Wright family plot, where she had found Sam.

"Hold on a second," she said to Jack, stepping around the headstones for a closer look. "Oh my gosh. Come here!" she said in a loud whisper.

There, looking contented and calmly staring straight at Rosemary, was the cat she'd seen earlier.

"Oh no," Rosemary said, grabbing Jack's arm. "It's that cat. It's the cat Ingrid talked about. She said it was Hortence's cat, and she somehow knew that I'd seen it. How could she have known that, Jack?"

"Ow! You're clenching!" He loosened Rosemary's death grip on his arm. "Now. What do you mean, she knew you'd seen it?" asked Jack. Then he turned his attention to the cat. "Awww. Poor little thing."

"I don't know how she knew," Rosemary whispered, as though she didn't want the cat to hear. "But when I was talking to Ingrid, she said something like, 'You saw Hortence's cat, didn't you?' and I had just seen this very cat! Then she talked about how that meant that Hortence's spirit was 'on the move,' like this cat is some kind of *harbinger of doom.* Jack, she said it meant there would be another death!"

With one quick movement, Jack stepped forward and scooped up the little creature.

"Jack! Have you lost your mind? Did you hear what I just said? About the doom and the death? Put that down!"

"Be quiet! Next thing you know, Weaser will arrest this little one." Jack smiled at the cat, who seemed to be quite pleased with its current situation. "And we can't let that happen, can we now?" He tucked the little tortoise shell cat under his arm and began to pick his way out of the churchyard.

Rosemary stood stunned for a moment, then ran to catch up with Jack. "So, who'll take on the mayor's duties, now that he's gone?" she asked as they made their way to the bricked sidewalk that led around the village green.

"I assume Benedict Thatcher. City managers do all the work anyway, so he can certainly handle it. Actually, Thatcher made a run for mayor himself a while back. He ran against Sam that first term, believe it or not. I guess it was eight years ago? Of course, that was long before Charlie and I were on the scene, but with the elections coming up later this month, the *Paperwick Chronicle* did a whole feature about Sam's years in office—and how he was expected to run unopposed this year. Anyway, the article talked about the election two terms ago.

When Ben Thatcher didn't win, Sam tapped him for the city manager position. He knew he had what it took to do the work and wanted him as his right-hand man. It was kind of written up as an act of benevolence on Sam's part, but if you ask me, it was a shrewd move. Thatcher has the experience and background for that kind of work. Sam was more of a—rest his soul—a pretty face."

"You said city managers do all the work. What did you mean?"

"Oh, I was half joking. Mayors here are elected. Managers are appointed. The mayor is the face of the town. He does ribbon cuttings, has his picture taken a lot, kisses babies, marshals parades . . ."

"Acts like a ghost in cemetery crawls."

"Exactly. The manager, on the other hand, works behind the scenes, handles disputes and red tape and paperwork."

"So, the mayor gets all the glory, so to speak?"

"Well, yes, sort of."

"I wonder if Mr. Thatcher ever resented that."

"Doesn't seem like it. They're known around town to be best friends. The Thatchers and Sam were like family."

"Mr. Thatcher was a mess at the meadow. His hands were shaking and he was sweating—even in this cold," said Rosemary. "Poor man."

"Well, he just lost not only his friend but his colleague. It's understandable. And Becky—well, Sam was her friend, too, and her boss."

"Tight-knit group," Rosemary said, as Jack stopped in front of a small, red brick building.

"What's this?" she asked.

"We're taking this little sweetie to see Dr. Sims," said Jack, nuzzling the kitten. "We'll drop her here while we go to lunch, pick her up after. I want to get her checked out and take care of her shots."

"You're keeping the—the cat?"

"Well, Izzy could use a baby sister, couldn't she? And frankly, I think this cat likes you, Rosemary."

"How can you say that? It's been spying on me all morning." Rosemary lowered her voice and leaned closer to Jack. "And maybe I'm reaching here, but I feel like it's been glaring. A lot."

"Or maybe it was just adoring you from afar, because this precious wittle sweetie knows that deep down, you're a good person," said Jack, giving the kitten a peck on the nose.

They had a brief visit with Dr. Sims, who promised to take good care of the kitten, and then they headed on to the café for lunch.

"I think you should be the one to name her," said Jack.

"What? Why me?"

"Because I think that cat was following you."

"*Stalking* me is more like it."

"Watching over you," said Jack. "Protecting you. Don't forget, there might've been a killer in those woods today. You could've even been in danger."

"But Jack, the curse! Remember what Ingrid said?"

"You don't believe in things like curses, do you? I mean, what well-adjusted, intelligent adult believes in curses these days?" said Jack with a snort, stinging Rosemary with her own words.

He was right, of course.

There was a logical explanation for the appearance of the cat and for the funny feeling in Rosemary's gut, and even for Sam's horrible death.

"*Name the kitty*," Jack urged.

"No," said Rosemary.

"Come on," insisted Jack.

"I think I'm hungry," said Rosemary, trying to change the subject.

"You'll come around. Wait and see," said Jack.

Rosemary answered this remark with a roll of her eyes.

"Come on. I'll buy you lunch," he said, and they linked arms and walked on to the café.

14

On this visit to Potter's Café, it was Abbey who served them lunch, instead of Gabby. Creamy mac and cheese and a cup of thick tomato bisque left Rosemary feeling comforted and satisfied.

"I'm done with class for the day, so we're going to the museum," said Jack.

"Do you think the festival will still go on—I mean, what with the mayor dying?"

"It'll go on," said Jack. "Visitors will be arriving, and locals are counting on the extra business. Sam would be the first one to insist upon it."

"Then we still have a lot of work to do," said Rosemary.

The shops along Chestnut Street—one of the main streets around the town green—were festooned in colorful fall decorations. Every lamp post was wrapped in swag, every shop window featured oranges and reds and yellows. The smells of fresh bread and pastries wafted down the street from the open bakery door and mingled with the aroma of freshly ground coffee from the coffee shop. People wearing chunky sweaters and scarves hurried along the sidewalks, children played hide and seek among the trees on the green, and shopkeepers swept leaves away from front doors, waving to customers as they passed.

Life went on. That was what Rosemary was thinking about when they approached a tiny, white, clapboard building with an American flag flapping in the breeze out front, and lights that looked like gas lanterns flickering on either side of the door. Above the door, a hunter green sign was carved with gold letters: "Paperwick Historical Society Museum."

"This is the cutest museum ever, " said Rosemary as Jack pushed open the front door with a jingle and ushered her inside.

"And it's chock full of historical intrigue," he said. "Paperwick has been around since the 1600s, so a lot has happened between then and now."

"Old Ballybrook? Is that near here?" asked Rosemary, examining an old town sign featured in a lit glass case on the wall near the entrance.

"That was the name of the original colony," said Jack.

"The whole *state* was a British colony, though," said Rosemary, moving from one display to another, lost in thought. "Quinetucket."

"Quine—what?" asked Jack.

"That was what the Native Americans called this little corner of their world. It means *beside the long, tidal river.* The French mispronounced it, and we ended up with 'Connecticut.'"

"And the set of Puritans who settled this area started out in one big group, Ballybrook, but then eventually divided up into a smattering of villages, including Paperwick."

"So, the Founders Day Festival will celebrate that heritage."

"And celebrate the founders," said Jack, pointing at another glass case that held an ancient-looking piece of parchment.

"The town charter," said Rosemary, squinting to make out the old handwriting. "Filbert. Anderson. Graves. Potter. Clark. Martin."

"Yep. These were the original families of Paperwick."

"So, Matthew Graves—the cursed judge who wanted to condemn Hortence . . . His was one of the original families."

"Yep. The Graves were active in politics right from the beginning."

"Are there still any of them around?"

"Not in Paperwick. But there are some in the area. I've been told that some of them moved in the direction of New Haven. They don't have a stellar reputation as a group, if you want the truth—neither back in history nor at present." Jack stepped over to one of the large display cases, took out a small key, and carefully opened the lid. "And this," he said as he lifted a crinkle-paged volume out of the case with great care, "is Mercy Clark's record book."

Rosemary's eyes widened as she recognized the handwriting. It was the same as that on the note from Jack's barn.

"Wow," she breathed. "There it is again."

"There what is again?"

"That feeling I get when history comes alive. I felt that way this morning when I saw Hortence's grave. History has this way of sneaking up and punching you right in the stomach, you know?"

"Takes your breath away," agreed Jack, nodding.

"Look," said Rosemary, pointing to an entry in the book. "Here, Mercy is talking about a visit she and Hortence made to someone named Hannah Smith, eight months pregnant. And here, she talks about the ingredients for a tincture to fade freckles."

"I love freckles," said Jack.

"That must be what first drew you to me," said Rosemary with a chuckle.

"Oh, yeah. It was your freckles. The way they're sprinkled right across your little button nose. That, and the wild, curly hair."

Rosemary laughed and gingerly turned a group of pages in the old book.

"Just want to check . . . Ah! Yes. This last section, where the handwriting changes. That's when Elizabeth Graves took over as midwife, right? After Hortence and Mercy were gone?"

"That's right," said Jack. "Amazing, isn't it?"

"Can we take this home? Just for tonight?" Rosemary asked.

"I had a feeling you'd request to check it out," said Jack with a wink. "Normally that would be out of the question, but since you happen to know the president of the Historical Society—and he happens to know you're a reputable historian—we might be able to pull a few strings."

"That would be wonderful. I can curl up with this and read all night."

"You're a wild woman, you know."

"You can tell by my hair."

"It's for the best that we take it home anyway," said Jack. "With all the commotion this afternoon, we were late getting lunch, and now it's almost time to go home and fix dinner. Charlie's grilling fish, and we're making my mother's potatoes."

"Ooh—the scalloped ones, with all the butter? The ones she used to catch your dad? It's been years since we made those."

"The very ones. And don't forget, we've got company coming."

"Oh yeah. Seth." Rosemary tried not to let Jack see her small smile.

"Yes, Seth. Oh—and also the cat-without-a-name. We need to head back to Dr. Sims' place before she closes up shop for the day."

After Jack had carefully wrapped Mercy's journal and sealed it in a plastic bag and then nested the bag inside an heirloom storage box, they locked up the museum and headed outside just as the sun was beginning to get low in the sky.

"I'm worried about Ingrid," said Rosemary as they walked along the sidewalk.

"Really? Why?" asked Jack.

"Because they took her in for questioning."

"She's a definite suspect, Rosie."

"I just don't see her as a killer."

"Rosemary, you just met her. And she's had some crazy outbursts, even since Charlie and I have lived here. I think she has a long history of that sort of thing."

"But I just don't think she's the type. I can't explain it. I know in my gut."

"Your gut? The same gut that loves to mix marshmallow cream with potato chips? *That* gut? Look, Rosie, you may be right. Or you might be letting your sympathies for Hortence and Mercy color your opinion of Ingrid. Let's let the police do their job and trust that they'll nab the killer."

"I'm not very good at letting things lie, you know," said Rosemary.

"Are you kidding? You're the *worst* at letting things lie. But even though you're inquisitive in the extreme, and even though we both love a good mystery, we're not detectives."

"Yeah, but you saw the detective. He's not what I would call . . ."

"The sharpest pencil in the box? The brightest bulb? No," Jack admitted. "Barney Weaser would never be accused of that."

"I just want to try to find out more, just ask a few questions—"

"Rosie, we're letting the police handle it. All kidding aside, somewhere there's a killer on the loose, and we'd be wise to play it safe this time."

"Okay," Rosemary said. "I'll just keep my ears open, though. Okay?"

"Agreed. And I'll do the same."

They stopped in at the veterinary clinic and Dr. Sims handed them a small pet carrier with a sleepy kitten inside.

"She's in good shape," said the doctor. "I'll need to see her back in a few weeks, for her second round of shots."

"We'll be here," said Jack.

Once they got to Holly Golightly, Jack handed Rosemary the carrier.

"I can't hold this," said Rosemary.

"Just for a second, while I unlock Holly," said Jack.

Rosemary reluctantly took hold of the handle and held the carrier as far away from her body as she possibly could. She glanced down once, and saw those green eyes, calmly looking out at her.

“Could you stop staring at me?” she asked the cat.

“I’m telling you, this cat likes you,” said Jack. “I know what let’s do. Let’s just pretend that she’s a puppy. You’re not afraid of puppies.”

“Well . . .”

“Come on, Rosemary. Name the cat.”

15

Charlie was already home when they arrived back at the farm.

"Look what Rosemary got today," called Jack cheerfully.

Charlie's head poked around the corner from the kitchen.

"What did you get, Rosemary?"

"Mercy's journal! Can you believe Jack let me bring it home?"

"I was talking about *this*," said Jack, holding up the little pet carrier.

"Oh. Right," said Rosemary. "And we got a . . . um, cat," she mumbled.

"What? A *cat*?" Charlie hurried over, Izzy following at his heels. They both peeked inside the carrier.

"Well, hello, little one," Charlie cooed. "What's your name?"

"Rosemary hasn't decided on a name just yet," said Jack.

"Well, I know you and cats haven't always gotten along," said Charlie, putting a hand on Rosemary's sagging shoulder. "But maybe this one is different? This does look like an unusual cat."

"Unusual in a horrifying way?" asked Rosemary, looking into the carrier at the steady green eyes. "She looks like Hortence's cat. Am I the only one who can see it? Has the whole world gone crazy? Is Ingrid Clark the new standard for sanity around here?"

"No! This cat is unusually intelligent. You can see it in the eyes," insisted Jack.

"Really?" Rosemary leaned in to look a little closer.

"How about we let Izzy be the judge," said Charlie.

Jack set the carrier on the floor and they all watched Izzy closely.

The little dog sniffed around the complete perimeter of the carrier, then put her nose up to the bars as if in greeting, wagging her tale. The kitten, in turn, returned the greeting by touching noses, batting her lids, and purring softly.

"Look at that," said Charlie "Have you ever seen anything like it? They're fast friends!"

"Of course they are," said Jack, bending to pat Izzy on the head. "You should've seen her there, Charlie. This brave little creature, all alone at the cemetery. We had to save her. I just know this cat is special."

"Right. And how do you know that?" asked a skeptical Rosemary.

"I have a knack about these things," Jack said sagely.

"What is it with you people? Is that like the Paperwick town motto or something?"

"What?" asked Jack, holding up his hands innocently.

"I have just about been *knacked* to death here," cried Rosemary. "Is it something in the air? In the water? Do you all think you're clairvoyant?"

"We're highly intuitive at the very least," said Jack.

Charlie laughed and slowly opened the little carrier door to see what the animals would do.

The cat put a tentative paw out, then emerged entirely and looked around, as if sizing up the place and finding it quite to her liking. She and Izzy touched noses again, and then the kitten wandered into the living room, hopped up onto the couch, and proceeded to lick her paws as though she'd made the command decision that this was an acceptable throne.

Izzy seemed to be just fine with this decision, and trotted happily back into the kitchen.

"A bright spot in a hard day," said Charlie, putting a comforting arm around Rosemary's shoulders.

"So, you've heard all about it?" asked Rosemary. "Everything that happened with Sam?"

"It's all over town. Of course, Jack filled me in too. But it's all anyone is talking about. I'm so sorry for poor Sam. And for you—finding him like that. It must've been awful."

"It was one of the worst experiences of my life," said Rosemary. "I hope he didn't suffer."

"Do they know how it happened?" asked Charlie.

"I think the jury's still out on that," said Jack. "From what I can gather, they haven't decided yet if he had an accident or if he was murdered. But the cause of death was a blow to the head."

"What's this I hear about Becky Thatcher being there?" asked Charlie.

"She was there before I got there," said Rosemary. "I heard her scream, ran over to see what was happening, and she pointed to where Sam was."

"So, she must've been first on the scene," said Charlie.

"She said Ingrid Clark was already there when she arrived, but that she ran away," said Rosemary. "And Becky . . . I've never seen anyone so shaken. She was almost delirious."

"The Thatchers were very close friends with Sam," said Charlie. "And Becky has always struck me as a sort of shy, quiet type. I can't even imagine how shocked she was."

"Still can't believe Sam's gone," said Jack, shaking his head.

Rosemary sighed and looked thoughtfully at the ground. "I don't see how his death could've been an accident," she said.

"Why?" asked Charlie.

"The witch's mark," said Rosemary.

"Oh, that's right," said Jack. "I'd forgotten about that."

"The witch's mark?" asked Charlie.

"When I found Sam, he was lying face down. His shirt was torn slightly at the right shoulder. I saw a mark. I swear it was the witch's mark. Like a smear. Sort of a blue-black color."

"Like a bruise?" asked Jack.

Rosemary thought about this.

"Maybe it was a bruise," she said slowly. "I was so upset. Maybe my imagination got the better of me. I don't know anymore. I think I'm just overwhelmed."

“We still have plenty of time before dinner,” said Jack. “Why don’t you go take a nice, long bubble bath. Put on your coziest sweats. And then meet me in the kitchen and we’ll whip up some comfort food?”

“And I’ll marinate the fish and build a fire,” added Charlie.

“And we’ll all have a glass of wine,” said Jack.

“That sounds absolutely perfect,” said Rosemary. She started off toward her bedroom, but then stopped and looked back at the guys, who were fawning over the kitten.

“I want you both to know something,” she said with a smile. “Even with all that’s happened today, there’s no place I’d rather be than here with you two.”

16

Rosemary felt like a new woman after a long, hot, vanilla-scented soak in the tub. She washed her face, brushed out her hair and pulled it into a ponytail, and donned her softest sweatshirt and broken-in pair of jeans. With Seth's visit in mind, she swiped on a bit of tinted lip balm and headed to the kitchen.

Fires were crackling merrily in both the living room and the little kitchen fireplaces, a bottle of white wine was chilling, and the table was set for four.

"Ready to cook?" asked Jack as Rosemary entered the kitchen.

"Ready," said Rosemary. "I'll slice the potatoes."

"And I'll melt the butter," said Jack.

They'd made Mrs. Stone's butter potatoes together countless times. They'd even been known to eat them right out of the pan while watching a movie. But tonight, for Seth and Charlie's sake, they'd have to be more civilized.

"Let's make a big salad, too," said Jack.

"Sounds perfect," said Rosemary.

Just then, the little kitten came into the kitchen, yawning sleepily. She greeted Izzy first, who was sitting at Jack's feet in hopes that someone would drop a crumb. Then she sauntered over to Rosemary and wound between her legs, purring happily.

"What did I tell you?" asked Jack. "That cat loves you."

Rosemary was so relaxed after her bath that she was able to take a deep breath and stand very still until the little creature walked out of the room.

"Don't cats require things, like food and . . . other cat things?"

"Dr. Sims packed us a little goody bag," said Jack. "And for the few other things we still need, Seth's stopping by the store on his way over."

"You're pretty good friends, huh? You and Charlie and Seth?"

"We get along famously," said Jack. "He comes over every Tuesday and we usually get together on weekends, too. On

Tuesdays, we have a little pot luck dinner and then usually either watch a movie or play a board game."

"Where does Seth live?"

"Over by the campus, in a cottage."

"Speaking of cottages, that reminds me. Who lives in the cottage down by the pond?"

"Oh, the old caretaker's cottage, you mean?"

"Is that what it is? I saw a red truck there—"

Suddenly, there was a knock on the door.

"Ooh, Rosie, can you get that?" said Jack, who was just sliding the potatoes into the hot oven.

"Sure," said Rosemary, and she hurried to the door and opened it to find Seth juggling grocery bags and a tin foil-covered dish.

"Let me help," Rosemary offered, taking the bags out of Seth's hands.

"Thank you," he smiled. "I wasn't sure what your cat would need, so I got a little of everything."

"*Jack's* cat, you mean," said Rosemary.

"Right," said Seth, following Rosemary into the kitchen and greeting Jack and Charlie.

"Although," Seth continued, "in my experience, cats choose their people. Not the other way around."

In the grocery bags, there were small food and water bowls, kitten chow, a dainty green collar with a tiny bell on it, a couple of cat toys, and a small brush, presumably with which to groom the little creature.

"That's one lucky cat," said Rosemary, admiring the haul and filling the bowl with Kitten Crunchies, which caused the cat to come running.

"Wow, she's a beauty," said Seth. He bent down next to the kitten, who glanced at him and then went right back to eating. "I remember you, from the meadow this morning. You look just like Hortence's cat."

"Thank you!" said Rosemary.

"What are you going to name her?"

All eyes turned to Rosemary.

She shifted from foot to foot, and finally gave a long sigh.

"Fine. I give. I'll name her Smudge," she said.

"Smudge?" said Jack. "I like it."

"It suits her," said Charlie, who was just picking up the marinated fish and heading out to the grill.

Rosemary filled the kitty water bowl and set it down beside the food. Smudge looked up at her and blinked. Rosemary thought she almost looked like she was smiling. Maybe she liked her new name.

"You planned it this way, didn't you?" asked Rosemary, reaching a tentative finger out to touch the kitten's head. "I guess you're here to stay."

The marinated, grilled fish was delicious, the potatoes were rich and crisp and buttery, the salad was refreshing and tasted like fall, with toasted nuts, sliced pear, and dried cranberries on top.

Seth had brought vanilla bean ice cream and a pan of brownies, which were warming in the oven, and Jack and Rosemary got out the coffee things while Charlie ground the aromatic beans. Soon, the smells of coffee and chocolate mingled, and Rosemary took a deep breath and smiled.

"Heaven," she sighed.

"Let's go sit by the fire. We can set up the card table for our board game," said Jack.

They gathered around and sipped coffee and enjoyed warm brownies topped with melting ice cream as they talked about the day and Charlie set out the pieces to play Clue.

"It's especially tragic that the mayor died when he'd just gotten engaged," said Seth.

"Get out of town!" said Charlie. "I didn't know he was engaged."

"Neither did I," said Jack, surprised. "He was definitely the most eligible bachelor in Paperwick."

"In all of Connecticut," added Charlie.

"Hey!" said Seth.

"Present company excluded, of course," said Jack quickly.

"Apparently, he'd been dating this woman for some time, but she's not from Paperwick. They met back in school. Reconnected and started dating a few years ago. It's been a long-distance thing. He'd go visit her periodically. But he invited her to town a couple days ago, and finally popped the question. He'd just announced it this morning down at City Hall."

"The pretty blond woman from the café," said Charlie. "I bet that's the fiancé!"

Rosemary and Jack both agreed, remembering the woman with the shiny hair and fetching outfit.

"He didn't act engaged," said Rosemary. "I mean, he was a big flirt. Or I guess it's possible that was just his personality."

"No, I don't think so," said Seth. "When I got to the cemetery this morning and walked up on you two, I thought he looked smitten."

He shifted in his chair a little. Charlie and Jack said nothing, but both turned to look at Rosemary, and she instantly felt her cheeks getting warm.

"Well, then there you have it," she said, feeling self-conscious. "That's unusual behavior for a man who's just gotten engaged, don't you think? By the way, I wasn't interested—though I might've been flattered. And I don't know that he was *smitten*," she eyed Seth, "but he was overly friendly. I'm a little out of touch, but I know when someone is coming on. I assure you, Samuel Wright was not my type. A little too charming for me. And if I was his brand-new fiancée, I don't think I'd be comfortable with that kind of behavior."

All three men nodded in agreement, and Rosemary might have been imagining it, but she thought Seth breathed a little sigh of relief.

"I had a very interesting conversation with Ingrid Clark today," Rosemary told Seth.

"She talked to you?" he answered, surprised.

"Right after you left to go to class, I saw her wandering around in the trees."

"Watching the mayor," Jack reminded her.

"Yes, okay. She was watching the mayor and Mr. Thatcher. She's very protective of the meadow, and she's furious that they want to develop it."

"Exactly what you and I were talking about earlier, too," said Seth.

"Yep. I can understand why she's upset. She feels like the mayor and his supporters want to capitalize on her family's story."

"And it's not like Hortence Clark Gallow invented the cotton gin or was a famous author," said Seth. "She was wrongly accused of witchcraft."

"I think if presented the right way, Hortence's story could be a wonderful lesson in history and would inspire admiration because she was, for all intents and purposes, an early American medic," said Rosemary. "I'm going to read through Mercy's medical records tonight and try to learn more about the sisters' work here. If there's a story worth telling, it's that one."

"I agree," said Jack. "It's all in the presentation. On the one hand, you have a statue of a cartoon witch, holding a broom. On the other, you have a dignified portrait of a misunderstood woman and a snapshot of history that shouldn't be forgotten."

"We really ought to write our book," Rosemary said, looking at Jack.

“Let’s do it,” said Jack with a nod. “But only if you promise not to go on a yearlong tour with it. I want you settled.”

Rosemary laughed. “I’m feeling pretty settled tonight, even in the wake of this crazy day.” She picked up the tiny lead pipe from the Clue game. “But I sure would like to know who killed Samuel Wright.”

17

After three games of Clue—all of which Seth won—and an hour-long fireside chat, Jack yawned and stretched and declared it bedtime. Rosemary agreed, because she wanted to dig into Mercy's journal as soon as she was snuggled up in bed.

Charlie took Izzy and Smudge outside for a potty break, and then came back in, pulling the back door closed against a strong wind, which could be heard whistling through the trees.

"That time of year," said Charlie, locking the door. "Looks like another little storm is blowing in. Before you know it, we'll be in for our first dusting of snow."

"I just love it when he talks weather," said Jack, winking at Rosemary and Seth. "Well, I'm going to hit the sack, and

Charlie, didn't you say you still had a few chapters to write tonight?"

"Nope. All caught up," said Charlie, rejoining Rosemary and Seth on the couch.

"Well, then." Jack looked at Charlie with insistent eyes. "I need some help in the bathroom, with that broken, um, cabinet . . . hinge."

"What? Oh! Right. I'd forgotten about that," said Charlie, finally getting the not-so-subtle signal that Jack, matchmaker that he was, wanted to give Rosemary and Seth some alone time.

Of course, this was abundantly apparent to everyone else in the room.

As soon as Jack and Charlie had disappeared down the hallway, Seth chuckled. "I think they're trying to tell us something."

"That, or they're just really mad at you for kicking our booties at Clue." Rosemary laughed.

In the moment of silence that followed, Seth looked down and smiled to himself. "I should feel uncomfortable right about now, but for some reason, I don't," he said.

"Why would you feel uncomfortable?"

"Oh, you know. Alone with a pretty woman. You probably already figured out I'm not exactly a lady's man."

"Well, that's one of the things I like about you," said Rosemary. "And thank you."

Seth just smiled and then looked back at the fire, in no big hurry to leave. Rosemary was glad of that, since she was in no big hurry for him to go.

"I hope you find something of interest in Mercy's journal tonight. I'll be looking forward to hearing all about it," said Seth.

"Probably stay up way too late again," said Rosemary. "Want to peruse it with me for a while?"

"Wish I could," said Seth with a regretful sidelong glance. "But I have an early class tomorrow. But hey, if you find you have any anthropological questions, don't hesitate."

"Oh, I'll know who to call," said Rosemary.

She turned to face him on the couch. She didn't know why she did it. And he swiveled to face her, and looked at her as though he was about to say something, but then didn't.

"What is it?" she smiled.

"Oh, it's nothing really. I just thought—I mean, I just had this thought. Funny. It's been a long time."

"A long time since . . ." Their voices kept getting lower and lower, and now Rosemary was almost whispering.

"Since I've wanted to kiss someone," he answered, and they slowly leaned closer to one another, closing the little bit of space between them.

The moment their lips touched, Rosemary felt enveloped in warmth. Warmth from the fire, from the coziness of this room and the candles flickering with the wind whistling outside, and from the smell of this wonderful man—a mixture of the pine trees that grew all around and the books he loved and the brownies he'd made himself. And maybe just a hint of chalk dust.

She nudged a little closer, vaguely surprised at her own readiness to move deeper into the kiss, when there was a sudden clatter from the hallway, followed by whispers.

"Oh, my gosh," said Seth.

"Jack!" called Rosemary. "Tell me you two are not spying on us!"

Quick footsteps scuttled down the hallway and a door softly closed.

"Can you believe them?" said Rosemary.

Seth shook his head and laughed. "I think I can hear giggling. They're quite a pair," he said.

"They're stealthy," agreed Rosemary. "They meddle."

"And they spy," said Seth, nodding. He looked back at Rosemary. "But it's late. I'd better get going anyway."

They both stood.

"Hold on. Let me get your jacket," said Rosemary, turning to make a quick run to her room.

Seth grabbed her arm and pulled her toward him, enfolded her in his arms. "Keep it a while longer. Maybe it'll smell as nice as you when I get it back."

"How about I bring it to you tomorrow? I could swing by the university."

"I'd like that," he answered. "Jack and I always have lunch on campus on Wednesdays because we only have half an hour between classes. Would you come?"

Rosemary pulled out of his arms just a little bit, so she could see his eyes. "Love to," she said, smiling.

Seth kissed her cheek. "Nice dimple right there," he said.

"See you tomorrow," said Rosemary.

"I'll be looking forward to it," said Seth, and he stepped out into the blustery night.

Rosemary closed the door behind him, smiling dreamily before walking back to the couch. "You can come out now," she called in the general direction of the bedrooms.

There was no sound for a moment, but then Jack and Charlie slowly peeped out, looking as innocent as they could pretend to be.

"How's your bathroom cabinet handle?" Rosemary asked flatly.

"Good," Charlie answered quickly. "It's really good."

"Sorry about that, earlier. We were just on our way to the kitchen," said Jack. "And then there you were, in a passionate embrace with Dr. McGuire. We tried to sneak away without disturbing you."

"Right. So, tell me, why were you on your way to the kitchen—both of you? Together?" asked Rosemary.

There was a pause.

"I needed to get—" Charlie began, and at the same time, Jack was saying, "I was going . . . I mean we—"

"Next time you think of an excuse to leave me alone with a man," Rosemary interrupted them, "make it at least *slightly* believable."

"I can't help it! I'm clearly not very good at lying on the fly," said Jack. "And Charlie here can't even lie at all."

Charlie shrugged and nodded in agreement.

"Well, it's a good thing for you that I like Seth, or you'd be in big trouble." The stern look on Rosemary's face finally cracked into a big smile.

"So . . . you like Seth?" asked Jack, a gleam in his eye.

"Wait," said Charlie. "Do you like him? Or do you *like* him-like him?"

They plopped down on either side of her on the couch.

"Both," said Rosemary. "Man, this has been one heck of a day."

"How was the kiss?" asked Jack, unable to subdue the hint of giddiness in his voice.

"None of your beeswax!" said Rosemary, swatting him in the arm.

She paused, and a slow grin spread across her face. "It was good," she said. "Really good."

"Don't worry," Jack said to Charlie across Rosemary. "I'll get all the juicy details out of her tomorrow."

"I'm going to crawl into bed and read," said Rosemary, heaving herself up off the couch. "See you both tomorrow."

Jack and Charlie stood as well, and they all walked toward the bedroom hall.

"And guys?" said Rosemary, opening her door. "Thanks. I love you both."

"We love you, too," said Charlie, and they hugged her and said goodnight.

While Rosemary was brushing her teeth, she caught a glimpse of Smudge nosing open the door and soundlessly hopping up onto the bed. Rosemary closed the bathroom door except for one small crack and watched as the little creature chose one of the fluffy pillows, stepped up onto it, and proceeded to pad it with her paws, then walk in tiny circles and settle down into a tight, purring ball. She opened one eye when Rosemary finally approached the bed, and then closed it again.

"Are you pretending to be asleep? Because I know that trick," she said. "Okay, listen. If you're anything like those *Lady and the Tramp* cats, this isn't going to work out. I don't have any milk. And if you're thinking of smothering me in my sleep, well then, you're out of here. So, the only way this thing between us is going to fly is if you stay on your pillow and don't touch me or freak me out in any way during the night. Okay?"

Smudge opened the eye again, then closed it, which seemed to Rosemary to mean they had an understanding.

Mercy's journal was one of the most valuable things Rosemary had ever held in her hands. Honestly, if she had found it in a cave full of jewels, à la Indiana Jones, with only moments to grab something before the whole place exploded, she still would've saved the journal over anything else.

Sitting on her bed, she carefully laid it out on the cloth Jack had wrapped it in, and slipped on a pair of white, cotton gloves he had given her so that none of the oils from her hands would get on the precious pages. Rosemary had handled valuable artifacts many times before, so Jack knew he could trust her to take the utmost care. But even for Rosemary, this book was exceptional.

She was amazed by the forward thinking displayed by Hortence and Mercy in their administrations. In a period in history where medicine was marked by bloodletting, purging, and trying to rebalance the body's "humors," Hortence was prescribing good food and fresh air. She used honey to sooth sore throats. Made poultices to calm itchy skin. There were lists of ingredients for various maladies—some of them, Rosemary suspected, had been picked up from Native Americans in the area.

Rosemary smiled when she saw the name "Potter" listed repeatedly in the records. In fact, Hortence had delivered no fewer than twelve Potter babies—among them two sets of twins! Twins apparently ran in the Potter family.

While many area people probably couldn't afford to be seen by a doctor even when one could be summoned, Hortence and Mercy had accepted payment in the form of things like salt pork, squash, corn . . . The Potters had once paid for the care of one of their sick children with a linen handkerchief, and others hadn't been able to pay at all, but that didn't keep the sisters from making repeat visits.

Mercy wrote of cultivating and collecting basil, horehound, mint, and rosemary, among other herbs and plants. Rosemary marveled at the fact that she had probably done so on this very land that surrounded Jack and Charlie's house.

It was way past midnight by the time Rosemary deciphered a particularly hard-to-read passage in the journal about bruises Mercy herself had treated on Hortence's throat and wrists. There was an entry where Hortence's eye had swollen shut from bruising. Rosemary clenched her jaw as she read about symptoms that certainly smacked of spousal abuse. She thought of Jonathan Gallow, buried respectably in the church-yard. And Hortence, alone in the meadow. Then she realized Hortence would probably have preferred the beautiful, peaceful meadow as a final resting place anyway.

The wind moaned outside, and Rosemary got up and walked to the window. She saw only darkness and distant lightening, so she pulled the curtains closed and returned to bed.

A few pages later, Rosemary read about the death of a man identified only as J. in late August of 1668. A knife wound. This entry was different from the others. As Rosemary was quickly learning, anytime a patient passed away, Mercy simply wrote "God save" in neat, curling letters. But this time, she did not. Instead, in very tiny, almost illegible print, she had scratched the words "Truth and justice no more intertwined. Justice did the deed." Could this be Jonathan Gallow's death Mercy was describing? Rosemary scanned the entry again. Late summer, 1668. August.

Rosemary searched her memory for Jonathan Gallow's headstone in the First Church graveyard. "Died August 1668." She was sure of it. So, the timing was right.

Was Mercy saying that it was *just*—fair—that Jonathan Gallow had been knifed down in cold blood? It seemed a logical conclusion, though of course, there was no way to be sure.

And "Truth and justice no more intertwined." That phrase! Rosemary quickly took out the tin box with the note Mercy had written before running away with baby Lilly. And there it was: the very same phrase.

What was Mercy getting at? One thing was sure in Rosemary's estimation: An intelligent, careful woman like Mercy knew what she was writing. It meant something to her. She might not have been able to speak of such things, but she had to release them somehow. So, she did the one thing she could do: She wrote them down.

Rosemary gingerly closed the book and wrapped it carefully in the fabric, then returned it to its box; she did the same with the note.

She fell back into bed, where Smudge yawned, stood up, walked around in her little circles again, and to Rosemary's great relief, laid back down on her pillow and fell instantly asleep.

Rosemary's eyes were burning as she finally let them flutter closed, the sound of a light rain falling steadily on the metal roof, thoughts of Hortence and Seth and Ingrid still swirling in her mind.

She decided she would find her way back to the Potters' farm in the morning, and talk to Mrs. Potter about all of this. The Potters' history, after all, was connected to the Clarks'. Mercy's journal proved that.

If she and Jack were going to write a book about all of this, they'd need to get at the truth. And Mrs. Potter herself had said that the family had saved everything—old records and letters. Rosemary could even visit their family burial site while she was at the farm if it was okay with Mrs. Potter.

But it was more than the book that she and Jack would write that was on Rosemary's mind as she tried to sleep. She was restless with questions. What did Becky Thatcher mean when she said to her husband that Sam had died because of the curse? Had someone used the 350-year-old curse—and the witch's mark—to cover up a murder? All of these deaths that Seth had mentioned in the Graves family line—deaths that spanned hundreds of years and seemed to be tied to the curse . . . If curses weren't real, then what was the truth behind all of those? Were they merely coincidences? Were they deaths that all had happened for logical reasons and then been embellished for the sake of good storytelling over back fences and in local rumor mills?

In the end, there were three main questions that made it almost impossible for Rosemary to fall asleep: Who killed Hortence? Who killed Jonathan Gallow? And who killed Samuel Wright?

And then there was the fourth and even more intriguing question: Why?

18

The sunrise on the farm the next morning was golden and glorious. Rosemary had also risen early, but was neither golden *nor* glorious after only a few hours of sleep. She was energized, though, by thoughts of getting out and visiting Mrs. Potter, and of digging deeper into the history of Paperwick. And also, by the thought of seeing Seth at lunch and the memory of his kiss.

She pulled on jeans and a sweater, walked outside and down to the pond, to the little dock, where she curled up comfortably in one of the Adirondack chairs that overlooked the water.

She'd been sitting and thinking for some time when Jack strolled up behind her, carrying two steaming mugs.

"How about a nice hot cup of coffee to go with that view?"

Charlie was close behind, carrying his own coffee plus a small basket covered with a kitchen towel.

"Pumpkin scone?" he asked, taking a seat and passing the basket.

"Yum! Thanks, guys. This is just what the doctor ordered for a night with very little sleep."

"Let me guess: You stayed up too late reading," said Jack.

"Well . . ."

"And then you couldn't get your mind to settle down."

"Something like that," admitted Rosemary. "But it's all such a tangled web. And how bizarre is it that the murder of Hortence Gallow is connected to the deaths of both Matthew Graves, hundreds of years ago, and Sam Wright, here in the present time?"

"What? How so?" asked Charlie.

"Connected by the curse," said Rosemary. "Hortence dies, leaving a curse on the family of the judge who was about to condemn her. Then he mysteriously dies a year or so later, and is seen to bear the so-called witch's mark. Then Samuel Wright dies here this week—and even though he's not in that family, and so it would seem thus not in line for the curse—his murder is made to look like it's the curse that killed him, too."

She looked earnestly at Jack. "I've rethought it a thousand times," she said. "And I'm through second guessing myself. Samuel was lying there, facedown, the shoulder of his shirt torn, and there was a mark. I'm sure I saw it. And this part I'd forgotten in all of the chaos yesterday—but Becky Thatcher must've seen it too, because she was crying on her husband's shoulder, saying it was all because of the curse."

"Let's hope the detective gets to the bottom of things," said Charlie.

"I don't have a lot of faith in Barney Weaser," said Jack. "When we left, I heard him whispering with Benedict Thatcher, saying the whole thing was probably some kind of accident."

"Why would he think that?" asked Rosemary.

"He's not the brightest bulb," said Charlie.

"And he's lazy," added Jack. "If he decides it was an 'accident' and tries to bend the evidence to point to that conclusion, then it's either because he doesn't want the trouble of a full-blown murder investigation, or he doesn't want any negative publicity staining our perfect little town. Or I guess he could be in cahoots with whoever killed Sam, but that seems unlikely."

"Trying to protect a murderer? That could end his career and land him in jail," said Charlie.

"Does he seem like the ladder-climbing type, trying to advance his career at all costs?" asked Rosemary.

"He seems like the self-absorbed type. Whatever else he has in mind, rest assured Weaser's in it for himself and what he can get out of it, I guarantee," said Jack.

"Could he be schmoozing Benedict Thatcher because he wants to be on the good side of the next mayor?" asked Rosemary. "I mean, maybe he would even, say, overlook a few clues in order to make this all go away . . . to protect said future mayor?"

"Do you think Ben Thatcher needs protecting?" asked Charlie, leaning forward in his chair. "Does that mean you're thinking *he* killed Sam? And that Weaser suspects it but isn't willing to point a finger because of Thatcher's position?"

"No. I mean . . . maybe. From an outsider's viewpoint, Thatcher would have motive and opportunity."

"Go on," said Jack.

"He wanted to be mayor eight years ago, remember? He became city manager instead. So, he does all the work while Sam gets all the credit. Add to that the fact that Mr. Thatcher was probably the last person to see Sam alive. They had a meeting in the Witch's Meadow. I saw them, wandering through the trees. And I keep remembering little things. Like could swear I heard them arguing. I think Ingrid heard them, too."

"So, there's suspect number one. Ben Thatcher. But I can't help but wonder if Ingrid is the killer," said Jack, shaking his head. "She hated Sam and what he was trying to do in Paperwick. And she's a bit of a loon. So, there's your motive. And she, too, was in the park at the right time. And didn't you say she was spying on the mayor and Ben?"

Rosemary took a bite of her scone. "Yes," she admitted finally with a sigh. "And the other odd thing is that Ingrid predicted there would be another death," she said slowly. "I'm trying to remember her words. She talked about me seeing Smudge. She said something like, 'You saw Hortence's cat, didn't you?' She said it meant there would be another death."

"Oh, man, that isn't going to go off well with Weaser. Ingrid predicts another death and then sure enough, a few minutes later, there *is* one? Did anyone else hear her say that?"

"Other than me? I don't know for sure. We were basically alone in the meadow. Except Sam and Benedict were definitely there, too. And I can't say whether or not there was anyone else around. I wish I could go back in time and be more observant."

They sat in silence for a few minutes, enjoying the coffee and scones and the peaceful morning. A small flock of ducks glided down and landed on the far side of the pond, and once again, Rosemary was amazed at the beauty of this place. She noticed the old red truck driving up to the cottage that sat next to the pond.

"I keep meaning to ask about that place," Rosemary said. "Who's that in the red truck?"

"That's Bert Ander," said Jack, getting up. "You'll meet him."

"Nice guy," said Charlie, also standing.

"Well, I've got class in half an hour, so I'd better get going," said Jack.

"And I have an online meeting with my editor," said Charlie. "What are you up to today, Rosemary?"

"I'm having lunch with Jack and Seth on campus," said Rosemary. "But before that, I'm going to take a little drive out to the Potters' farm. I want to ask Mrs. Potter a few questions about the old days. Maybe get a look at their family burial plot."

"Great," said Jack. "And this afternoon, I thought we'd start hanging the lanterns in the trees at the churchyard, for the festival."

"Perfect," said Rosemary, feeling a surge of energy thanks to the coffee and having lots of interesting things on her agenda for the day. "See you at lunch."

Now that Rosemary was learning her way around Paperwick, it only took a few minutes to drive back through town, across the covered bridge, and along the creek until she arrived at Potter Farm. She'd given Mrs. Potter a call before heading that way, and was warmly encouraged to come right over.

"How are you, my dear girl?" Mrs. Potter called, hurrying out to meet Rosemary at her car, which she'd parked in the small lot near the farm stand. Before she could answer, Rosemary was caught up in a tight embrace.

"I heard about you finding poor Mayor Wright," said Mrs. Potter. "To think that we were just talking about him a mere two days ago! And now he's gone!"

"I know. It's a horrible business," said Rosemary. "He was such a nice man."

"The nicest. A terrible loss for the village. I understand poor Benedict Thatcher will be taking over as mayor for now," said Mrs. Potter as the two of them walked past the big red barn toward a cozy house that stood on a slight rise just a short distance behind the farm stand. Little paths wove all through the property, from the farm stand to the barn and the house, and then back through the orchard and beyond. The house was a large, old, traditional two-story, with gray siding and black shutters, and a wraparound porch. Smoke rose picturesquely from its two stone chimneys. Rosemary followed Mrs. Potter up wide porch steps to the front door, which was painted a deep burgundy color.

"That's my understanding," said Rosemary. "But Jack and Charlie say Mr. Thatcher is definitely capable of doing the work. Small comfort, I know. But sounds like the town is still in good hands."

"Oh, most definitely. Benedict ran for mayor himself some years ago, you know. Let's see . . ." Mrs. Potter thought for a moment. "Yes, it was eight years ago, when Mayor Wright ran that first time. Benedict had been working his way up in the community—doing a lot of good around here."

"And when he didn't win, the mayor appointed him city manager?"

"That's right. They've been quite a team."

"But I hear Mr. Thatcher was also close friends with the mayor. I mean, in addition to being his colleague."

"The closest. Those two worked together *and* played together. Like brothers. I can't imagine how Benedict and Becky will get along without Sam."

By now, they'd entered the house, and Mrs. Potter took Rosemary to a comfortable room just off the front entrance hall that appeared to be a study or library. The walls were lined with bookshelves which were packed to the brim with books. There was a large wooden desk with papers and books strewn about on its surface. The room looked lived in, and Rosemary liked that. Mrs. Potter motioned her to one of two cushy, oversized chairs next to a huge picture window that overlooked the orchard.

"I'll get us some tea. Be right back," said Mrs. Potter, who scuttled out of the room and was back almost instantly carrying a tray laden with a teapot, cream, sugar, teacups, and a plate of delicate-looking sandwich cookies filled with what appeared to be jelly. She set the tray on the table between the two chairs. "We'll just let that steep for a few minutes," she said.

"Hot tea will be wonderful. It's chilly out today," said Rosemary. "So, you were saying the Thatchers were really close with Mayor Wright?"

"The three of them were like peas in a pod. They all grew up together here. Of course, Becky dated Samuel first—before she fell for Ben. But when Sam went off to college, she took another look at Ben, and the rest is history."

"Becky dated Sam? That's hard to believe."

"Doesn't quite fit, does it?" said Mrs. Potter. "Becky has always been a shy one. And Sam was a rambunctious young man. A party boy. But then again, they do say opposites attract. It's better for both of them it didn't work out. Ben, on the other hand, was the perfect choice for Becky. Solid.

Decent. A very kind man." She looked down sadly. "And of course, poor Sam had just finally gotten around to getting engaged himself."

"I heard," said Rosemary. "Only a few days ago. So sad. Do you know anything about his fiancée?"

"Victoria Winthrop. Comes from a well-to-do family over in Hartford. She and Sam met back in their college days, at Yale. She's been living and working in New Haven ever since. The story goes, they dated in college, but broke up when Sam moved home to Paperwick. But they never lost touch and apparently rekindled the flame a few years ago."

"Have you seen her? The guys and I think we might've caught a glimpse of her. Is she a very beautiful blond woman? Tall, thin, well-dressed?"

"That's her, all right. Gabby waited on them at the café a few days ago, and came home with the scoop. Victoria is beautiful, educated, and rich. The honest truth is—and this is not gossip, because I got it right from Gabby—that Victoria is a bit of a snoot. She made that clear by the way she treated my girl. Apparently felt herself above the likes of a lowly small-town waitress."

"You can tell a lot about people by the way they treat the wait-staff at a restaurant."

"Exactly. I imagine if she'd known Gabby's family *owns* the restaurant, that might've made at least a small difference."

Rosemary nodded.

"Gabby got an earful as she was refilling their drinks and such. Seems Victoria wasn't really interested in living in a little place like Paperwick, but Sam had finally won her over. And then on her first visit to town, he died. Tragic!"

"She must be heartbroken," said Rosemary, accepting a cup of steaming tea from Mrs. Potter and plunking in a couple of sugar cubes and a dash of cream.

"You'd think," said Mrs. Potter, offering the plate of cookies.

Rosemary bit into one of the cookies and was momentarily stunned by how delicious it was. The thin white cookies were buttery and tender, and the red jelly filling tasted sweet and tart at once.

"Oh my gosh, Mrs. Potter. What is this filling?"

"Ah! That's my autumn-olive jelly. The bushes grow wild here. Do you like it?"

"I love it. It's the perfect balance with these delicate little cookies."

"Well, help yourself, dear," said Mrs. Potter, pleased with the compliment.

"But go on, about Victoria," said Rosemary, getting back on topic. "I'm surprised she didn't rush over to the crime scene. Did she already leave town?"

Mrs. Potter glanced around and lowered her voice a little. "Apparently she was off getting a manicure when it happened. Or so she claims. I checked with George—Officer Harris, that is—and he filled me in. And now, Victoria's moved her things out of Sam's house and is staying at our inn," said Mrs. Potter. "Seems she felt spooky, being in that house all alone. I'm sure she'll stay on through the memorial service tomorrow, and then hightail it out of town."

"Wow. You own an inn, too?"

"Right on the green, just a hop, skip, and a jump from the café. Potter's Bed and Bakery. The inn is just above the bakery, there on Chestnut Street," said Mrs. Potter. "Listen, when you've been in a town as long as we Potters have been in Paperwick, you drop a lot of hooks into the water."

"So that *was* Victoria Jack and Charlie and I saw at the café the other day," said Rosemary. "We were actually having lunch there when Gabby waited on the happy couple. They looked stunning together."

"No doubt," said Mrs. Potter. "But I'm not sure they would've been happy." She looked into her teacup and frowned.

"What do you mean?" asked Rosemary, taking another cookie. "Because of Victoria's snootiness?"

"It's more than that. After dating for years, Mayor Wright would've known all about that, I feel sure. He must've made his peace with it or seen past it. No, this is really just an observation *since* Sam's death. I have a knack about people, you know. I'm very intuitive. And the young lady doesn't seem to me to be . . . well . . . as heartbroken as she should be."

"Really?"

"She just got engaged, for heaven's sake. She must've been in love, since she said yes and was prepared to pick up her life and move to Paperwick. It just seems to me that she should be more . . ."

"Upset?"

"Yes. Her fiancé—presumably the love of her life—has been murdered, for goodness sake!"

"So, you don't think it was an accident?"

"Good heavens, no."

"A minute ago, you said Victoria 'claimed' she was off getting a manicure when Sam died. What did you mean by that?"

"It's not for me to go around accusing people of murder," said Mrs. Potter, leaning in a bit closer. "But don't you think it's suspicious? She comes to town, and Sam dies? I mean, I know the people of Paperwick. If we had a murderer in our midst, I think I'd have at least an inkling. No one knows this Victoria, but going off of what little I've seen of her, I can tell you the woman has a seriously bad temper. What if she and Sam had some sort of fight and things got out of hand?"

"I guess it could have been her and Sam I heard arguing in the woods just before he died," said Rosemary thoughtfully. "I honestly couldn't make out the voices. I know at least one of them was male. But I can't be sure about the other."

"And trust me when I tell you, based on the way Victoria acted when she checked into the Bed and Bakery last night . . . Well, let's just say I don't have a high opinion of the woman."

"And you do have a knack for knowing people," said Rosemary, beating Mrs. Potter to the words.

"I do indeed!" Mrs. Potter leaned even closer and lowered her voice even more. "The woman was drunk when she checked in last night. I mean falling-down drunk. And she had awful manners. Talked to me like I was her servant. She had me carry her suitcase to her room, for crying out loud! And all the way to the room, she was mumbling about that 'son of a b-word' Sam!"

"It definitely sounds like Victoria is more put out than she is devastated," said Rosemary. "But have they officially ruled Sam's death a murder yet? I heard that Detective Weaser said it might be an accident—"

"That man is a dud. There's just no nice way to say it. He's a dud. *Accident*, my fanny!"

Just then, one of Mrs. Potter's twin daughters running came in.

"Mom, we've got the corn maze done! Come out and see!"

"Dear, you can see we have company here," said Mrs. Potter, motioning toward Rosemary. "Slow down for a second and say hello!"

"Oh, hello. Miss Grey, right?" The girl twisted one of her many long, brown curls around her finger and smiled.

"Hello…Abbey?"

"Fooled you! I'm Gabby."

"Gabby, tell your brother and sister we'll be right out," said Mrs. Potter. "That is, if *Doctor* Grey wouldn't mind taking a peek at the corn maze."

"Oops. Dr. Grey, sorry about that," said Gabby.

"That's okay. I'd love to see the corn maze."

They set down their teacups and walked down the orchard path, through a group of Honeycrisp apple trees, and then veered to the right and were soon standing before a huge cornfield. Abbey and a young man who looked to be about twelve years old were installing a large wooden sign which read "Get Lost in Potter's Corn Maze!" with another, smaller banner tacked onto it that read, "Can you defeat the DRAGON?"

"Dr. Rosemary Grey, you already know Abigail and Gabriella," Mrs. Potter began.

"Mom!" both girls said at once.

"Alright, alright," said Mrs. Potter. "Abbey and Gabby, then." She cleared her throat. "You haven't met my youngest, Henry."

"Very nice to meet you, Henry," said Rosemary, smiling at the freckle-faced boy.

"He's really Bubba," said Abbey.

"You should definitely call him Bubba," said Gabby.

Rosemary looked at the boy and raised an eyebrow.

"Yep, you should definitely call me Bubba," he said, shrugging his shoulders a little.

"Bubba it is, then," said Rosemary.

"So, you've got the maze all trimmed, then?" asked Mrs. Potter.

"Yep," said Bubba.

"This is a*maz*ing," said Rosemary, eliciting a little laugh from the children. "It's huge!"

"Biggest in this county," said Mrs. Potter. "We used to be the biggest in the state, but then our rivals, Fillpot's Family Farm, expanded theirs by three yards. Three measly yards! We do still hold the distinction of having the maze with the most options, though. You could spend all day in there! And we have five levels, too."

"Ours is the best!" said Gabby.

"Levels?" asked Rosemary. "What are levels in a corn maze?"

"Ooh, let me tell her!" said Abbey. "So, level one is for the little kids. They use this entrance over here." She ran over to an opening in the corn maze and pointed. "Level two is for older kids, level three is for teenagers and grownups who don't want to spend all day in there."

"And level four is for crazy people," said Bubba. "Nobody's getting out of level four without help."

"Then what's level five like?" asked Rosemary.

"Level five is for people who want the ultimate challenge," said Gabby. "You better pack a lunch if you go in there."

"This is so cool," said Rosemary. "Is it open all through the fall?"

"It officially opens this weekend at the Founders Day Festival," said Mrs. Potter. "And then it stays open all month. After that, we shift into Christmas mode. You'll have to come back during the holidays for Potters' Christmas Tree Farm Holiday Fair and Gala!"

"You also grow Christmas trees?" asked Rosemary, who was beginning to think the Potter family knew no bounds.

"Oh, of course!" said Mrs. Potter.

"That way," said Bubba, pointing to where the orchard path curved even further away and disappeared over a small rise. Sure enough, rows upon rows of evergreens were visible in the distance, growing all the way up the next hill.

"Dad dresses up like Santa," said Abbey.

"And Mom dresses up like Mrs. Santa," said Gabby.

"I'm the elf," said Bubba.

"I'll definitely come," said Rosemary, giving Bubba a wink.

"So how do you make a corn maze?" asked Rosemary, looking back at the corn. "Do you plant the corn and then cut the paths into it?"

"Nope. We plan the maze from day one," said Mrs. Potter. "We actually create our design on a grid, then stake it out with little orange flags, then plant our corn accordingly."

"I had no idea," said Rosemary.

"And then we keep it trimmed and neat," said Abbey.

"This year's design—if you could view it from the sky—is a huge castle, with turrets and a drawbridge," said Mrs. Potter.

"And a dragon!" said Bubba.

"And we have a wooden stand, right in the middle, just in case anybody gets lost," said Abbey.

"Then we can tell them where to go," added Gabby.

"Wow," said Rosemary. "I can't wait to try it out."

"Why wait?" said Gabby with a giggle. "Mom, you could take Miss—I mean *Dr.* Grey through level one right now."

The other two kids made noises of approval, and Mrs. Potter looked at Rosemary and gave her a sort of "might-as-well-do-it" shrug.

So, Mrs. Potter and Rosemary trooped good-naturedly into the maze.

"Mrs. Potter, I have to tell you about what I saw at the cemetery. About how I found Sam's body," said Rosemary, pushing aside an ear of corn and looking at the fork in the path ahead of them, wondering which way they'd go. "Because it's really disturbing, and I don't know what to make of it. Maybe you can offer some insight."

"Go on, dear," Mrs. Potter said, taking the left path while listening intently.

"He was facedown, in his own family's plot in the graveyard, and on his shoulder . . . Please don't think I'm crazy. But there was a tear in his shirt, and there was a mark."

Mrs. Potter's eyes grew wide and she sucked in her breath and stopped walking. "The witch's mark?" she gasped.

"Yes."

"So, the curse strikes again."

"That's exactly what Becky Thatcher seemed to think. But why would the curse strike Samuel Wright? I mean, I don't believe in curses. But even if I did, unless I've misunderstood the story of Hortence Gallow, the curse was leveled against the judge's family. The Graves family."

"Yes, exactly," said Mrs. Potter, who was walking again and veering right at the next fork in the path. "Against that Matthew Graves, who accused Hortence of witchcraft and was set to condemn and execute her."

"But I don't understand, then."

"Don't understand what, dear?"

"The curse was for the *Graves* family. And from what Seth—Dr. McGuire—told me, the supposed victims of the curse through the years have all been people who were somehow sitting in the judgment seat *and* were in that family line."

"That's correct," said Mrs. Potter, nodding and pausing at a three-pronged fork and looking a bit puzzled. "Don't remember this being here," she muttered, before nodding to herself and confidently setting off down the middle path. "And the curse will not be lifted until Hortence's killer is identified, proving her innocence and setting her spirit free."

"So why Samuel Wright, then?" asked Rosemary, feeling exasperated.

"Because as mayor, he was a kind of judge—a city official. And as a descendent of Matthew Graves—"

"Wait. Hold on," said Rosemary, stopping in her tracks. "Samuel Wright was a descendent of Matthew Graves? How is that possible? The Wrights didn't even move to Paperwick until the 1700s. Sam told me."

"Well, it's a bit of a twisting path, not unlike this one," said Mrs. Potter, turning back to Rosemary. "But I can show you family tree charts and bloodlines from the founding families. Like I said, we Potters never throw anything away. But let me make it as short and sweet as I can. Matthew Graves died—a suspicious death, and thus he was the first victim of the curse—'round about 1669. A year after Hortence. That left Elizabeth Graves a widow, but she'd had five children by Matthew before his demise. She actually took up midwifery in Hortence and Mercy's stead after Hortence died and Mercy fled. Did you know?"

"Yes. That part I knew," answered Rosemary.

"Anyway, Elizabeth's youngest child was a girl, named Faith. In the early 1700s, Faith Graves married the newly arrived Jed Wright. Their first child—a son—was Elias Wright."

"Elias Wright was the character Sam was going to play at the cemetery crawl!" said Rosemary. "He thought Elias was the first Wright born in Paperwick."

"Well, technically, of course, he was."

"So, Sam is related to the Graves family—and to one of the founding fathers of Paperwick. Why did he not know this?"

"He never seemed interested in digging into his past, and we Potters never talked about that connection because to be honest, I wouldn't want to tell *anyone* they were related to that Matthew Graves."

"But why?"

"He was crooked. And a womanizer. This isn't something you'd ever find in any history book, mind you. All of those say he was a good man and an important member of society. But we Potters know better. The story has been handed down from generation to generation. There he was, married to poor Elizabeth, and taking mistresses all over town. He made a play for our own dearest Maggie. How's that for scandalous?"

"Maggie, as in *Maggie's Pride*? The apple namesake?"

"The very same. She was a strong, bold, and prideful woman. When I say prideful, I mean in the good way. Confident. Self-assured."

Rosemary nodded and thought of Hortence, who'd had similar character traits.

"Matthew Graves was handsome. Powerful. Used to getting what he wanted. Anyway, he took a try at Maggie, and she told him where to get off. Then she came home and told her brothers what had happened, and believe me, they made sure it never happened again. But Matthew Graves would've compromised our Maggie's honor without giving it a second thought if he could've gotten away with it."

"And so that's the bad blood between your family and Sam's," said Rosemary, fully understanding at last. "That's the feud you spoke of the other day."

"That's the bad blood," confirmed Mrs. Potter as they strolled deeper into the maze. "We never brought it up with Samuel because he was a good man, and even the modern-day Graves family's reputation isn't the best. It's not as though he'd want to look up any long-lost cousins if you know what I mean. But like I told you before, it was all water that had passed under the proverbial bridge hundreds of years ago as far as we're concerned. The Wrights were good folk. And who wants to go around digging up three hundred fifty-year-old skeletons?"

Mrs. Potter stopped walking and shook her head. "And now you can see why Sam's death was on account of the curse," she said. "As a Graves in the judgement seat, he couldn't escape it."

"Or maybe someone just wanted it to appear that way."

Mrs. Potter looked at Rosemary thoughtfully for a moment.

"Well, if it's not the curse, my money is on that horrible Victoria Winthrop," she said. "But if it *is* the curse . . . Well, you're the historian. Use your skills to find out what happened to Hortence Gallow. Break the curse before anyone else falls victim."

"I still don't know that I believe in curses, Mrs. Potter, but you have my word. I'll try."

"That's all I can ask, my dear," said Mrs. Potter with a smile. "Now. Where in tarnation are we? Gabby! This is *not* level one!"

Giggles could be heard coming from somewhere in the maze.

"I mean it, you three!" Mrs. Potter yelled. "Get us out of here!"

19

Because she and Mrs. Potter had spent so long lost in the corn maze, Rosemary had to say goodbye and be on her way before seeing the Potter family's burial plot. Mrs. Potter was happy to extend an invitation for Rosemary to return the following week, which Rosemary gladly accepted.

With the top still down on her trusty convertible, Rosemary enjoyed the fresh fall air on the drive to Paperwick University. The leaves were brilliant against a blue sky, and Rosemary slowed down as she drove through town, admiring tree-lined streets and beautiful old homes. She smiled as she passed the old courthouse, Potter's Café, First Church, and the Bed and Bakery. She was tempted to stop the car and spend some time on the green, where ducks were gliding on the pond and several couples were chatting while walking around the fitness trail that wove its way through the trees.

But a glance at the clock told Rosemary that she only had an hour until she was to meet Jack and Seth for lunch, and she wanted to spend some time at the university library before then. So, she made the turn at the Village Market, where piles of pumpkins and colorful gourds were on offer outside, and drove toward the university. A few minutes later, she was pulling into a visitor's parking spot near the library.

The library, like many of the buildings on campus, looked very old and historic from the outside. But when Rosemary pushed open a huge wood and glass door, she found a well-appointed, modern facility inside. The place was full of light thanks to huge windows, and rows of bookshelves were surrounded by comfortable sitting areas, computer kiosks, and study carrels. Small glassed-in meeting rooms and classrooms were scattered here and there, and it enlivened the whole atmosphere to be able to see students leaning over tables sharing ideas, classes being taught, and people huddled up with their noses in books.

Jack had told Rosemary to go to the front desk and ask for Jane Snow, who would be expecting her.

"Hello," Rosemary said to a pretty, older woman whose silver hair was pulled back into a ponytail. "I'm Rosemary Grey. I'm looking for Ms. Snow."

"Ah! Hello, Dr. Grey. I am Mrs. Snow, but if you don't let the kids hear you, you may call me Jane." She gave a little wink, and Rosemary immediately knew that she and Jane would get along just fine.

"Now," Jane continued, "I believe you are here to spend some time with the genealogy collection?"

"And any local history you have would be great, too," said Rosemary, nodding.

"Let's get you settled in, then," said Jane, motioning for Rosemary to follow her.

They entered a room at the back of the library which had the word "Genealogy" written in gold lettering on the glass door.

"You'll find most of what we have on the local families over here in this section," said Jane, pointing to a couple of shelves along the wall. "And as you can imagine, there's not a huge amount of material available on the history of this tiny village, but I do have one volume, which I will bring you."

Jane left Rosemary to browse the shelves and returned shortly with a small hardbound book entitled, *Paperwick: A History*.

Knowing she couldn't check books out of the genealogy collection, Rosemary started with family records. Most of them were very dull lists. The Kings were leaders of the church. The Filberts and Andersons were farmers. The Martins had a brewery, which sparked Rosemary's interest—although she knew from her studies that the idea that Puritans didn't drink beer and wine was only a popular myth. The

Graves family had been into politics, government, and dispensing justice from the beginning. The Potters—much like the modern-day Potters—were into everything from shop-keeping to farming. And the Clarks were also land owners, farmers, and upstanding citizens in general.

Someone other than Rosemary had obviously taken an interest in the Clark family, as their history was marked with an avocado-green sticky note that had been left behind. There were also light pencil underlines on certain passages. Rosemary removed the sticky note and crumpled it up, thinking that people really should be more respectful of library property.

She then opened the Paperwick history book that Jane had brought her. Evidently, the same sticky-note-leaver had handled this book, because the same unusual green sticky notes were stuck here and there. Always in passages that mentioned the Clark family.

Passages about Hortence and Mercy were lightly underlined, and in the section that talked about Hortence being accused of witchcraft, Rosemary found another sticky note—but this one had writing on it: *Meadow View = Witch's Way. Statue in meadow. Celebration on Halloween: inaugurate statue and Witch's Meadow officially. Alert state tourism board. Ads in Visit Connecticut Magazine?*

Someone, it seemed, had plans to capitalize on Hortence Gallow's tale, and Rosemary wondered who the sticky-note bandit was. She pulled out every one of the notes, and took a peek at the clock on the wall.

Time to meet Jack and Seth.

She approached Jane with the books that had been marked up.

"A few of these have pencil markings in them. Thought I'd call it to your attention, Jane," said Rosemary.

"Why thank you," said Jane. "College kids these days. Although," she glanced at the titles. "There's only one person who's picked up these books in ages—other than you, of course." She shook her head sadly.

"Who would that be?" asked Rosemary, who felt she already knew the answer. "I mean, maybe this person and I can compare notes."

"Not possible, I'm sorry to say," said Jane. "It was Mayor Wright."

The little snack bar on the Paperwick University campus, as it turned out, made the best French fries Rosemary had ever tasted. Hot and crispy out of the fryer, they were seasoned to perfection and were just the right accompaniment to her bacon, lettuce, and tomato sandwich.

She'd met Jack and Seth downstairs at Langner Hall, and they'd strolled across campus together through cascades of falling leaves, talking about the morning's classes and enjoying the sunshine.

They'd stood in line at the snack bar and then taken their food to a quiet picnic table outside.

"So, Rosie, how was your visit with Mrs. P?" asked Jack, unwrapping a cheeseburger.

"Enlightening," said Rosemary. "The first time I met her, she'd told me that everyone knows everybody in Paperwick. Well, Mrs. Potter knows every*thing* about everybody. And then some."

"Anything juicy?" asked Jack, wiggling his eyebrows.

"Yep," said Rosemary. "Get this: The Wrights are related to the Graves."

"Hold on," said Seth, setting down his forkful of salad. "Are you serious?"

"The judge, Matthew Graves, had a daughter, named Faith. Faith married into the Wright family when they came here just after the turn of the 18th century. Sam didn't know this because he wasn't really interested in the whole genealogy thing. And Mrs. Potter didn't tell him, because the Graves family has an unsavory history, and she didn't think this knowledge would do Sam any good—personally or politically. She would've explained it all to him if he'd asked, of course . . ."

"But he never did," said Seth.

"So, the curse—" Jack began.

"Yep. It would seem that Hortence's curse struck again."

"But curses aren't real," said Jack.

"I don't think they are either," said Rosemary. "But I'm not feeling sure of anything right now."

Seth had to hurry off to his next class, but promised to stop by the churchyard afterward. Jack had sent his afternoon class to do research in the library, so he and Rosemary headed over to the cemetery to work on hanging lanterns in the trees for Friday's festival.

"So, Sam had been researching the Clarks' history at the library?" asked Jack as they set up the ladder and moved it into place under a tree.

"It would appear so. And if his notes are any indication, Ingrid was right: He was thinking about the idea of capitalizing on her family's history."

"So, Ingrid's theories might not be as far-fetched as people think."

"Exactly," said Rosemary. "These are beautiful, by the way," she added, taking one of the lanterns out of a packing box and admiring it. "They're really made to look old."

"And flip the switch on the bottom," said Jack, who was climbing a ladder with a length of fishing line in one hand.

Rosemary flipped the switch and the lantern glowed, a little faux flame flickering merrily inside the bubbled glass. "Nice! I can't wait to see how these look in the dark," she said.

"And they're all remote control operated," said Jack, reaching down so that Rosemary could hand up the lantern. "So, all we do Friday night is press one button, and they'll all come on."

"Wonderful."

"Once we're done with these, we can line the path with luminarias. And then we'll bedeck the maple tree in the meadow with a dozen of these lanterns and surround it with extra candles—battery-operated, of course."

"And what about the costumes? Did you get my notes about what everyone should wear?"

"Yep. Dropped those off at school this morning, and Madame Petit assures me she has everything we need. Our 'spirits' will get costumed at the university before coming over here on Friday."

"Madame Petit is . . ."

"Head of the theater arts department, yes," said Jack.

"It's all coming together. We can put the finishing touches on the scripts tonight, and do a run-through before showtime."

"It's going to be the hit of the festival," said Jack.

"No doubt about that," said a voice, coming up behind them.

They turned to see Seth approaching, a big smile on his face as his eyes met Rosemary's.

"Done with class for today?" asked Rosemary.

"All done," said Seth. "I'm at your disposal."

"Great. We'll keep hanging lanterns, and you start in with the luminarias. Rosie, hand him the ordered list of spirits, so he'll know how to illuminate the path."

"Sure thing, boss," said Rosemary with a grin.

While Jack went on securing a lantern to a low-hanging bough, Rosemary dug in her bag and took out a slip of paper with the list of headstones Seth would need to locate.

"Thanks," he said, purposely brushing her hand as he took the list.

"You're welcome," she smiled. "And the luminarias are in that box over there. Each bag gets a battery-operated candle and a stone from the basket, to weigh it down in case the wind decides to come back. We'll wait until Friday to arrange the candles in the meadow. Jack's got everything set to one remote control, and we'll do a test run with the actors early Friday evening before the event gets underway."

"Maybe you and I should stop by tonight after dark—you know, to make sure the lights are in working order," said Seth, a smile in his voice.

"Sounds nice," said Rosemary. "Romantic, even."

"If you two are done with your idle chatter, I could use some help moving this ladder," called Jack.

"Oh! Sorry," said Rosemary, hurrying over to help him.

The three of them kept at it until the last lantern was hung.

"Not bad," said Rosemary, standing back and taking in the whole churchyard. "Can we light candles in the church windows, too?"

"That would be a nice touch," Jack said, nodding.

"Wow, this place looks great!" said Charlie, jogging up. "Good work!"

"Thanks, Sweetie," said Jack. "Not bad, huh?"

"I would've expected nothing less from you three. And good thing the luminarias are weather-proof. We're due another storm, if you can believe it."

"Oh no. Tell me you're kidding," said Jack. "I checked the forecast! It's supposed to be clear."

"By Friday it will be, so don't worry. There's a scattering of storms bumping around tonight and tomorrow night, but nothing that would hurt any of this."

Jack breathed a sigh of relief.

"We'll keep an eye on things," he said, then turning to Charlie, asked, "What brings you downtown? I thought you were working all afternoon."

"Thought you'd want to hear the news," said Charlie. "They just arrested Ingrid Clark."

"They say she didn't go quietly," said Charlie. "They'd questioned her yesterday. But they must've gotten something substantial on her, because they took her in today. They had to handcuff her. It wasn't pretty, from what I hear."

"I still don't think she did it," said Rosemary.

"I hope she didn't," said Jack.

"She's refusing to say anything. I just talked to George Harris," said Charlie.

"As in Officer Harris?" asked Rosemary.

"Yep. Ran into him at the market. He was there buying a package of those tiny donuts and a giant cup of coffee—so you know he's upset."

"He always eats garbage when he's upset," Jack told Rosemary. "So, Ingrid isn't defending herself at all?"

"Apparently she's just completely clammed up," said Charlie. "Won't speak to Weaser."

"Can't blame her for that," said Jack with a snort.

"Meanwhile, Weaser's been spouting off, saying he's got all the evidence he needs to convict. Scaring Ingrid half to death. But George isn't so sure. In fact, he was pretty shaken up about the whole thing."

"I knew I liked that George," said Rosemary. "He's a good note-taker."

"Always the professor," said Jack, giving her a nudge.

"I wonder if Ingrid would talk to me," said Rosemary.

"Do you think she would?" asked Jack.

"Well, she talked to me yesterday. She knows I agree with her about protecting the meadow. And we were both there—we both saw the mayor and Mr. Thatcher. She was watching them pretty closely. Maybe she knows something she's hesitant to say."

Rosemary looked from Jack to Charlie to Seth.

"So, you want to give it a try?" asked Seth.

Rosemary nodded.

"Then I'll take you down to the police station," said Seth.

"I need to stop by Jack and Charlie's first," said Rosemary. "I have to pick something up."

20

The Paperwick police station was a small building right next to the courthouse. When Rosemary and Seth arrived, the first officer they saw at the front desk was George, who looked relieved to see them.

"I guess Charlie told you about Ms. Clark," he said, standing and brushing powdered sugar off his fingers—residue from the tiny donuts, no doubt.

"Yes," said Rosemary. "Do you think we could speak to her, George?"

George looked around. The office was quiet. A door in the corner with a nameplate that read *Detective B. Weaser* was closed. One other uniformed officer sat at a desk, engrossed in paperwork in the other corner.

"I think it's worth a try," said George. "Come with me."

He escorted Rosemary and Seth down a short hallway to a sterile-looking little interviewing room—which probably doubled as a sort of employee lounge, because it housed a small refrigerator, a coffee maker, and a vending machine. They took seats at the table.

"I'll be right back," said George.

He returned shortly with Ingrid Clark, who was wearing handcuffs and looking frail.

"I'm sorry about the handcuffs, Ms. Clark," said George. "It's the only way I could get you out and bring you here. But look, here's Rosemary and Seth. They want to help you."

Ingrid took a seat at the table across from Rosemary and Seth, and gave George a nod, as if to tell him she understood.

"I'll be right over here in the corner," said George. "If you should need anything."

"Thank you, George" said Rosemary. "Ms. Clark," she began. "Ingrid. Can you talk to us about what's going on?"

Ingrid looked at Rosemary and then Seth.

"Oh, pardon me. This is Dr. Seth McGuire. He's a professor at the university. Anthropology."

"Funny. I had him pegged for archaeology," said Ingrid, giving Seth the once-over.

Rosemary looked at Seth who seemed taken aback.

"I did my undergrad work in archaeology," he said, amazed. "How did you guess?"

"I have a knack about these things," said Ingrid. Her eyes shifted to Rosemary. "Give him back his jacket yet?"

"How did you know it was his?" asked Rosemary.

"I know things. We'll leave it at that."

"Do you know who killed Sam?"

Ingrid's lips formed a thin line and her eyes fell.

"Because I don't think he was the victim by some curse," Rosemary continued.

Ingrid looked up at Rosemary again. "The curse isn't magic, you know," she said.

"It's not?" asked Rosemary.

"Curses are funny," said Ingrid. "We bring them on ourselves."

Rosemary fell back in her chair. Ingrid was right, of course. And maybe she wasn't as batty as she seemed, either. She was certainly one of the most fascinating people Rosemary had ever encountered.

"So, tell me, then: How did Samuel Wright curse himself?"

"By being a jackass," said Ingrid.

"And that got him killed?"

"Yep."

"Did you kill him?"

"Nope."

"Then tell me who did. Because Ingrid, you were seen standing over Sam's body. That doesn't bode well."

Ingrid looked down again and shuddered.

"So, you did find him, but you didn't kill him?" asked Rosemary quietly.

"That is correct," said Ingrid wearily. "Awhile after I talked to you, I went looking for him. And there he was. I checked his pulse. He was already gone. And then that Becky showed up and screamed and you know the rest. No one believes me."

"We do," said Rosemary.

"Is there any real evidence that you killed Sam beyond the fact that you were there right after he died?" asked Seth.

"No. There couldn't be. Because that's all that happened."

"There must be something we can do to get you out of here," said Rosemary.

"This is what happens when you separate justice from truth," said Ingrid, reminding Rosemary of Mercy's words. "And with someone like that Detective Weaser acting in the place of justice . . . Well, he's not really interested in the facts. He doesn't seek the truth. He just wants to butter up the right people and make a splash—put away a witch."

A single tear rolled down Ingrid's weathered cheek, and Rosemary thought she had never seen anything more heartbreaking—this proud woman who was as tough as a boot, looking so vulnerable.

"I want to show you something," said Rosemary, opening her bag.

She carefully took out the little box, opened it, and laid Mercy's note on the table in front of Ingrid.

"Jack found it in the old barn on the Clark farm. It was in this box, sealed with wax."

Ingrid leaned forward and marveled at the little scrap of paper.

"Just like her journal," she said, smiling softly.

"Her journal?"

"Mercy's journal."

"Her medical notes, from the museum, you mean? Yes—she uses that same phrase about justice—"

"Not that relic. I'm talking about her personal diary."

"What? Mercy also kept a diary?" asked Seth.

"She was an avid writer. Wrote everything down. That was her way of dealing with things. Yes, she kept a diary."

"I'd love to see it someday," said Rosemary.

"If I didn't want you to see it, I wouldn't have told you about it, would I?" said Ingrid, regaining a hint of her usual feisty spirit.

"Do you have any idea what this means?" asked Rosemary, pointing to Mercy's note.

"Yes, and you will too, when you read her journal. Look for the entries from just after this note was written."

"Wait. But Mercy wrote this note right as she left town. So, you're saying the journal is from *after* that?"

"Handed down for generations. From mother to daughter, all these years. The family donated some things to be shared with the public . . . And kept some things to ourselves."

"But why?"

"Would you want your personal business laid out for the whole world to see?" asked Ingrid.

"No, I guess not," admitted Rosemary.

"And are you the last of the Clark women?" asked Seth. "Is that why you're the caretaker of Mercy's journal now?"

"I am not the last. But I am the last in Mercy's line."

"Mercy's line? But aren't you Hortence's eleven-times great-granddaughter?" asked Rosemary, confused.

"Eleven-times great-*niece*. I am of Mercy's line. You see, Mercy left Paperwick in those dark days, but even though her sister's life had ended, Mercy's life went on. She moved north. Met and married a good man—a doctor by the name of Jonah Mills. Raised Lilly and had a daughter of her own. She loved this place, though. Loved that farm your friends own now. Loved that old barn. That's why we Clarks came back when that witch nonsense had finally blown over. For better or worse, this area is our home. Heck, I've got cousins fifteen miles up the road."

"So, the Mary Clark who returned here: The story is that she was Lilly's daughter," said Rosemary.

"She was not. Mary was Rose's daughter. Rose was Mercy's child."

Rosemary let out a deep sigh.

"And why is your name still Clark?" asked Seth. "Since all of the generations of women must've married and had children. Did they not take their husbands' names?"

"It is our tradition. The Clark women keep the name."

"I'm so glad to hear that Mercy was okay. The Historical Society only knows her story up until she left town." Rosemary felt a tear sting her eye as she smiled at Ingrid and reached out a hand—though she assumed Ingrid wouldn't take it. "You have a very proud heritage. Mercy was a survivor and a writer and an incredibly strong woman."

Ingrid's fist unclenched, and she laid her hand atop Rosemary's.

"Like you," she said gruffly.

"Like *you*," said Rosemary.

"You say you don't know who killed Sam," Seth said quietly. "But I have a feeling you have at least an inkling. How did Sam's curse kill him?"

Ingrid's gaze turned to Seth.

"That old curse." She paused thoughtfully. "But they're connected, of course, those two," she muttered to herself. "I'll tell you a story about two spoiled boys who were cut from the same piece of cloth. Samuel Wright was a glutton. Matthew Graves was a glutton. Vastly different generations. Same. Old.

Story." Ingrid tapped the table with her finger at each of these three words. "They got a little power, then they wanted more power. They got a little money, then they wanted more. They each captured the heart of a woman, but then they had to have another, and another. They both always wanted whatever was just out of reach. Neither could ever be content. Not with what they owned. Not with just one woman. That was their shared curse. And that is why they also shared the same fate."

"Who was the woman Matthew Graves wanted?" asked Rosemary. "He was married to Elizabeth. She was the good woman whose heart he'd captured. But she wasn't enough for him."

"It's not important," said Ingrid.

"Was it Hortence?" asked Rosemary.

Ingrid said nothing.

"Sam was a flirt," said Rosemary, shifting the subject. "But he'd just committed himself to one woman. I mean, he'd *just* gotten engaged."

"That's right. And how do you think that woman felt when she saw the way he conducted himself around here? Don't you think it's odd that this woman whom he proposed to had never been to Paperwick before? Or that no one here had ever heard of her before? That was no accident! That was by design. Samuel Wright's convoluted design. She would've cramped his style."

"But surely he was on his best behavior with Victoria around," said Rosemary.

"She'd have to be pretty blind not to see the women swooning everywhere he went," said Ingrid with a hint of disgust in her voice. "Or not to feel them jealously glaring at her."

"But then why would he bother to get married at all?" asked Seth. "He could just stay single. Play the field."

"My guess is he finally caved to pressure. That, or he needed to keep up appearances and was just using this poor girl."

"But then," said Rosemary, "Victoria had known Sam for a long time. She must've had at least a hint of what she was getting herself into."

"Who knows?" Ingrid continued. "Maybe they each decided it was worth it to give marriage a try. But she would've been none too happy once she put two and two together and realized how he operated here at home. No one wants to be made a fool of."

"So are you saying you think she accepted his proposal, came here, saw how it was, and then . . ." Rosemary lowered her voice and leaned forward in her chair. "And then killed Sam?"

"Hell hath no fury," said Ingrid.

"Let's think about this," said Rosemary, looking at Ingrid. "Whoever killed Sam did it in the meadow. You were there that day, just like I was. You were watching Sam and Benedict Thatcher. Remember? Did you see anyone else? Because I think . . ." Rosemary lowered her voice even further, to a whisper. She glanced quickly at George. "I think it makes more sense that it was Thatcher—not Victoria—who did it."

"Jealousy," said Ingrid with a knowing nod. "Either way, the murderer would've been fueled by jealousy. You could be right."

"I was hoping you picked up on something that morning. Something that I missed. Maybe something the police don't even know."

Ingrid said nothing.

"I'm pretty sure I heard them arguing," said Rosemary. "Sam and Mr. Thatcher. Back in the trees? While you and I were talking. I'm almost positive."

Ingrid thought back and nodded slowly. "Yes. That's true."

"Could you hear what they were saying?"

"Nope."

"Then what can we do to help the truth along?" asked Rosemary, who was beginning to feel frustrated. "What can we do to see that truth and justice are united again?"

"If Weaser has his mind made up, maybe they'll just decide I killed Sam." Ingrid gave a little sniffle.

"But Ingrid, you didn't do it," Rosemary said. "And circumstantial evidence might be enough to bring you here, but it isn't enough to *keep* you here."

"But there is something . . . Well, there's something in my house that would look pretty bad if Weaser found it." There was a note of guilt in Ingrid's voice.

"Are they going to search Ingrid's house?" Seth asked, turning to George.

Ingrid looked at George and gave him a little wave, signaling him to come closer.

"You don't have to stand over there, young Mr. Harris," she said. "I trust you. You might work with a dishonest man, but you're good, through and through."

George looked at his feet, embarrassed. "Once Detective Weaser obtains a warrant, yes," he said. "They'll search your house, Ms. Clark. As of now, he doesn't have one. You are here because you were seen watching the mayor in the park just before he died, and because you were found with the body. And, well, also because it's widely known that you didn't care for the way Mayor Wright conducted business."

"Never should've thrown that rock through his window," Ingrid muttered.

"That's all circumstantial evidence, though," said George. "They'll need more than that to go any further with this."

"So why hasn't Detective Weaser gotten a search warrant yet?" asked Rosemary. "Seems like he'd be in a big hurry to get over to Ingrid's house to try to find something incriminating."

"I believe he's trying to collect more evidence that would, well, warrant a warrant," said George. "Detective Weaser is at City Hall right now, meeting with Becky Thatcher."

"Becky Thatcher?" asked Seth. "Why?"

"Becky seemed convinced that Ingrid killed Sam," said Rosemary.

"That's right. And she said she has some kind of evidence," said George. "Something at the mayor's office she wanted to show Detective Weaser."

"What could it be?" asked Rosemary, turning back to Ingrid.

"I don't know." Ingrid looked as confused as anyone.

"I don't expect Detective Weaser will delay with the warrant once he gets back," warned George. He looked pointedly at Ingrid.

"Go to my house," said Ingrid, looking at Rosemary and Seth, a sense of urgency now in her voice. "You have to get there before the police. There are two things you should get. First, get Mercy's diary. It's in a box, in a secret compartment behind the painting of the meadow. Start with the section from the fall of 1668—just after Mercy fled with baby Lilly. You'll see who Mercy suspected of killing Hortence. You have to prove that and release Hortence's spirit."

"But what does that old murder have to do with the one you're tangled up in now? Ingrid, we want to help *you*," said Rosemary.

"Trust me, they're connected. Remember the story: A man wins the heart of a good woman. Then his eye wanders to another. Then the good woman finds out. And the old curse comes alive. The good woman does a thing she never would've thought herself capable of. Mark my words. History repeats itself. Samuel Wright's fiancée would've been furious when she saw who he really was. And now this murder, like all of the others since Matthew Graves, has been laid at Hortence's feet."

"Because people are claiming Sam was a victim of the curse," said Rosemary.

"So, it all goes back on Hortence," said Seth.

"She wasn't a witch, for crying out loud. She was just angry and trapped and frankly, I would've cursed Matthew Graves too. She can't be free until her legacy becomes one of healing instead of killing. Just go read the journal. Start with the entry dated November 13, 1668. Then read October 11, 1669. Get it out of the house before Weaser has a chance to get his greasy hands on it."

George automatically whipped out his little notebook, scribbled down the dates, and handed the page to Rosemary.

"And what's the second thing we're supposed to get?" asked Seth.

"Open the bottom left drawer on my desk. You'll know it when you see it."

"We better get you back to your cell, Ms. Clark," said George. "I haven't broken any rules letting you speak to these . . . counselors . . . but it would be better if you were in your cell when the detective gets back."

Ingrid stood, pitiful with handcuffs around her boney wrists. She met Rosemary's eyes, but said nothing.

"We'll go to your house right away," said Rosemary. "You have my word."

"The address is 331 Meadow View. The key is under a flower pot on the front porch. You'll know it when you see it."

With a nod to Rosemary and Seth, George hurriedly took Ingrid out of the room.

"We'll find our way out, George," Rosemary called after him.

"Hold up, George," said Seth, jogging over and handing George a business card. "My cell number's on here. Please be in touch if you have any news. And thank you."

As they went back down the hall to exit the police station, Seth took Rosemary's hand and gave it a squeeze.

"We have to help her, Seth," said Rosemary.

"Then we'd better hurry."

As they made the short drive to Ingrid's house, Rosemary thought back over everything that had been said at the police station.

"Ingrid said, 'A good woman does a thing she never thought herself capable of.' She talked about jealousy being a powerful motive for murder. She's implying that all those years ago, Elizabeth Graves killed her husband out of jealousy because the judge had a wandering eye, isn't she? And now, Ingrid thinks the same thing has happened with Sam—that Victoria is the prime suspect because she was fueled by the same kind of jealousy."

"Like she said, history repeats itself," said Seth. "Maybe the clue that points to Sam's killer is buried somewhere deep in the past."

21

Ingrid's house was catty-corner from the meadow, and if a house could look like its owner, this one did.

It was a small place, with a rickety fence around a front yard which was basically just one big garden—and an impressive garden, at that. There were herbs and a few hardy fall blooms, each one lovingly marked by a tiny stake in the ground that identified it.

"Goldenrod. Autumn Crocus," Rosemary read.

"Sneezeweed? Tickseed?" Seth frowned.

"Well, at least she has an organizational system in place," said Rosemary.

Just then, she spotted a large rosemary bush, and remembered the little bouquet that Ingrid had left on Hortence's grave.

"She said the key is under a flowerpot on the porch," said Seth, pointing wide-eyed at Ingrid's front porch. "But look!"

Ingrid's craftsman-style cottage boasted a generous front porch which was covered up in flowerpots, each one home to a different, well-tended herb or green or bloom.

"We'd better start looking," said Seth, going up the front steps. "This may take a while, and we need to be out of here before Weaser shows up."

Rosemary stood looking at the pots thoughtfully. "Wait. Try the pot with the yellow flowers first," she said. "Those were the ones that were tied up in the bundle with the rosemary, remember?"

"That's right," said Seth, lifting the heavy pot overflowing with the yellow blooms.

Sure enough, the key lay beneath the pot. Rosemary slipped it out and gave Seth a victorious look.

"Smarty pants," he said, setting the pot back down and straightening. "Lucky guess."

"Ah-ha! But Ingrid said we'd know the right pot when we saw it. And she was right. Hey, while we're here, what's the name of that flower? I asked Ingrid about it, and she said she didn't know what it was called. But now, seeing her garden, I'm having a hard time believing that."

Seth bent down and shifted the flowers to reveal the little plant stake.

"Huh. It's called Birds-foot."

"What an interesting name," said Rosemary. "I'll open the door. You check on your phone and see what it symbolizes."

"You know, it might not symbolize anything. Maybe she just likes the looks of it alongside rosemary."

"She knew the rosemary meant remembrance. She's an expert gardener. She knows the language of flowers," said Rosemary, jiggling the key in the old lock.

Finally, she was able to turn the key and the door opened into a comfortable, well-worn living room.

Shabby furniture was arranged around a woodstove, and a large desk faced the picture window that overlooked the back yard—which was a riot of flowers and plants just like the front yard. The desk was littered with papers.

"You check the bottom left drawer. I'll look around for a painting of the meadow," said Rosemary.

"Good. We've got to hurry and get out of here," said Seth.

"Getting antsy, are you?"

"Aren't you?"

A moment later, just as Rosemary was headed down a hall still in search of the painting, Seth called her.

"Can you come here a second? I think you're going to want to see this," he said.

Rosemary came to the desk where Seth sat looking through a file which was stuffed with newspaper clippings—all of them featuring Mayor Wright.

"There are literally eight years' worth of articles about the mayor in here," whispered Seth, digging through the collection. "Was she obsessed?"

"Oh wow," Rosemary whispered back, feeling her stomach turn over. "Look at that one where she drew devil horns and a pitchfork on his picture. Or that one where she scratched out his face. Ingrid is right. This looks pretty bad."

"To say the least."

"Wait, why are we whispering? We're the only ones here." Rosemary cleared her throat. "Okay, this does look bad, but I think Ingrid was worried and angry. Not obsessed."

"But the whole meadow development deal didn't even happen until this year. Why would she have articles going back through his whole history as mayor?"

"I can't imagine. Unless—"

"Unless what?"

"Ingrid is a member of one of the founding families here. She knows the history of this place inside and out, just like Mrs. Potter. Maybe like Mrs. Potter, she knew that Sam was a descendant of Matthew Graves—the man she blames for disgracing her family and changing the course of their lives."

"I'll bet that's why she said they were cut from the same cloth," said Seth.

"Exactly. Maybe she didn't trust Sam Wright from day one. So, she watched him closely. These are all articles clipped from the newspaper. It's not as if they have anything to do with Sam's personal life. I mean, Ingrid wasn't spying on him at home. She was just following his actions as mayor."

"And judging by her recent artwork, she didn't approve," said Seth, holding up another clipping of the mayor, this time with a ridiculous mustache and a monocle drawn onto his face.

Rosemary couldn't keep herself from laughing out loud.

"And then there's this," said Seth.

He held out his cell phone, and Rosemary took it.

"Birds-foot, *Lotus corniculatus* . . . means *revenge*." Rosemary took a few steps backward and let out a long sigh.

Seth's cell phone buzzed in Rosemary's hand and she automatically looked at it.

"Oh no," she said, handing it back to Seth.

The text had come from George. Detective Weaser was back at the station after meeting with Becky Thatcher, who had presented him with a recent note she'd received at the mayor's office—a threatening letter written by none other than Ingrid Clark.

"The evidence is piling up against Ingrid," said Seth.

"There has to be some mistake," said Rosemary.

"Rosemary, I like Ingrid, too. She's a character. I don't want her to be guilty. But this," he said, holding up the file, "is just plain weird. Add to that a rock through the mayor's window and a threatening letter? It's not looking good for Ingrid."

"I just don't think she did it. I'll admit—and she would too—that she didn't like Sam."

"Didn't *like* him? She clearly despised the guy."

"But I know she didn't kill him."

Seth's cell phone buzzed, and he glanced at it.

"Oh boy. It's George. Weaser's on his way over. Find that painting!"

22

Twenty minutes later, Seth and Rosemary were back at the farm, sitting around the table with Jack and Charlie, Mercy's diary laid out in front of them. They'd found it exactly where Ingrid had said it would be, in a small cabinet which was hidden behind a painting of the Witch's Meadow. Rosemary had smiled when she'd noticed that the little brass plate beneath the painting simply read, *The Meadow*, and she wondered if Ingrid was the artist. There was no signature on the piece, but then, Ingrid didn't seem the type to care whether anyone knew of her accomplishments. She was most definitely a person who lived her life with little concern for what people thought of her.

Rosemary had grabbed the diary, Seth had tucked the file of articles under his arm and closed the desk drawer, and they'd locked the front door, leaving the key under the pot of bird's-foot. As they drove away, just as they'd turned off by the meadow, in his rearview mirror Seth could see Weaser rounding the opposite corner. Their escape had been far too narrow for comfort.

"Before we look at this, I have to tell you about Sam's fiancée, Victoria Winthrop," said Jack. "I happened to run into her after you two left the churchyard."

"You ran into her?" asked Rosemary, skeptical. "Probably more like curiosity got the better of you, and you made a *point* of running into her."

"Well, was it my fault she showed up at the church?" asked Jack.

"Seriously?" asked Seth. "Why would she be there?"

"Because of course that's where Sam's memorial is going to be held. She was there meeting with Reverend Bob. They were talking about the order of the service, and let me tell you, I got an earful."

"You eavesdropped on a bereaved person?" asked Charlie.

"*Eavesdrop* is a funny word. I was adjusting a few of the lanterns outside the church in the cemetery. The church window just happened to be opened a crack, so I could hear what they were saying, and then they came outside to the Wright family plot where, I assume, Sam will be laid to rest."

"Oh, my gosh," said Charlie. "I still can't get over the idea that Sam is gone."

"Well, Miss Victoria Winthrop is over it," said Jack.

"What makes you think that?" asked Rosemary.

"Well, for starters, she asked how long the service would take on Thursday," said Jack, raising a critical brow.

"That seems like it could be a relevant question," said Seth.

"She said she had a massage appointment she had to get to and didn't want to be late."

"Well . . . that is, admittedly, a little cold," said Rosemary.

"And then there was the part where Reverend Bob was saying what a sad loss this is, and what a good man Sam was. And she scoffed."

"She *scoffed*?" asked Charlie.

"Yes! She made that scoffing sound!" said Jack.

"How rude," said Charlie.

"Reverend Bob thought so too, I could tell," said Jack. "By then, they'd come outside, and I could see everything from the ladder."

"You were literally hovering over them!" said Rosemary. "Didn't they notice?"

"That Victoria is a piece of work. She looked at me for a split second and dismissed me like I was a servant or something. Probably thought I was the maintenance man."

"That lines up perfectly with Mrs. Potter's impression of Victoria," said Rosemary.

"Oh, Mrs. Potter sugar-coated the woman, I assure you!" said Jack. "She's *way* worse in person. Nothing even slightly resembling the classy-looking lady we saw with Sam at the café. But I'm just getting to the juicy part. There they were—Victoria and Reverend Bob—looking over the Wright family plot, where Sam was found dead a day ago, no less. I mean, the police tape was *just* taken down! And Victoria says, 'Shouldn't you bury him over there, with that Graves lowlife?'"

"Get out!" said Rosemary.

"I'm totally serious. Victoria Winthrop was seething with barely contained rage, and she knew that the Wrights and the Graves are related."

"What did Reverend Bob say?" asked Charlie.

"He didn't know what to say. He just looked at Victoria, all confused. And then she said, 'Sam and I did that genealogy thing years ago,' and that as a 'rising political star,' he didn't want people to know about that particular family connection. That if they did, the press could start digging deeper and find out that the Graves family was notorious—still is notorious—for being a bunch of scumbags. I mean, literal skeletons in their closets. Apparently, the pedigree is extremely important to Ms. Winthrop. The way she talked, she would've been stooping to marry Sam, and now that he's up and died, she's feeling very inconvenienced by this whole mess."

"I can't believe this. He said he didn't know his family's history before the early 1700s when the Wrights moved to Paperwick. That scoundrel!" said Rosemary, immediately feeling a pang of guilt for calling out a dead man.

"And get this: Victoria said that Sam had aspirations of running for the United States Senate after his next mayoral term, that *that* was why he wanted to single-handedly put Paperwick—or as she called it, 'this hick village,' on the map. Can you believe it? She said Sam had his sights set on the White House down the line."

"And she would be the cherry on top," said Rosemary, shaking her head.

"This is astounding," said Seth. "Ingrid might be right."

"About what?" asked Charlie.

"She suspects Victoria killed Sam in a jealous rage because of his flirtations with other women. And then she drew all of these parallels between Sam and Matthew Graves, and said they'd suffered the same fate for the same reasons—that both had been killed because of wanting what they couldn't have," said Seth. "She said this diary holds part of the answer, but that we need to prove that it was Judge Graves who murdered Hortence. She thinks that will set Hortence's troubled spirt free."

"If Ingrid's family hasn't been able to do that in all these years, I don't see how we can," said Rosemary.

"Are you kidding?" said Charlie. "You're all academics and I'm a writer. Research is what we do. The answer might be as plain as day if we can just figure out where to look."

"Hold the phone," said Jack. "Judge Graves had accused Hortence of witchcraft—I mean, basically the whole town was after her in the panic, but he was the one who made the accusation."

"And he was also the one who had the power to condemn her," added Charlie.

"But then I don't understand. Why murder her?" asked Jack. "Why not just pass his judgement and have her executed right out in the open?"

"That is the question," said Rosemary, opening the journal and carefully turning the pages. "And of course, Ingrid didn't say it outright, but I think she implied that Hortence and the very married judge were *involved*, and that was why he needed to get rid of her. Either to avoid disgrace or because he wanted her land."

"Maybe both," said Jack.

Rosemary checked the little scrap of paper George had given her back at the police station and found the page she was looking for.

"Here it is. November 13, 1668. This is where Ingrid said to start reading."

"Wow. Look at that handwriting," Charlie marveled.

"Can you make this out?" asked Jack.

"I can," said Rosemary. "I've looked at so many writings from this time period. Early American Puritan English. Not the easiest, but once you get the hang of it, it flows pretty smoothly." She began scanning the words. "I'm going to paraphrase, okay?"

"Of course," said Jack.

"Mercy says that she and Lilly have arrived safely at her cousin's house, in Hartford. She is thanking God for their safe passage. She says the baby is fussy, but she thinks it's because she's confused as to where her mother is. How will Mercy ever replace her? And will the specter of the accusation follow them forever, like a shadow, like a ghost?"

Rosemary paused and read further.

"She is heartbroken at the loss of her sister. Here she says, 'justice and truth, torn apart.'"

"Similar to the note from our barn!" said Jack. "Is it some kind of code?"

"And Ingrid also said something just like that today at the police station," said Seth. "Almost the same words."

"Here, Mercy is saying Hortence was so beautiful, so bold . . . She says it's not that shocking that Matthew fell in love with her. And Mercy can also understand how Hortence, who'd been so lonely in her marriage to Jonathan Gallow, had fallen under Matthew's spell. "

At this, Rosemary looked up with wide eyes. Jack's jaw dropped. Charlie put a hand to his forehead. And Seth fell back in his chair.

"So Hortence really was having a full-blown affair with the judge," said Jack.

"Mercy talks about the price of Hortence's beauty and spirit. And—oh my gosh."

"What? Go on!" said Jack.

"She says that it was Matthew who killed Jonathan Gallow. With a knife, in a fight. Jonathan challenged Matthew when he found out that—" Rosemary exhaled as though she'd been punched in the stomach.

"That what?" all three men said at once.

"That Lilly was Matthew's child. Not Jonathan's."

"Whoa," said Seth. "So, Matthew and Hortence had a baby. Wow."

"But if Matthew loved Hortence like Mercy said, why would he accuse her of witchcraft? Or kill her?"

Rosemary read further and shook her head sadly. "He allowed her to go to jail so that he could rescue her. Here it says that Mercy got there that night—that awful night—to offer prayers and comfort to her sister. She had planned to beg Judge Graves to show leniency at the trial the next morning. But when Mercy arrived at the jail, Matthew was already there. He'd used his key—"

"Justice holds the only key!" Jack interjected excitedly.

"Unlocked her cell, took her out, and tried to convince her to run away with him. She refused. He threatened her. Said he'd lock her back up and she'd face the noose. She told him he couldn't kill the mother of his child, confirming to him that Lilly was his, and saying that she could not be Jonathan's. Hortence had been married to Jonathan all those years with no babies, after all. Seems the sisters had long suspected Jonathan couldn't father children."

"So that's why Jonathan knew she'd had an affair. He couldn't have children, but his wife was pregnant nonetheless."

"Exactly," said Rosemary, pausing to scan further down the page.

"Mercy was shocked. She hadn't known about her sister's affair until that moment, that night at the jail. But Hortence refused to leave her farm or her patients or her sister. She wanted to stay here and raise her child with Mercy's help, and she swore she'd never tell a soul that Lilly was Matthew's baby. In return, she asked Matthew to lift the stigma of his accusation, 'lest she live in disgrace' for the rest of her life. Matthew grabbed Hortence by the arm, pulled her to him, and she uttered something in his ear that Mercy couldn't hear. Then she snatched her arm away, pointed at him, and screamed, 'I curse you, Matthew Graves!' and ran off. Mercy stayed hidden and saw Matthew go back inside to his chambers within the jailhouse. She watched her sister disappear into the shadows and the rain, hoping that she would find a safe hiding place. Mercy was still determined to speak to the judge. But just as she was about to come out of hiding and approach him, she saw Elizabeth Graves hurrying up, carrying a basket. From the distance, Elizabeth had seen Hortence running away like a lunatic. So, she ran inside, found her husband, and told him that Hortence had escaped."

"Which he took down in his journal, like a good boy," said Seth. "It all falls into place."

"But there's more," said Rosemary. "Mercy waited outside, hiding, listening, hoping that she could still speak some reason to the judge—and maybe even use this new information about his affair with her sister as a bargaining chip to plea for Hortence's safety."

"Poor Mercy," said Charlie. "Outside all alone, in the rain."

"She was supposed to be the quiet one," said Rosemary. "But I suspect she was the smart one, and every bit as brave as Hortence."

"So, what happened next?" asked Jack.

Rosemary read further, turned the page, and read to the end of the passage.

"She waited there outside until Elizabeth Graves hurried out, upset. She heard the judge tell his wife to go home, that Hortence would eventually return there. Elizabeth walked off in the direction of their home—which was right next to Mercy and Hortence's farm—*this* farm. Mercy waited a few minutes longer, trying to formulate what she would say, and finally gathered the courage to approach Judge Graves. She was horrified."

"Understandable," said Seth. "After all, she could easily be accused of witchcraft herself. And the judge would certainly sleep better at night with her out of the way, knowing that there was a decent chance Mercy knew everything."

"But when Mercy knocked on his chamber door, there was no answer. She knocked again. Waited. And when she went back out into the rain, she saw that he'd left by the back door, and was galloping off on a horse into the darkness. *Not* in the direction of home."

"Oh, let me guess," said Jack. "He was going toward the meadow, just like Hortence had."

"Yep. Mercy ran in the same direction, on foot. But when she got to the meadow, it was too late. Her sister was dead, her bodice torn, revealing the birthmark on her shoulder blade. No sign of Matthew Graves or anyone else. In a panic, Mercy ran home and started packing. As she writes this, she says she'll never forgive herself for leaving her sister's body there in the meadow, but she wanted to protect the baby above all else."

"So, Mercy believed the judge killed her sister that night," said Charlie.

"Yes. But in a fit of passion. In a twisted effort to control her. Not because he ever really thought she was a witch," said Rosemary. "He let her sit in that jail cell long enough to frighten her. He was betting that from that awful place, she would see him riding in like a knight, as her savior—as the *only* one, in fact, who could've saved her," said Rosemary. "And when she refused his terms, he killed her and doomed her memory by casting the shadow of that bogus confession. Everyone for many years would believe Hortence really was a witch."

"Sick," said Jack. "But it does sound like Graves was ready to leave his wife and the farm and his position to take Hortence and run away."

"Sounds like obsession to me," said Charlie.

"What was the other date Ingrid said to look for in the journal?" asked Seth.

"October of the next year," said Rosemary, carefully turning the pages, wishing she could hurry, but knowing she had to be extremely careful with the old book. "October 11. Here it is."

"We have just received the news . . ." she read. Then paused, reading further. "Oh. Matthew Graves is dead. Mercy prays for his soul and for Elizabeth. She says that the townsfolk believe Judge Graves died of the curse as he had feared he would for nearly a year." Rosemary looked up. "Mercy says that after Hortence's death, Matthew was haunted. That he spoke often of the curse—blamed it for every malady, every stroke of bad luck that befell him. Until the end, he claimed that Hortence had cursed him from her jail cell before she mysteriously escaped through the locked bars. Mercy says that the worst thing Matthew did to her sister was to turn her into a witch in the eyes of the people of Paperwick. She fears that this is how Hortence will always be remembered, and that their family will never be able to return to the land they loved. She says that the world is better off without Matthew Graves, and that she and Elizabeth both know it wasn't Hortence's curse that killed him."

"She and Elizabeth?" asked Jack. "Why Elizabeth?"

"The final thing Mercy says on the matter is that Elizabeth understood what the sisters had taught her very well." Rosemary smiled. "I have a theory. Elizabeth was a quick study, and took over as midwife after Hortence and Mercy were gone, right? They'd taught her all about herbs and medicines —what to use and what to stay away from. What was healing . . . And what was toxic. Elizabeth was no fool. She had her husband's number. She could have poisoned him, chalked it up to the curse, and moved on with her life. After all, the only medical record we have of Matthew Graves' death is the one his wife wrote, in Mercy's record book."

"And that one says he died quite suddenly, as if stricken down by a curse," said Jack. "It's one of my favorite entries in the whole Elizabeth Graves section of the book."

"*A good woman does a thing she never thought herself capable of*," said Seth. "Just like Ingrid said."

"Yes," said Rosemary.

"Poor Hortence—caught up between Jonathan and Matthew," said Charlie. "Two selfish men."

"Whatever killed Graves, he brought it on himself," said Jack.

"Would you say the same of Sam?" asked Charlie.

"That's definitely what Ingrid thinks," said Rosemary.

"She says that these murders, hundreds of years apart, could be tied together," said Seth. "That Sam's death echoes Matthew's. She seems to think that in examining the past, we'll figure out what's going on here in the present."

"And in the process, set Hortence's spirit free," added Rosemary. "I don't know if Ingrid means that literally or figuratively. Like maybe she's saying that it's time to set the story straight. Clear the family name."

"Or maybe she thinks Hortence's actual ghost still walks the land, waiting for someone to prove whodunnit," said Jack in his spooky voice.

"It's an old story, this business of deceit and jealousy leading to a crime of passion," said Charlie. "Been told a million times."

"But I can't see how we could ever *prove* anything about any of this. Yes—at least in light of Mercy's eyewitness report—it's probable that the judge killed Hortence. But no one actually *saw* the murder take place. It's not like we can travel back in time and look for clues. What if the mystery is unsolvable?"

Jack let out a long sigh. "Let's hope the same isn't true in the case of Samuel Wright."

23

"Let's take a break," said Jack. "I'm hungry."

"Me too," said Charlie. "We need comfort food."

"Stay and eat with us, Seth," said Jack.

Seth caught Rosemary's smile and quickly agreed to stay.

"Pizza. Deep-dish," said Jack. "We've already got the dough rising in the kitchen."

"Chicago-style, baby," said Charlie. "And a big salad. And then we can whip up a batch of my famous snickerdoodles."

"Famous snickerdoodles?" asked Rosemary.

"As in, he won the grand prize at the county fair last year," said Jack. "They're that good."

"I love a good snickerdoodle," said Seth, grinning at Rosemary.

"Oh, me too," said Rosemary.

Jack and Charlie uncovered a bowl that was almost overflowing with yeasty dough, which smelled like heaven. Charlie kneaded the dough and then Jack attempted to toss it into the air in an expert fashion. Eventually, though, Charlie handed him a rolling pin. Jack floured the dough, rolled it out, and then pressed it into the big, cast iron skillet which Charlie had coated in olive oil.

Rosemary and Seth were in charge of toppings.

"I'm going to insist on sausage," said Seth.

"And extra cheese. And diced tomatoes. And mushrooms?"

"Definitely mushrooms."

"Aren't they cute?" Jack said, nudging Charlie.

"They're almost as cute as us," agreed Charlie.

"They'll never be as cute as us," said Jack. "Do you think they'll fall in love?"

"Hey! We're right here in the room," said Rosemary, feeling her cheeks heating up. "Don't you think you should wait until after we're out of earshot to talk about us?"

Jack and Charlie looked at each other.

"Nah," said Jack, while Charlie shook his head.

Once the pizza was in the oven, Jack and Rosemary put together a salad while Charlie showed Seth how to make his famous snickerdoodles.

"First off, the facts," Charlie said as Rosemary and Jack listened in and tried not to giggle too loudly. "One: The snickerdoodle is the state cookie of Connecticut. If you're going to win awards with this cookie, you'd better get it right. And two: It is incredibly hard to go up against all of the frosted, fancy, dipped, and chipped cookies in the world—and to do it with this modest little cookie."

Seth nodded obediently.

"If you're going to make a prizewinning snickerdoodle, it needs to be thick, it needs to be chewy, it needs to be moist. Yes, there are those who like them thin and crispy, but that's not gonna fly in this house."

"Wow, he's really serious about his snickerdoodles," Rosemary whispered to Jack.

"He's like a drill sergeant," Jack answered. "Look at how he's wielding that wooden spoon."

"I would not want to meet him in a dark alley with that spoon," said Rosemary.

At this, Seth turned and looked at her and then at Jack. "Do you mind? I'm trying to learn how to make these cookies," he said.

"Sorry," whispered Rosemary. "Come on, Jack. We'll take our salad to the table and build a fire."

Still giggling, she and Jack carried the salad bowl and a carafe of dressing into the next room. As Rosemary helped Jack build a fire, she paused for a moment and looked around.

The sun was just setting, casting a deep crimson light across the pond. The room was aglow with lamps and firelight. Wonderful smells were coming from the kitchen, along with voices and occasional laughter.

Home. Rosemary realized that this was what home felt like. This might even be what peace felt like. She was so used to feeling restless that she hadn't even realized she *was* restless. Until she wasn't.

Within a few minutes, they were all seated around the table, enjoying hot, cheesy slices of pizza and cool, crisp salad. Hints of vanilla and cinnamon drifted in on the air from the kitchen where the cookies were baking in the oven.

"I'm stuffed," Jack groaned.

"Me too, but don't worry, I'll still have room for cookies," said Rosemary.

Once the dinner dishes were in the dishwasher and the cookies were cooling on racks in the kitchen, the four friends gathered around the fire, and eventually, the conversation shifted back to Mercy and Hortence and murder.

"Talk about a tangled web," said Jack.

"No kidding," said Rosemary. "But it goes to show that the same problems have plagued mankind forever."

"*Nothing new under the sun*, as the Good Book says," said Jack.

"At least it sounds like Matthew Graves lived with terrible guilt about killing Hortence—I mean, assuming he did kill her," said Seth. "Mercy said he was haunted . . . that he was convinced he'd actually been dealt a deadly curse."

"He even thought he saw Hortence's cat just before he died, remember?" said Rosemary, who was now beginning to relax with Smudge curled up on one side of her, Izzy on the other.

"I bet he did have a seriously troubled conscience, and that it eventually got to him," said Charlie. "I mean, can you imagine the guilt? In his own twisted way, it sounds like Matthew loved Hortence. So, once she was gone, he had to deal with both his own guilt and the loss of her."

"But he couldn't talk about either. To anyone," said Jack. "That would mean risking his reputation and disgracing himself. It must've been a heck of a thing to keep it all bottled up." Jack shook his head. "And in the days before therapy!"

Suddenly, Rosemary sat upright and gasped.

"What is it, Rosie?" asked Jack.

"The judge's conscience. Of course! And Josias King."

"What are you saying?" asked Seth.

"Graves felt guilty. He was *racked* with guilt, in fact. He lived with it for almost a year. Imagine it: He'd killed the woman he loved. His child by her was living out there in the world somewhere. Meanwhile, he'd seized the Clark's land, and every day, looked out on that land and faced the woman he was married to and lived with his memories. Don't you think he would've wanted to release some of that guilt?"

"Of course. He probably carried it to the grave, though," said Charlie.

"Or maybe not," said Rosemary. "What if he confessed? What if he tried to relieve his conscience by seeking the counsel of his priest?"

"What if he did?" asked Jack. "That would just be one more thing we'll never be able to prove. And besides, did Puritans even go to confession?"

"But what if Josias King, pastor of the First Church, *did* offer counsel to his sheep? And what if Judge Graves did confide in him? This is a longshot, but hear me out. Sam told me that he has a book. It was given to him as a gift from the historical society eight years ago—before you guys moved here. It's a reproduction of the journal of Reverend King. It seems the good priest kept detailed records of his conversations with his parishioners. He wrote things down as a way of keeping track of his flock and knowing how best to pray for each one of them. His records were supposed to be destroyed upon his death, but his wife just couldn't do it."

"How is it possible that I don't know about this?" asked Jack in amazement.

"The original is tucked away in a museum at the capitol. This is a bound reproduction, and Sam has the only copy."

"Any idea where it is?" asked Seth.

"It's at his house," said Rosemary. "In the little outbuilding that was his home office. Where did he live?"

"You've actually seen the place. It's on Maple Leaf Drive. That's the street that runs behind the courthouse, a short walk from the green," said Charlie. "You can just see Sam's house from the churchyard. It's literally around the corner."

"Nice evening for a walk, don't you think?" asked Jack.

"Or a cup of cider at Potter's," said Charlie.

"Wait, guys," said Seth, holding up his hands. "We're not going to break into Sam's home office. This is nuts. We can't get the book tonight." He thought for a moment. "But then again, we could go down to the churchyard, test out the lanterns and make sure everything's in working order."

"And then if we just happened to walk by Sam's and checked in there and it just happened to be open . . ." said Jack. "Or, you know, we jiggle the doorknob, and it turns out not to be locked?"

"Sam did offer to lend me the book, after all," said Rosemary. "So, we know he wouldn't have objected. We wouldn't be stealing it. Just borrowing it."

"But we won't break any laws or anything like that. Are we all in agreement?" insisted Seth.

"Of course," said Jack. "Let's go."

24

The rain and the wind from the past few days had given the town a reprieve, and it was shaping up to be a lovely, moonlit night as they all piled into Holly Golightly, drove into town, and parked along the green.

Charlie pronounced it, "Nippy, but not cold."

"Sweater weather," agreed Rosemary.

They walked past warmly lit shop windows filled with pumpkins and notices for the upcoming festival, and the café and coffee shop, which were doing a brisk business in weather that begged a warm drink shared among friends.

Shortly, they arrived at the church and Jack produced a pocket-sized remote control.

"Drumroll, please," said Jack, clicking the button.

The whole churchyard was instantly illuminated. The lanterns in the trees flickered on, and the luminarias along the path glistened and winked in the light breeze. Rosemary was caught off guard by the sight. She hadn't expected the churchyard to look this beautiful. She closed her eyes and smiled.

"How can you see it with your eyes closed?" asked Seth, putting an arm around her shoulders.

"Oh, I can see it," said Rosemary. "It's the most beautiful thing I've ever seen."

She opened her eyes and looked at Seth, who was smiling at her.

"Me too," he said, grinning his endearing lopsided grin.

"She always closes her eyes at the sight of something breathtaking," said Jack. "Why does she do it? The world may never know."

"I have an idea," said Charlie in his louder-than-normal, not-very-convincing stage voice. "Let's stroll over there to the courthouse. Rosemary hasn't really seen it yet. And it's so pretty at night, all lit up."

"Yes. Let's!" Jack responded.

They walked the short distance and soon stood before the courthouse, a charming building, three stories high, of red brick lined with large windows that overlooked the center of town.

"Notice the colonial flair," said Jack loudly, gesturing to the building's façade. "And as you can see by this placard, it was built in 1790."

"I just love these 18th century buildings," Rosemary said for the benefit of any passersby—although there were none, aside from the occasional coffee shop patron hurrying past. Otherwise, all was quiet and closed up tight.

"So which way to Sam's house?" asked Rosemary under her breath.

Jack glanced around stealthily and then pointed, and they all walked quietly past the courthouse, where they took a right and headed to the back side of the block. The street that ran along there was called Maple Leaf Drive, and even in the early evening light, Rosemary could see why: it was lined with huge, colorful maple trees. The houses were lit from within, and though they were on a mission to sneak into a dead man's office, Rosemary couldn't help feeling a mix of cozy warmth—at the sight of the people inside their houses, going about their evening activities—and the excitement of finding the priest's book of confessions. Sure, they could've waited until the next day to search for it. Sure, they could've called the courthouse and asked Sam's secretary, Becky Thatcher, about it. But it was just so much fun to see the town at night, and to sneak over to look for the book, like a bunch of twelve-year-olds.

Probably, they'd arrive at Sam's house and it would be locked up tight, and they'd just walk on by. Probably, they'd lose their nerve or come to their senses.

But as they scurried down the road, dodging from one tree to the next, Rosemary couldn't remember the last time she'd had so much fun. This felt like a historical treasure hunt.

"Here we are," whispered Jack, as they approached a particularly charming house with an inviting front porch, framed by large trees.

"Holy smoke!" said Seth. "Someone's coming!"

They all scampered further down the sidewalk, past Sam's house, but then snuck back and hid behind a row of large bushes that had been planted alongside the porch.

Sure enough, someone was there, moving through the shadows up the front walk.

"Can you see who it is?" whispered Rosemary.

"Not yet," said Jack.

The person stumbled a little on the first step up to the porch and cursed under their breath. Rosemary could see now that it was definitely a woman.

"Figures even your house would be a trap," the angry voice grumbled. "Just another trap," she called loudly, as if announcing it to the empty street.

"Oh lord. It's Victoria," said Jack.

By this time, Victoria Winthrop was fumbling with a loaded keyring, trying this key and that, cursing every time the chosen key didn't fit the lock on Sam's front door.

"Just like our engagement," Victoria said, her voice slurring a bit. "Trap, trap, trap."

"She's been drinking," said Charlie.

"You think? I can almost smell the scotch all the way over here," said Jack.

"A big, fat trap!" Victoria lamented loudly.

"I get the feeling she thought their engagement was a trap," said Seth.

"Very intuitive," said Rosemary, elbowing him.

Finally, Victoria found the correct key, pushed open the front door, and went inside. Lights came on in the front room and then subsequent rooms, and even from outside, Victoria could be heard, slamming doors and cursing.

"I have an idea," said Rosemary. "Let's knock on the door. Let's go in there and talk to her."

"Seriously? She might be a killer!" said Jack.

"But there are four of us. And she's clearly inebriated. I mean, we go in there, all friendly and sympathetic, and who knows? Maybe she'll fess up and Ingrid will be off the hook. Or maybe she'll at least let us go and get the book from Sam's office out back. I can tell her he offered to lend it to me."

"Good plan," said Seth with a deep breath. "Let's do it."

They all went up the front steps and gathered at the door. Rosemary gave a nod and rang the bell. When no one answered, she rang it again.

Finally, the door swung open and there was Victoria Winthrop, looking decidedly less pulled-together than she had a few days before at the café.

"Who are you and what do you want?" she asked.

It was at this point that Rosemary noticed Victoria was wearing mismatched socks. She had on shorts, an oversized t-shirt, and sneakers with one blue sock and one red. And her hair was nothing like the shining golden coif she'd had when she'd breezed by their table at the café. It was a frizzy mess. And then there was her makeup, which had most definitely seen better days. Rosemary wondered if Victoria's mascara was smeared because she'd been crying, or if it was simply because she hadn't washed it off the day before.

"We're here to offer our condolences," said Rosemary quickly, hoping to keep the door open. "We're so sorry for your loss."

"Do I know you?" asked Victoria, squinting at the four of them.

"No. We've never met," said Rosemary. "We knew your fiancée, and well, we just felt bad for you."

"Yeah, I bet *you* knew him," Victoria said, giving Rosemary the once-over. "You felt bad for me, huh? Why? Because I dodged a big ol' bullet named Samuel Wright?" And then Victoria made a sound that was something like, "Bah!"

"Well, then, maybe we should be congratulating you," said Jack in his most charming voice.

"You look familiar," Victoria said, attempting to focus on Jack. She thought for a moment, and Rosemary held her breath, hoping Victoria wouldn't remember Jack from the ladder in the churchyard. "No. Never mind. You don't." She snorted at her own remark.

Rosemary glanced at Jack, who was breathing his own sigh of relief.

"So, you're off the hook, then," said Seth.

Victoria looked at him and a slow smile spread across her face.

“I am off the hook,” she said, “And available. Please come in.”

She stepped aside and let the four of them enter the house, although Rosemary suspected she really only wanted Seth to come in. He was awfully cute, after all.

“So, are you staying here? At Sam’s house?” asked Rosemary, trying to sound casual.

“I was staying at a B&B in town. But thought I’d come over to Sammy’s place. You see, he keeps a supply of the most wonderful brandy. If you’ll help me find it, I’ll be glad to share.”

Was that a wink she’d just given Seth?

“Sure, we’ll help,” said Rosemary quickly. “We should probably also look out in his office.”

“Yes, definitely,” said Jack. “I think I remember that he kept some brandy there. Do you have the key?”

“It’s one of these,” Victoria said, thrusting the keyring full of keys at Jack. “How about you three go look out there in the office, and *you*,” she smiled at Seth, “can stay here and look in the house with me.”

“Great!” said Jack, grabbing the keys and hurrying toward the back door along with Rosemary and Charlie. Rosemary glanced back over her shoulder as they left. Seth gave her a look that said, "*Hurry!*" and she winked and nodded.

It took a while to find the key that opened Sam's little outbuilding.

"He really should've labeled these," said Charlie.

"Why does one man need this many keys?" asked Rosemary.

They pushed the door open and switched on the light, revealing a quaint little room with a large, well-appointed desk, a cushy couch next to a woodstove, and bookshelves lining every wall, loaded with hundreds of books.

"Wow. Who knew Sam was so tidy?" said Jack, taking in the perfectly aligned stacks of files on the desk.

"Even his books are lined up perfectly. Not one out of place," said Charlie. "And this is quite a collection. Wonder if they'll donate it to the library."

"He may not have been very organized about his keys," said Rosemary, coming to stand beside Charlie and looking over the books. "But the bookshelves are immaculate. Look. Reference books over there. Nonfiction in this section—and it's categorized by subject matter. Fiction over here, all arranged by author's last name . . . Yep, he's a believer in the Dewey Decimal System."

"You have to respect the man," said Charlie. "Jack, can we get some of these tiny brass shelf labels for our bookshelves at home?"

"Absolutely. In fact, we need to reorganize our whole library *tonight*," said Jack, admiring the shelves.

"So, the book we're looking for, if it's on these shelves, is with local history . . . What did he say it was called . . ." Rosemary ran a finger along the spines.

"Could it really be that it's going to be that easy to find it?" asked Jack.

"Yep," said Rosemary, pulling out a beautifully leather-bound volume. "*Paperwick: The Original Sins, A Cautionary Tale.*"

"Sounds scandalous!" said Jack, taking the book. "I can't wait to dig into this."

"And good news," called Charlie, who'd wandered over to Sam's desk. "I found the brandy! He has a little cabinet over here which is basically a minibar."

"Ooh, are there any mixed nuts?" asked Jack.

"Shouldn't we go rescue Seth now?" said Rosemary.

"Or should we stay here and look into this little baby for a few minutes?" asked Jack, waving the book.

"We couldn't do that," said Rosemary. "Seth needs us in there."

"Maybe just a tiny peek?" said Jack.

Unable to resist temptation, Rosemary took the book and began flipping through the pages hurriedly.

"Find late 1669—probably just before Judge Graves went off to that great courtroom in the sky," said Jack.

"Here it is," said Rosemary. "Gosh, I love these seventeenth century people. So, organized. Everyone wrote everything down. No wonder they called this town Paperwick."

"Because of all of the paper they used?" asked Charlie.

"And candle wicks they burned, staying up late, reading and writing," said Rosemary, laughing. "But seriously, culturally speaking, the Puritans were very big on literacy, because they wanted everyone to be able to read the Bible."

Jack nodded approvingly. "Very good, Dr. Grey," he said with a smile.

Rosemary scanned the words—easy to read, because they'd been typeset in a simple font.

"Let's see . . . what does Josias have to say on October 1, 1669 . . . Looks like the Potters had another baby. Reverend King writes about the upcoming baptism. He mentions the need to fix the leaky roof, because the fall has brought forth abundant rain."

"Just like this fall," said Charlie.

"There are lists of things he wants to obtain for people in need. He has written down some sermon notes. Ah! October third. He talks about giving counsel to two of his flock: one, a farmer with the initials A.L., who is contemplating purchasing ten acres to plant in corn next year. And the other . . ." Rosemary looked up with huge eyes.

"Matthew Graves? *Shut the front door*!" Jack said, almost unable to contain his excitement, and leaning closer to take a look.

"A person with the initials J.G. did seek Reverend King's help," continued Rosemary. "Seems he was deeply troubled because he'd been unfaithful to his wife and . . ."

"Oh. My. Gosh," said Jack, bending to read over Rosemary's shoulder. "He confessed he'd committed a plethora of mortal sins. Reverend King actually numbered them!"

"Whoa," said Charlie. "You know you're in trouble when the priest has to number your sins to keep track of all of them."

"He'd killed a man in self-defense, and, holy cow! He killed his mistress. He confessed! He couldn't stand the guilt!" exclaimed Jack.

"Reverend King was deeply troubled and advised J.G. to immediately take the matter to the council," said Rosemary, reading further. "He said that he must confess publicly. Even if he faced death for his actions, and even though J.G.'s soul was already predestined for either salvation or damnation, he might be able to receive a measure of grace by confessing and facing up to his crimes," said Rosemary.

"But J.G.," said Charlie. "I suppose that *could* be someone other than Matthew Graves. Are you sure it's a 'J'?"

"I bet he's referring to Judge Graves," said Rosemary.

"Or Justice Graves," said Charlie.

"Justice and truth . . ." said Jack.

At that moment, the door flew open, and there stood Becky Thatcher, with a look that was a mix of rage and horror on her face.

"*What* do you think you're doing?"

25

"Who let you in here?" asked a red-faced Benedict Thatcher, coming up behind his wife. "What's going on?"

"Sam's fiancée, Victoria, let us in here," said Jack, stepping forward. "And Sam himself had offered to let Rosemary borrow a book. We're researching some local history for both the cemetery crawl at the festival on Friday night, *and* for a book we're going to be writing." He smiled proudly at Rosemary.

"Victoria Winthrop? That phony," said Becky. "She never even loved our Sam." She looked sadly up at her husband, who put a hand on her shoulder.

"Well, you'll have to take that up with Victoria," said Jack. "We'll just be on our way."

They started to move toward the door, but Benedict stepped in front of it.

"You're taking Sam's brandy?" he asked, clearly appalled. "Are you going to tell me he said you could borrow that too?"

"Not at all," said Charlie. "This is for Victoria. She asked us to get it."

"That woman traipses in here and starts stealing Sam's things," said Becky, who was starting to cry. "And we're just supposed to stand by and do nothing?"

"Excuse me for asking," said Rosemary, "but why are you here yourselves?"

"We live next door," said Benedict. "We were in our backyard, saw the lights on in Sam's office, and thought we'd better check. And a good thing we did. Let's get into the house before that woman wrecks the place."

"Of course you live next door," mumbled Jack, shaking his head as they all trooped out of Sam's office behind the Thatchers.

Rosemary gave him an elbow in the ribs as a warning, and tucked the *Cautionary Tale* into the oversized pocket of her sweater.

When they got into the house, a relieved Seth hurried over to stand next to Rosemary.

"Great!" spat Victoria. "More *Paperwick* people. Just wonderful. Did you find the brandy? Because I had *no luck* in here." She gave Seth a pointed look, which Rosemary took to mean he'd resisted Victoria's flirtations and Victoria was none too pleased about it.

Charlie came forward with the bottle, but Benedict Thatcher held out an arm, stopping him.

"Now wait just a minute here," he said. "What right do you have to rifle through Sam's things?"

"What right do *I* have?" asked an incredulous and still very drunk Victoria. "Seriously? I'm Sam's fiancée. What right do *you* have to come into what would have been *our* home and question *me*? As if the police haven't already questioned me enough today." She mumbled this last part under her breath.

"We are Sam's friends," Becky choked out.

"Well, I am the love of Sam's life, so *stick it*, sister!" At this, Victoria lunged forward, snatched the bottle of brandy out of Charlie's hands and stalked toward the kitchen.

The normally sweet, demure little Becky looked ready to take a run at Victoria, but her husband again put a steadying hand on her shoulder.

Meanwhile, cabinet doors in the kitchen could be heard slamming as Victoria presumably searched for a glass. She returned to the room, the bottle tucked up under her arm, taking a swig from a glass half full of the amber liquid. She looked surprised to see them all still standing in the living room.

"What? You're all still here? Time for you to go away." She stumbled toward the door and reached for the knob.

"We'll go away," said Benedict. "But you need to go, too. I'll escort you back to your hotel."

"Why? So, you can knock me off like you knocked of my Sam?"

Benedict sucked in his breath and took a step backward, as though he'd been burned.

"Ben didn't kill Sam, you horrible woman!" said Becky, who had just seconds before managed to stop crying but was now starting up again. "That witch Ingrid Clark killed him, and everyone knows it, and that's why she's in jail."

"If the police really think Ingrid killed Sam, then why did they question me all day long?" yelled Victoria. "Like I had anything to do with it," she said in a more subdued tone. "And we both know it wasn't the witch who did it either, don't we, *Ben*?"

She took a drink, found that her glass was empty, and fumbled to get the bottle open to pour herself another.

"I don't know what you're talking about," said Ben, whose face had turned almost purple as he tried to hold himself together.

"Oh, but don't you, though?" said Victoria, a sickly sweet smile spreading across her face. "Sam told me all about you. How you wanted to be the mayor. How you were jealous of him. How you'd been arguing lately about *every, little, thing.*"

"Shut up!" Becky yelled, stepping protectively in front of her husband. "The killer is safely behind bars, and that's the end of it! Ben would never harm Sam. They were like brothers."

At this, Victoria said, "Pffft! Cain and Abel, maybe." She wobbled a little, as though she was getting dizzy. "But the witch in the jail cell didn't do *squat*," she went on, and then walked over and flopped onto the couch. "Unless it's a crime to think Samuel Wright was an ass. She's not in there for murder, anyway. She's in there for being a kook. And I heard that Officer Harris talking to Weaser today, saying that the coroner's report came in and Sam's head was bashed in by a rock. And guess what, Benedict? They're doing all kinds of testing—DNA testing—and soon they'll know *exactly* who did it. And that's not all. Some of those security monitors you installed in the trees? Turns out they were actually working. The quality of the recordings was so bad they had to be sent off to a specialist to be clarified. But it won't be long now."

At this, Benedict had to sit down.

"My darling," said Becky, rushing to her husband's side and kneeling down next to him. "Your heart. You know what the doctor said. You have to calm down. Don't listen to this awful woman. She doesn't know what she's talking about."

"Oh, but I do," said Victoria. "And he knows it. And I know it. Even *these* losers probably know it." She pointed wildly at Jack, Rosemary, Seth, and Charlie. "And the police will soon know it too—unless you have that Weaser in your back pocket like Sam did. But keep in mind, Benedict Thatcher: Weaser goes to the highest bidder. So, you'll have to make plenty of deals with that devil if you're going to get off scot-free and actually get to be the mayor of this pathetic, little, backward, backwoods, ancient, boring town! I was supposed to be the first lady, for crying out loud! That was the plan!"

With that, Victoria stood up, stumbled across the room, and threw open the front door. "Lock up for me, would you?" she said, flinging the ring of keys back over her shoulder. Jack, thankfully, ducked just in time, before they narrowly missed his head and hit the wall behind them.

With a slam of the door, Victoria was gone.

There was a beat of silence, and then all eyes slowly turned to Benedict Thatcher, who was still sitting with Becky at his knee, head in his hands.

"Are you okay, Mr. Thatcher?" asked Seth, approaching the couple and trying to get a look at Ben's face.

Ben let out a long, sorrowful moan. “No. I’m not okay. I’ll never be okay again.” He lifted his head and looked at his wife. “Go on home, Becky. I have something I have to do.”

“Ben, you come home with me,” Becky pleaded. “It’s late. What could you possibly have to do tonight?”

He stood, wavered a little, then took a deep breath as if to fortify himself. “You’ll know soon enough,” he said.

“Then I’m coming with you,” said Becky. “Whatever it is, we’ll do it together.”

“No. Not this time,” he said, looking at her sadly.

“Ben, I’m—”

“No, you’re not. Go home.”

There was such a note of finality in his voice that Becky nodded, stood, and without even looking at the others, quietly left the room.

“Mr. Thatcher, do you need to get to the hospital?” asked Jack. “You don’t look well at all. We can give you a ride. Charlie will go get the car.”

“No,” Ben answered quickly. “I need to be alone now.”

With that, he trudged out the door and disappeared into the shadows.

Rosemary closed the door quietly and turned around to face the others. “Where do you think he’s going?” she asked.

“Who knows,” said Jack. “I’ll call City Hall and check on him in the morning.”

“Did you find the book?” asked Seth.

“Yes—we found it exactly where it should’ve been, as a matter of fact,” said Rosemary. “Sam might’ve led a double life, but he was seriously organized. You should see his office. Everything in its place.”

“And you’ll never believe this,” said Jack. “We think we found the confession of Matthew Graves.”

“Seriously? So, his conscience did get the better of him,” said Seth.

“Big time,” said Rosemary. “He couldn’t live with what he’d done, and he told the priest everything.”

“That is, we’re pretty sure it was Matthew Graves who told the priest everything,” said Charlie, taking a seat. “Josias King only used people’s initials, not their full names, in his records.”

“And he called this person J.G.—which we think is probably Judge Graves,” said Rosemary.

Seth sat down next to Rosemary and thought for a moment. “So Reverend King kept records of everything in his writings, right?”

“Yep,” said Rosemary. “Weddings, baptisms, births . . .”

“Deaths?” asked Seth.

Rosemary met his eyes. “Good idea!” she said, reading his thoughts. She flipped forward a few pages in the book. “Quick, Jack,” she said. “What day did Matthew Graves die?”

“Hold on . . . give me a second . . . let me think . . .” Jack put his hands to his temples and closed his eyes in concentration. “October 1669 . . . October 5th!”

Rosemary flipped a few more pages.

“Where is it, where is it . . .” She quickly scanned the pages. “Here it is. October 5th. Josias is riding out to visit Jolly Smith, who’s taken ill . . . He’s reminding himself to take the loaf of bread Mrs. King baked . . .” Rosemary turned to the next page. “A death! ‘J.G. has passed away. He will be missed by his wife *Elizabeth*, but his troubled soul is troubled no more.’”

Rosemary snapped the book shut and looked at the others in amazement.

“So, that’s it, then!” said Jack. “J.G. *is* Matthew Graves.”

"And Matthew Graves had confessed to the priest. And who knows? Maybe he went home and confessed to his wife after that," said Rosemary.

"It would make sense," said Seth. "If he was about to turn himself in, like the priest had advised, he might've wanted to tell his wife first. It would've been his only chance to apologize."

"And then it would also make sense that either he took his own life or Elizabeth, who'd probably had it up to here with him by now, poisoned him, like Mercy implied she did," said Charlie.

"I can imagine that Elizabeth was a little bit miffed if her husband told her he'd cheated on her and then killed her friend and neighbor, Hortence," said Rosemary. "But do you all realize what this means? It can all come out into the light now. If we combine all of these different primary sources, a very clear picture of the past comes into view. Hortence wasn't a witch. And now everyone will know it."

"Let's get out of here," said Jack. "We'll head back out to the farm and eat those cookies."

"Good idea," said Charlie. "A really good snickerdoodle will set us all right."

They switched off the lights and locked the door, leaving Sam's house quiet and dark, and made their way down the front steps and walked along Maple Leaf Drive back in the direction of the courthouse.

"Wow," said Charlie, pointing at the sky. "Would you look at that moon?"

A thin sliver of a moon glistened in the night sky, a sprinkling of stars scattered around it.

"Did you see that?" asked Rosemary suddenly.

"I saw it," said Seth, smiling at the sky.

"What?" asked Jack.

"A shooting star," said Rosemary. "So beautiful. Look! There's another one!"

"And there's another," said Charlie, pointing. "I've never seen so many at once."

"Almost like a sign," said Jack, putting an arm around Rosemary.

"Do you think?" she asked, smiling at her friend, and then closing her eyes and turning her face back up to the glorious sky.

"I think that just like you, Hortence is smiling."

26

The snickerdoodles didn't disappoint. And they were perfect with a cup of warm milk, with just a hint of chocolate melting into it.

"I have decided that I will have this snack every night at bedtime from now on," said Rosemary, biting into her second cookie.

"Good idea," said Seth. "And now that I know how to make them…" He looked at Rosemary, then quickly looked down and smiled to himself.

"This has been quite an eventful evening," said Charlie.

"Found a three hundred fifty-year-old confession and set a restless midwife's soul at ease, as per usual?" said Jack.

“All in a night’s work,” agreed Rosemary, dusting crumbs from her fingers and picking up her mug.

“I’d better be getting home,” said Seth, standing to go. He looked down at Rosemary. “Walk me out?”

Rosemary smiled and nodded, getting up and following Seth to the door.

“Thanks for the best time ever, guys,” Seth called back to Jack and Charlie.

“Anytime!” Jack said.

Once outside, Seth took Rosemary’s hand.

“It’s getting chilly,” he said, as they walked toward his car.

“Charlie tells me storms could roll in tomorrow night, but then we can expect sunshine and clear skies Friday night for the festival.”

“And Charlie’s never wrong,” Seth laughed.

“Nope. He’s foolproof.”

“Jack’s never wrong, either,” said Seth, stopping and pulling Rosemary close.

“Is that so?” said Rosemary, smiling up at him.

"That *is* so," Seth answered. "He told me you were wonderful. He told me you were beautiful. And he told me I should ask you out."

"Well, you should, you know," said Rosemary, feeling her heart kick up a notch.

"Rosemary?" he said softly. "Will you go with me to the Founders Day Festival this Friday night?"

"I'd love to."

Seth brushed a strand of Rosemary's hair out of her face, and then touched her cheek. When he bent to kiss her, softly and slowly, Rosemary felt a wave of warm energy run through her all the way to her toes. Then when Seth looked at her, grinning, his head still tilted slightly, the energy ran right back up to her heart.

"When I said I'd had the best time ever tonight?" he began.

"Yes?"

"I meant it."

Seth brushed another lock of hair behind Rosemary's ear.

"Me, too," she said, laying her own hand on top of his.

"Do you think those guys are watching us from the window right now?"

"Most definitely."

Seth laughed, opened his car door, and got in.

"See you tomorrow?" he asked, shutting the door and rolling down the window.

"Yes," said Rosemary. "We'll be at the memorial service for Sam in the morning—although after meeting Victoria tonight, I'm wondering if that will be more of a circus."

"I'm going too. I'll see you all there."

Seth gave a little salute toward the front windows of the house, and when Rosemary turned to look, a curtain shifted back into place.

"They're horrible!" she said.

"The worst," Seth agreed.

When Rosemary went back inside, she looked around at the deserted living room.

"Jack? Charlie?"

"In the kitchen," Jack called. "Where we've been all along, ever since the moment you and Seth went outside!"

"Right," said Rosemary, glancing down to see Smudge, who had suddenly appeared and was sitting at her feet, blinking up at her with knowing green eyes.

"Hello," she said, bending down to pat her on the head. "You know, I never would've ever thought in a million years that I'd voluntarily befriend a cat. I mean, no offense. And, well, you did make the first move. But you seem like a good soul."

Smudge looked at her as if she was returning the compliment.

"Let's go see if we can find you a treat," Rosemary said, going to the kitchen, the kitten following at her heels.

Rosemary had slept like a rock that night and woke the next morning with pink light streaming into her window. She pulled on her robe, stepped into her slippers, and hurried into the kitchen. She wanted to be the one to make coffee for the guys today.

Soon, the smell of freshly brewed coffee must've wafted its way down the hall, because Jack emerged from his room and joined Rosemary in the kitchen.

"Good morning, sunshine," he said. "You're up early today."

"I slept so soundly last night. I'm feeling refreshed and ready to go," said Rosemary, pouring Jack a cup of coffee and setting the cream and sugar in front of him.

"You're all aglow. Seems to me you're in love," Jack teased.

"Let's not jump the gun, Cupid," said Rosemary. "But I do have to admit, this time, you picked a good one."

"*This* time? When have I ever led you astray?"

"You're kidding, right? Remember that Bobby Stanforth? Junior year? And that guy, what was his name? Phillip Brunswick, when we were twenty-two?"

"Well, those didn't count," said Jack, waving her words away.

"I agree," said Rosemary. "Those didn't count." She glanced out the huge kitchen windows. "The sunrise is glorious this morning. Let's go out and sit on the dock," she suggested.

"Great idea," said Jack, grabbing his mug and following her to the door.

"Where's Charlie?"

"Out for a run. He'll be along shortly."

They made their way down the gentle hill from the house to the pond, and snuggled up with their coffee in the Adirondack chairs overlooking the water. The sun was rising from behind them, but the clouds over the pond were turning a beautiful shade of deep pink, which was reflecting off the surface of the water, bathing the whole scene in pinks and mauves.

"This must be what it's like to look at the world through rose-colored glasses," said Jack.

Just then, Charlie jogged up.

“Good morning, all,” he said, punching a tiny button on his sports watch.

“Isn’t it, though?” said Rosemary, smiling up at him from her cozy chair.

“She’s in love,” sang Jack. “And the sunrise is incredible this morning!”

“That’s because a storm’s coming,” said Charlie.

“Are you kidding? It’s perfect out,” said Jack.

“Oh, I remember the rule: ’Pink sky in the morning, sailors take warning,’ right?” asked Rosemary.

“That’s right,” said Charlie. “Or some say, ‘Red sky in the morning, shepherds warning.’ But either way, it means the high pressure system has moved off, and a low pressure system is moving in. Don’t worry: by tomorrow’s festival, it’ll clear out.”

“That’s the main thing. We can check on our lanterns and everything early Friday, but they should be fine. They’re all waterproof. And the path through the cemetery is bricked, of course, so mud isn’t a big concern,” said Jack.

“Good thing,” said Charlie.

“So, are you having to cancel class this morning for Sam’s memorial?” Rosemary asked Jack.

"Just my ten o'clock. Hey, come have lunch with me and Seth today, okay?"

"Great. I wonder how long the service will go on," said Rosemary.

"Why? Do you have a massage appointment to get to?"

"Ha, ha. Very funny. No. Just curious."

"Right. I'm on to you, my friend," said Jack, raising a brow at Rosemary. "I bet you're just aching to read more of those scandalous confessions Reverend Josias took down."

"Well . . ."

"Meanwhile, we should probably all have some breakfast and get cleaned up to go to the memorial service," said Charlie.

They whipped up a big pot of oatmeal and stirred in things like almond butter, honey, yogurt, and walnuts, and made another pot of coffee. By the time Rosemary stepped into the shower, the sun was rising into a cloud-scattered sky.

Was it irreverent that she was looking forward to the memorial service? Seth would be there, for one thing. And as an observer of human behavior, Rosemary thought it would be interesting to watch the other people who showed up, to see what kinds of friends Sam had kept company with.

Not surprisingly, First Church was full to bursting well before the service began. Rosemary, Jack, and Charlie had found Seth outside, and they'd all slid into the back row on the right of the center aisle, with Jack sitting at the end closest to the aisle. Looking around at the crowd, which sat somewhat hushed and waiting respectfully, Rosemary couldn't help but feel that Sam would've been pleased to have so many people come out to remember and celebrate his life.

"This is perfect," whispered Jack. "I can see everyone from here."

"Shhh!" said Charlie.

"But don't you realize," said Jack, leaning across Rosemary to talk to Charlie. "That the killer could be here?"

"That would require a high level of audacity," said Seth, leaning over Charlie to talk to Jack.

"But the killer always goes to the funeral in movies," whispered Jack. "They have to. They can't stay away."

"I bet Victoria Winthrop is hung over after last night's bender," said Rosemary. "Do you see her anywhere?"

"She's got to be up front," said Jack, straining to see. "Nope, she's not there."

"What about the Thatchers?" asked Rosemary. "Can you see them?"

Jack leaned slightly out into the aisle and scanned the pews.

"Yes. There's Becky, way up front. But I don't see Benedict."

"He's not with her?" asked Charlie. "That's odd."

"He looked awful last night," whispered Seth. "Maybe he stayed home."

"And missed his best friend's memorial service?" asked Rosemary. "Doesn't sound right. He'd have to be really sick."

"Becky mentioned his heart. Maybe he had a heart attack or something," said Seth, concerned.

"Look at Becky," said Jack. "Well never mind. None of you can see her. But let me tell you, her shoulders are shaking, she's crying so hard. Poor thing. Maybe something bad really did happen to her husband."

"That, on top of Sam's death might do her in," said Rosemary, shaking her head. "She's about ready to break down."

"Excuse me. Can I squeeze in here?" Officer Harris approached their pew from the little side aisle on the end opposite Jack.

"Of course," said Seth, and they all scooted further together.

"How's it going, George?" asked Charlie.

"Tough night, if you want the truth," George whispered.

"I like your uniform," said Rosemary, leaning across both Charlie and Seth, and giving George a little wave.

"The whole force is wearing dress blues today, out of respect for the mayor."

"Of course," whispered Jack, peering to see the other officers present. "All four of you look very professional." Then, leaning closer to Rosemary he explained, "The only reason Paperwick is up to four police officers is because one of them, Marleen Sanderson, was on maternity leave until a month ago, so they hired a stand-in. But then when Marleen came back to work, they just decided that all four could stay."

George looked down the row and raised an eyebrow.

"I would go sit in the front with the rest of the force," he said, "but I ran late. Had to stay at the office a bit longer. It's been crazy down there ever since Mr. Thatcher turned himself in."

"What was that, George?" Jack said, straining to hear. "I thought you said Thatcher turned himself in."

"I did," said George. "Late last night. He showed up around midnight. Confessed to involuntary manslaughter."

"He killed Sam?" asked Rosemary in a loud whisper, amazed.

"I'd better not say anything else for now. But you'll see it all in the paper."

"I can't believe this," said Jack, forgetting to whisper.

"Shhh!" scolded Charlie. "The service is about to begin."

“So was Ingrid released then, George?” asked Rosemary.

“Yes, Ms. Clark was released about an hour ago. Detective Weaser hadn’t found anything of interest when he searched her house, but was still holding her as a person of interest. But Mr. Thatcher’s confession changed everything.”

The organ suddenly came to life, playing a somber hymn, cutting short their conversation. Everyone stood as Reverend Bob processed up the aisle and turned to face the crowd.

“Please be seated,” he said as soon as the hymn came to a close.

There was a shuffling of shoes and a few whispers as the crowd settled in.

Reverend Bob looked out over the faces.

“We have come together today,” he began, in a booming voice that easily carried all the way to the back of the church, “to thank God for the life of Samuel Wright. As many of you know—"

Reverend Bob was interrupted by a blood curdling scream from the back of the church.

All heads turned to see Mrs. Potter, who had just burst in through the doors at the foot of the aisle, right next to Jack.

“Mrs. P!” said Jack, getting to his feet. “What’s happened?”

"Police! I need the police right away! She—she's dead!" Mrs. Potter turned white as a ghost and wavered slightly.

Jack hurried into the aisle and took Mrs. Potter's arm to support her.

"What are you saying? Who's dead?" he asked.

"Victoria Winthrop! She's dead!"

At this pronouncement, Mrs. Potter fainted into Jack's arms. Jack, who wasn't quite prepared to support Mrs. Potter in her entirety, sank slowly to the floor himself, as Rosemary, Charlie, Seth, and George hurried to help.

"At least you broke her fall," said Charlie, kneeling down next to them and checking Mrs. Potter's pulse.

"Help," choked Jack in a raspy voice.

Meanwhile, the entire congregation had risen to its feet, and an alarmed buzz filled the church.

"Don't panic," Reverend Bob's voice cut through the noise. "Let's all go down the outside aisles into the churchyard in an orderly fashion! Officer Harris has the matter in hand."

As most of the parishioners filed out, George knelt alongside Charlie, and together, they lifted Mrs. Potter enough so that a grateful Jack could slither out from under her.

"She's coming to," said George.

"Oh, Charlie, dear. It's you," Mrs. Potter said, her eyes fluttering open. "And George. Thank goodness."

"You said Victoria Winthrop is dead," said George, taking out his trusty notepad. "Are you sure?"

"Yes, of course I'm sure. She's as dead as dead can be! Help me up and we'll go back to the Bed and Bakery. I'll show you."

They helped Mrs. Potter to stand and slowly made their way out of the church. What basically amounted to the entire population of the village was milling about in the churchyard by now. Reverend Bob was announcing that the service would continue at the graveside a few yards away, and that the police had "the other situation" under control. Of course, all eyes watched as George and another one of the officers present escorted Mrs. Potter out of the churchyard and down the street in the direction of Potter's Bed and Bakery.

"That woman is solid as a rock," said Jack, who had twisted his ankle slightly when Mrs. Potter had fainted on him.

"Can you believe this?" said Charlie. "Benedict Thatcher left Sam's last night and went to the police and turned himself in? He killed Sam. Your instincts were right, Rosemary."

"I can't get over it," said Seth. "That's why he looked so sick. His conscience was getting to him."

"Just like in the case of Matthew Graves and the telltale conscience," said Jack.

"What about Victoria? Can you believe she's dead? We *just saw* her. And sure, she was drunk. But what happened, and how did she go from being drunk to being dead?" asked Seth.

"The thing that keeps bothering me," Rosemary said slowly, thinking about the night before, "is that Benedict Thatcher left us at Sam's house around ten o'clock. George said he turned himself in around midnight. So, what was he doing for two hours in between?"

"He told Becky he had to do something, and he had to do it alone," said Seth.

Rosemary nodded. "I know. But what if the thing he had to do was kill Victoria Winthrop?"

27

"This is surreal," said Charlie, as they all stood slightly dazed, in line for coffee and a bagel with cream cheese and lox. At a funeral.

"This was Sam's favorite," said Jack. "He got a bagel with cream cheese and lox and a coffee every Friday morning at the bakery."

"I don't mean the bagels are surreal. I'm talking about this *whole situation*," said Charlie. "There's no violent crime in Paperwick!"

"Well, not since that whole witch business back in the 1600s, anyway," mumbled Jack, elbowing Rosemary.

"And now, here we are, eating bagels, with two murders in as many days."

"We don't know that Victoria was murdered," said Seth. "You saw her stumbling out of Sam's last night. It's more likely she had an accident."

"I guess you're right," said Charlie, a little relieved.

"Look at Becky," said Rosemary, peering through the crowd to where Becky Thatcher stood, dressed in black, dark circles under her eyes, holding an untouched bagel in one hand. "Imagine how she's feeling. Her husband killed one of their dearest friends."

"George said involuntary manslaughter," said Seth. "So, he didn't mean to kill him, apparently."

"I heard them arguing. In the woods," said Rosemary. "I was talking to Ingrid. It was just after you left, Seth. I wonder why they were so angry at each other."

"Remember last night? Victoria said Ben was jealous of Sam. She really hit a nerve," said Jack.

"No kidding," said Rosemary. "I know that they were meeting to discuss the security cameras that were being installed around the meadow. Sam told me Benedict was in charge of the project."

"And when Becky arrived, looking for them, she only found Sam, already dead, and Ingrid Clark standing over him. So, Benedict must've argued with Sam, somehow killed him, and left…" said Seth.

"Then Ingrid showed up, found him…" added Jack.

"That would've been right after she left me," said Rosemary. "Then shortly after that, I packed up my things and was walking back toward the church when I heard Becky scream. The timeline makes sense."

"Let's talk more about this over lunch," said Jack. "I have to get over to campus for class."

"So do I," said Seth.

"Rosemary, want to come along?"

"I'll come over shortly," said Rosemary. "I want to check on Mrs. Potter first."

Even in the midst of police and paramedics rushing about, Potter's Bed and Bakery smelled like heaven. The bakery was downstairs, and customers were still being handed bags of cookies and carefully wrapped loaves of bread over the glass display cases that were filled with good things.

As Rosemary entered the bakery, George was just coming down the stairs with Mrs. Potter, another officer trailing behind.

Rosemary stood looking at the array of tarts, cookies, and pastries as though she was pondering what to purchase, all the while, straining to hear George and Mrs. Potter's conversation.

"We'll have to clear the place out, just for a bit," George was saying. "You understand."

"Of course I understand, George," said Mrs. Potter.

"The paramedics will move the body out, and then we'll be able to confine our investigation to the second floor in Ms. Winthrop's room. I'm expecting Detective Weaser within the next few minutes."

"I'm just so glad you're here, George. So upsetting." Mrs. Potter lowered her voice a bit. "It looks like she passed out drunk. Shoes strewn on the floor, an empty brandy bottle right there on the bed with her. Did she die in her sleep?"

"Too soon to tell," said George. "There may have been other substances involved. We found some prescription pills in the medicine cabinet that wouldn't have mixed well with too much alcohol. Perhaps Ms. Winthrop took something. It was probably accidental, from what I can tell, although we can't yet rule out suicide or, well, something else."

"Something else? What else could it be?" asked Mrs. Potter, alarmed.

"We'll know more when the coroner determines the cause of death," said George. "Until then, we'll have to keep the room exactly as it is. Sorry for the inconvenience, Mrs. P."

"Don't you worry about that, George. Meanwhile, have a cinnamon roll. I know they're your favorite."

Mrs. Potter shimmied behind the counter, grabbed a bakery bag and a pair of tongs, and put a giant cinnamon roll, gleaming with frosting and studded with pecans, into the bag. She folded the top of the bag closed and handed it to George.

"You go ahead and start clearing out the customers, dear," she said. "I'll take a few trays of donuts outside for your crew."

George thanked Mrs. Potter, who had just spotted Rosemary and waved her over.

"Can you believe this sad business, Rosemary?" she asked, shaking her head and sliding a couple of huge, donut-laden trays out from one of the glass display cases.

"Here. Let me help you take these outside, Mrs. Potter."

"Thank you, dear. I'm still having a hard time getting over a death in our little inn. This has never happened before! And we're all still reeling from the loss of Sam."

"So, you were the one who found Victoria, I take it?" asked Rosemary, taking one of the trays and heading outside along with the other customers who were vacating the bakery.

"Yes. Awful!" said Mrs. Potter. "I was all ready to walk down to Sam's memorial service. Thought I'd offer to walk over with the poor girl. I mean, as rude as she'd been, I thought maybe it was all because she was grieving, and I felt a wave of sympathy. But when I knocked on her door, there was no answer.

"We've been here at the bakery, of course, since very early this morning, baking and getting things ready for our morning rush. So, I knew Ms. Winthrop—assuming she was in her room—had not left for the service yet. What can I say? I had a bad feeling. I have a knack about people, and I know that woman was deeply troubled."

"So, when she didn't answer the door . . ."

"Well, the door was open a crack, so I decided to take a peek," said Mrs. Potter, showing Rosemary where to set down the donut-laden tray. "And there she was."

"On the bed?" asked Rosemary. "I mean—I don't want to pry.. . . ."

"Not at all. Yes, she was on the bed, still in her clothes. She hadn't even made down the comforter. It looked like she'd walked into the room, kicked off her shoes, and passed out cold."

"And never woke up again," said Rosemary.

"Exactly. I supposed she and Sam are together now," said Mrs. Potter, laying a hand over her heart and looking upward.

"I guess you heard that Mr. Thatcher confessed to killing Sam," said Rosemary.

"Oh, yes! Broke my heart! George told me. He said the man was on the verge of a breakdown when he arrived at the police station in the middle of the night. He'd been carrying the burden of horrible guilt."

"So, it was an accident, right? I mean, Mr. Thatcher didn't kill Sam on purpose." Rosemary wondered how far she could pry without crossing the line and sounding insensitive.

"Oh yes. George said that Ben and Sam had a horrible fight, Ben pushed Sam, and Sam hit his head on a rock. Benedict was horrified at what he'd done and ran away. He was so ashamed and panicked, he ran for a doctor instead of calling 9-1-1. In the meantime, Becky texted him, said she'd gone to the meadow to find him, but found poor Sam instead. And he was already dead! Can you imagine? All this time, Benedict knowing what had happened and not saying a word? Awful!"

"Becky got there and made the mistake of thinking Ingrid Clark had killed Sam," said Rosemary.

"Poor old Ingrid," said Mrs. Potter. "She made no secret of her feelings about Sam—and she's definitely crossed the line a few times. There was an incident with a brick and a nasty note that I won't go into now. But I don't believe she'd ever actually hurt anyone. I mean, have you seen her garden?"

"Yes, as a matter of fact, I have."

"She plants seeds. Helps things grow. The way she cares for those plants . . ." Mrs. Potter shook her head. "Ingrid's no killer, I'd bet my bottom dollar on it. Sad as it is that Benedict is in jail, I'm glad Ingrid was cleared."

"Me too," said Rosemary. "In fact, I think I'll pay her a visit or ask her to dinner."

"That would be very nice, dear. Well, I'd better go put on another pot of coffee before Detective Weaser arrives. Give my best to the boys. And in spite of all this mess, I hope you're enjoying your stay in Paperwick."

Rosemary smiled. "In spite of all of this, I am," she said.

"This is going to sound crazy," said Rosemary over lunch with Jack and Seth. "But what would you think of the idea of inviting Ingrid Clark out to the farm? I mean, so she can see where her ancestors lived?"

"I actually love that idea," said Jack.

"Really? Even though she's a bit of a nut?"

"Are you kidding? The nuttier, the better, I say. I'd like to make friends with Ingrid—and not just because we're going to need her for our book. I love it that she's connected to our land and the legend of Hortence Gallow. Let's invite her to come over tonight for dinner. It'll be a hoot."

"Wonderful."

"Do you think she'll accept the invitation?" asked Seth.

"I *think* so," said Rosemary. "We've established a little bit of a friendly rapport. And she is very dedicated to her family and its history. I think she'd love to see the place her eleven-times great-grandmother and aunt lived."

"Great. Call her up, and we'll make an evening of it," said Jack. "Charlie will be thrilled. As a writer, he loves meeting new characters. Seth, you come too."

"Are you sure you want me here three nights in a row?" laughed Seth.

"Absolutely," Rosemary answered for Jack. "Besides, I think Ingrid approves of you."

"But bring a pan of your brownies, just in case," said Jack.

28

Rosemary was glad the predicted rain was holding off as she helped Jack and Charlie in the kitchen that evening. Seth had offered to pick up Ingrid, who had considered their invitation with surprising tolerance. She'd even almost smiled. When Rosemary promised to show her the old barn, she'd agreed to come.

Rosemary was in charge of the cheese and crackers platter. Charlie was making a quick shepherd's pie, and Jack was throwing together a salad. The fire was lit, and the house was warm and inviting and ready for company. The sun was just starting to move toward setting, so there would be plenty of daylight left to show Ingrid around outside before dinner.

"They're heeere," said Jack, coming back into the kitchen after setting the table.

From the window, Rosemary smiled, watching Seth run around to open the door for Ingrid, who looked none the worse for wear after her time in police custody. She flung her door open just as Seth reached for it, knocking him aside.

"That woman is a force to be reckoned with," Jack said in genuine admiration, looking out the window over Rosemary's shoulder.

"She is that," agreed Rosemary.

Jack called Charlie, and together, they all hurried into the entry room and opened the door before Seth had even rung the bell.

"Hello, and welcome!" said Jack. He held out a hand to Ingrid, who frowned at his hand, but didn't shake it.

"Hello, Ingrid," said Rosemary. "So glad you're here."

"As are we," said Charlie. "Glad you're here and not . . . well, in jail . . . anymore."

"Thanks," said Ingrid, who actually smiled a little at Charlie. "So am I."

"Dinner's almost ready," he said. "How about we show you around before it gets dark?"

"But first, we'd like to return these to you," said Rosemary, handing Ingrid Mercy's diary and the file of articles about Sam that they'd found in Ingrid's desk.

"Well, you keep the diary for now," said Ingrid gently. "And these," she held out the file. "Let's recycle these. I don't need them anymore."

"Will do," said Jack, taking the items from Ingrid and running them down the hallway.

"I know you must've wondered about that file," Ingrid said, looking down at her hands and then up at Rosemary and Seth.

"Well, we could understand why it was better if Detective Weaser didn't discover them," said Rosemary.

"You really weren't a fan of the mayor," said Seth with a chuckle.

"No, I was not," admitted Ingrid. "When you've lived as long as I have, and your family has lived in the same place for generations, you know the families. You watch and wait and wonder if the descendants will favor the good or the bad in their own bloodlines. The Wrights were good folks. The Graves were not. I remembered Mercy's descriptions of Matthew Graves and couldn't help but see the similarities in Samuel Wright. Handsome. Ambitious. Charming. Always reaching. Always hungry. So, I followed what he was doing here in our town very closely."

"And the thing with the brick through his window?"

"Oh, if I had that to do again!" said Ingrid. "If I could've pulled that brick back in space the second after it left my hand

. . . I know that was wrong. I just . . . got so tired of him not listening to my concerns. Of him not meeting my eyes, you know? As though I was just some crazy old lady who could be brushed aside. So, I *made* him listen."

"Well, first," said Rosemary. "You're not that old."

"I'm seventy-five if I'm a day!"

"Seventy is the new fifty-five," put in Charlie, who'd been standing by quietly.

"And second," Rosemary continued, "I'd have been mad, too. And I discovered some notes in the library that Sam had written, and I think you were right about him planning to exploit your family's struggles."

Ingrid nodded gratefully and gave a little sniffle.

"So, seventy's the new fifty-five, is it?" she said, looking at Charlie.

"You've got a long life ahead of you, young lady," he said with a smile. "And you're going to be having lots of dinners here with us, and spending as much time on this land as you'd like."

Rosemary had never seen Ingrid smile with her whole face. She always half-smiled or seemed to be stifling a smile. But now, Ingrid grinned so broadly that her whole face lit up, and Rosemary's heart filled.

"Now let's get outside and look around before the sun sets," said Jack, who'd come back into the room and ran to open the back door.

Ingrid nodded, and they all stepped out onto the back porch that overlooked the pond.

They showed Ingrid the old barn, showed her where they'd found Mercy's note, walked through Jack and Charlie's miniature orchard, with its handful of apple and pear trees, and ended standing on the dock.

"It's my understanding that the Clarks—and others who farmed the land after them—used the water from this pond for everything from irrigation to drinking water," said Charlie.

"It's in the perfect spot, you see," said Ingrid, taking in the land around them. "Fresh rain would run off into this pond from all the land around it. It's one of the reasons this parcel of land was so valuable."

"The first thing that attracted us to this place was its history," said Jack. "And your family's history in particular."

"We truly want you to know that you're welcome here anytime," said Charlie. "And we'll always do our best to be good stewards of this land."

"Well, I appreciate that," said Ingrid, who'd softened up so much that she was almost unrecognizable.

"The sun's setting. We often sit here on the water to watch it, and I think the rain is still a good distance off," said Charlie. "Would you like to sit awhile?"

Ingrid nodded and took a seat. "You know, the people who owned this place before you weren't so friendly. This is actually the first time I've been on this land since my mother brought me here as a little girl."

"We didn't know you'd been here before," said Jack, smiling.

"Just that one time. And it's more beautiful, even, than I remember it—and that's saying a lot. You boys have done a lot with the house."

"It's been fun," said Jack.

"A labor of love," added Charlie.

The sky was now a riot of pink and lavender. A small flock of ducks glided over the pond, circled, and skidded into the water on the far side. Rosemary looked at Ingrid, who was watching them closely.

"She's almost free, you know," she said. "Hortence."

"Almost?" said Rosemary.

"Seth here told me all about your findings on our drive over. But I felt it even before he said a word. I felt it last night. You've found enough evidence to finally point to Hortence's killer. I feel she's slipping into the next world, just as she should. She'll be with Mercy and Lilly and all the rest." Ingrid met Rosemary's eyes. "My family is grateful," she said. "The ones who live in the world now. And the ones who came before. Thank you."

"We were glad to help," said Rosemary, smiling.

"And have you told Rosemary here about the little cottage?" asked Ingrid, looking at Charlie and Jack.

"What little cottage?" asked Rosemary.

"How did you know about that?" asked Jack.

"I could say I have a knack about these things," said Ingrid. "And it would be true. But really, I am a very observant and intuitive person. I listen to things around town. I might not say a lot, so no one really knows I'm listening, but I am."

"What cottage?" Rosemary asked again.

"That one," said Ingrid, pointing to the cottage by the pond.

"Amazing," said Charlie, looking at Ingrid.

"Not really," said Ingrid. "Bert Ander told me he's been over here working on the place, said you boys were hoping your friend who was visiting would decide to stay. Simple as that."

"Are you saying the man in the red truck doesn't live in that cottage?"

"No. He's the contractor. Bert Ander," said Jack, still surprised that Ingrid knew all about the cottage.

Rosemary looked at Ingrid. "Ingrid, that time you told me I was through wandering . . . that I was home . . . Is that why you thought that I'd stay in Paperwick? Because you knew about the cottage?"

"Nope. I thought you'd stay in Paperwick because you're loved here."

"I—I'm—"

"Loved. Jack and Charlie love you. This goofball loves you too, but he doesn't know it yet," she pointed a thumb over her shoulder at Seth, who turned bright red. "You're tired of wandering around—I can see that in your eyes. And you seem like a reasonable person," she went on. "A reasonable person wants to make their home in the place where they can be surrounded by love."

Rosemary was silent for a moment, not knowing what to say. She could almost feel her heart swelling with joy. "Jack. Charlie," she said, turning to face them. "Are you renovating that cottage for me?"

"We wanted to tell you at the right time. And Rosie, there's no pressure. It's a great little place, and if you don't want to live there, we'll use it as a guest house or maybe a B&B or get a renter in. It's just an idea. We thought that one day, you'd want to settle. And we're your family. So, we were hoping you might choose to settle here."

"Uh—" Seth raised his hand like a school kid. "I am also hoping you'll stick around."

"See?" asked Ingrid. "What'd I tell you?"

Rosemary looked across the water at the cottage, with its little railed porch overlooking the water. She could see herself on that porch. As clear as day, she could see herself, sitting in a rocking chair, drinking a cup of coffee, and amazingly, Smudge was curled up in her lap in this vision.

"Think about it," said Jack. "Remember. No pressure, Rosemary."

"I don't need to think about it," said Rosemary, a happy tear stinging her eye. "I'm home."

Before she could say another word, she was engulfed in a hug and then Jack was doing his happy dance, and everyone was laughing. Even Ingrid.

"This is the real thing," she said, as they started up the hill toward the house for dinner. "Not like what that Sam Wright had."

"What do you mean?" asked Rosemary.

"You are all true friends. This is true love."

"Oh, I think I see what you mean," said Rosemary. "Sam and Victoria Winthrop. You're right. That wasn't real love. And what a sad end."

"It was a ridiculous hoax," agreed Ingrid. "Not to mention his friendship with Benedict Thatcher."

"So, they weren't really friends?" asked Charlie, confused.

Ingrid scoffed. "Lord, no."

"Hold on," said Rosemary. "Do you suspect Ben killed Sam on purpose? The story we heard is that Ben and Sam argued, Ben pushed Sam, and Sam hit his head on a rock when he fell."

"Oh, I don't think Benedict killed Sam on purpose. But I told you that murder was riddled with jealousy."

"I'm not following," said Rosemary.

"Well, it's understandable that Thatcher was angry at Sam Wright. He'd just finally figured out that his wife—that Becky Thatcher—had been having an affair with Sam for God knows how long."

"Are you serious?" ask Jack.

By now, they'd all stopped dead in their tracks and were gathered around Ingrid.

"Ben Thatcher does not have the knack. He is not observant. He lives with his head down. If he would look around him once in a while, he'd learn a lot. *Of course* I'm serious. Becky was the mayor's secretary. She's been in love with him forever. Doesn't anyone notice these things anymore? It was obvious. They had a longstanding affair—and then when that no-good Sam announced his engagement the other day, and brought that piece of work Victoria Winthrop to town, Becky lost it. See, in that moment, she should've been happy for her boss and supposed friend. But she was clearly upset. That twit Benedict finally saw what had been right in front of his nose—heck, right in his own backyard. He confronted Sam, punched his lights out, and accidentally killed him to boot. Talk about your tangled webs!"

"So that's why Becky has been falling apart all week," said Seth.

"Yep," said Ingrid.

"She didn't just lose a boss or friend or neighbor, she lost the love of her life," said Rosemary.

"Bingo," said Ingrid.

"Unbelievable," said Jack. "I never would've thought that sweet little Becky would do such a thing—be unfaithful. She just doesn't seem the type."

"But she does, really. You just have to look a little deeper," said Ingrid. "She and Sam had dated as kids. She was moon-eyed over him back then, and she never stopped. She picked the better man, really. Samuel Wright wasn't husband material. But in her heart, she'd never ended it with Sam. The real surprise is that Benedict couldn't see it."

"Or maybe didn't want to," said Seth.

"So sad," said Rosemary.

They kept talking as they went inside, took their seats around the table, and Charlie spooned out generous portions of shepherd's pie, it's savory meat and vegetable filling seeping out from under steaming, buttery mashed potatoes.

"I wonder what will become of Becky," said Rosemary after they'd cleared away the dinner dishes and cut into Seth's brownies. "Will she wait for Benedict to get out of jail? I mean, how long will he be in there? Will they try to patch things up? Or get divorced?"

"They won't make it," said Ingrid. "The trust is destroyed, and it was misplaced from the start. Everyone was lying to everyone. No one was ever worthy of anyone else's trust."

"And now Victoria's dead, too," said Rosemary. "I went by the bakery while the police were still there and checked in on Mrs. Potter. She and George were talking, and he was saying that they weren't sure what killed Victoria. Maybe an accidental overdose, or maybe she mixed some kind of medication with too much alcohol."

"She was pretty upset when we saw her, not to mention drunk," said Jack. "What if she meant to end it all?"

"She didn't," said Ingrid in her usual confident fashion.

"What makes you so sure?" asked Jack.

"She wasn't depressed. She was just hopping mad. She was probably using Sam just as much as he was using her, and she was angry that her plans went wrong. All she needed to do was get a grip, and after the obligatory mourning period, go find another rising star to catch hold of."

"I keep wondering if Benedict left Sam's house that night and killed Victoria," said Rosemary.

"She had really upset him, and he's proved that he can't control his temper. After all, he got into a deadly fight with Sam," said Seth. "What if he confronted Victoria just like he'd confronted Sam?"

"George said they hadn't determined the cause of death yet when I was at the Bed and Bakery. I wonder if the investigation has brought any answers yet."

"I could give George a call," said Charlie. "He won't tell us anything that's privileged information . . ."

"But he might give a hint," said Jack. "Go call him, Charlie."

Charlie headed toward his study to make the call, and everyone else dug into the brownies as the first distant roll of thunder sounded off.

"Here comes the storm!" he called from the hallway.

"There's one thing that's still bothering me," said Rosemary. "Why would Benedict go to the trouble of drawing the witch's mark on Sam's shoulder? Was he trying to make it look like the curse had killed Sam?"

"The witch's mark?" said Ingrid, standing up so abruptly that her chair fell over behind her and clattered onto the floor. "What are you talking about?"

"I—I meant the mark on Sam's shoulder," said Rosemary. "Where his shirt was torn."

"I talked to George about that," said Jack, rising to pick up Ingrid's chair. "He said it was done in black marker. Drawn on with a Sharpie. Believe it or not, Benedict must've drawn it on Sam's shoulder and left the body that way so that it would appear that the curse had taken its toll on another member of the Graves family. Even if no one would buy it, it might have served as a point of a distraction. Maybe Benedict thought he could slip between the cracks in the confusion."

Ingrid, listening intently, a deep furrow in her brow, was still standing.

“Ingrid, are you okay?” asked Rosemary.

“When I found Sam’s body,” said Ingrid, leaning forward and planting both palms on the table. “There was no mark.”

29

The room was dead silent for a long moment, save the rumbling of the approaching storm and the crackling fire.

"But Ingrid," Rosemary finally said. "You knew there was talk that it was Hortence's curse that had killed Sam. How could you not have known that it was because of the witch's mark? That's why his death was being blamed on the curse."

"I assumed it was because of Samuel Wright's connection to the Graves family," said Ingrid. "They've been a cursed lot for forever."

"I want to get this straight," said Rosemary, going around the table and sitting in the chair next to Ingrid's. Ingrid sat down, and the two women faced one another. "Let's go back to that day. You and I talked in the woods. We both think we heard

Sam and Ben arguing. You left me, and went back toward the trees. Where did you go?"

"I was going to go home. I was thinking about our conversation, and what you said about writing a book to set the record straight about Hortence. I was thinking about showing you Mercy's diary even then."

"Okay, so you walked through the meadow, into the trees, and back toward your house, which as we know, is just across the street."

"That's right. I was lost in my thoughts about Hortence. And I also felt better knowing that you saw the importance of protecting the meadow, and maybe others did too. I had been so angry earlier. But I didn't feel angry anymore. I felt hopeful. And then that's when I got the call."

"What call?"

"Someone called and told me the mayor was in the meadow, and that he and Thatcher were planning to ruin the place. Of course, I already knew that. I had planned to wait until the right moment and approach them, but then I caught you taking my picture and got distracted."

Rosemary smiled at the memory. "I thought you were furious with me," she said.

"You'd probably never guess this," said Ingrid, "But I'm not always the friendliest on first acquaintance. Anyway, I didn't care for the mayor, and that went both ways. He wasn't too fond of me either. Didn't trust him from day one, although I had hoped he didn't bear too many of the Graves family traits. Anyway, I was surprised to get that call. The woman said she was worried about Mayor Wright messing up our beautiful meadow. She said I ought to try to catch him while he was still there. Of course, I'd meant to do that in the first place. What better time to have a word with both the mayor and the city manager about their cockamamie ideas? So, I turned right back around and went in the direction of where we'd heard them talking. I had to look around for some time before I found him, at the edge of the meadow. Looked like he'd been hit in the head. There was blood in his hair and all over the ground near his head. I bent down to check for a pulse, and that's when that Becky saw me."

"And screamed?"

"That was the odd part. She didn't scream at all. To look at her, I thought she was too stunned to scream. Her eyes were huge. But then there was a change." Ingrid stopped talking and frowned thoughtfully.

"A change in what?" asked Rosemary.

"In her eyes. Like some thought had crossed her mind. Like a shadow. She said, 'What have you done?' or something like that. I knew it looked bad. I panicked. You know I'm not great with people. I shouldn't have done it, but I ran away."

"So, you found Sam at the edge of the meadow."

"Yep."

"Face down, bleeding from the back of the head."

"Yep."

Rosemary looked at Jack across the table.

"Holy cow," said Jack.

"What is it?" asked Ingrid.

"When I found Sam, he was still face-down, but he wasn't at the edge of the meadow. He was in the cemetery, in the Wrights' corner, and he had the mark on his shoulder."

There was a moment of silence as this new information sank into everyone's minds.

"I came running because Becky was screaming," said Rosemary. "She was in the meadow. She pointed to the trail of blood. She knew about the mark, because I heard her telling her husband she'd seen it—that it was the curse that killed Sam. Then, of course, she switched her story and accused you, Ingrid. She led us all to believe that when she found Sam, you were standing over him there in the cemetery. That is how you know who killed Sam and left the witch's mark because, after all, you're a descendent of—"

"Of a witch," said Ingrid, nodding.

"And the person who called you and told you that the mayor was in the meadow?"

"A woman. Muffled voice. Now I see who it was."

"Becky," said Rosemary. "Ingrid, did you ever write a threatening letter to the mayor?"

"The thing with the brick? I didn't threaten him, I just—"

"Not the thing with the brick. Before Weaser searched your house, Becky Thatcher had showed him a threatening letter that you sent to the mayor *at his office*."

Ingrid looked taken aback. "I never wrote any letter like that," she said.

Just then, Charlie came rushing back into the room.

"Finally got hold of George," he said. "Victoria didn't die of a drug overdose or an accident."

"She didn't?" said Jack, standing.

"Suffocation," said Charlie. "She was smothered with a pillow."

"She was murdered," said Seth, amazed.

"Did Benedict confess to that, too?" asked Rosemary, a sick feeling growing in the pit of her stomach.

"Nope. In fact, George says Ben couldn't have done it, because Victoria had only been dead a couple of hours when Mrs. Potter found her and came running into the memorial service this morning. By then, Ben was already in custody. Seems that during the time between Ben leaving Sam's house and turning himself in, Ben was just walking around the village, trying to get his nerve up to go to the police."

"Charlie, call the police. Call George back," said Rosemary. "Jack, fire up Holly. We have to get to the Thatchers' house, and I have a bad feeling it's too late."

They all piled into Holly Golightly, Jack driving like a maniac, and Charlie calling the police on his cell phone. Within minutes they were passing the village green, the rain coming down hard, Holly's little windshield wipers beating furiously to little avail.

"I can barely see," said Jack, leaning forward.

"Why is it so dark?" asked Rosemary from the backseat, where she was squeezed between Seth and Ingrid.

"The electricity must be out all over town," said Charlie.

"A night as black as ink," said Seth, meeting Rosemary's eyes.

“It looks deserted,” said Jack, as they pulled into the Thatchers’ driveway.

A terrible clap of thunder boomed overhead and the sky broke open as they got out of the car and ran to the front door. While Seth and Ingrid banged on the front door, Jack, Charlie, and Rosemary ran around to the other three sides of the house, peering in windows and knocking.

“She’s not answering,” Jack yelled through the pounding rain as he ran past Rosemary. “I think she’s already made a run for it!”

“Ingrid and I will check next door at Sam’s!” called Seth over another clap of thunder.

“Hurry!” yelled Rosemary.

“I’ll go check on Charlie!” said Jack, disappearing into the darkness.

Rosemary looked in the direction of Sam’s house, which, of course, was just as dark as all of the other houses on the street. That was when she saw it. Or thought she saw it. A slight flicker of light in Sam’s backyard. It was coming from his office.

Rosemary ran through the pelting rain to the little building behind Sam’s house.

She tried the door, and it opened. She stepped inside, and closed the door behind her, relieved for a moment to be out of the storm.

The moment didn't last long.

There, sitting on the couch, a candle burning on the table beside her, was Becky Thatcher.

30

Rosemary pushed wet strands of hair out of her eyes.

"Hello, Becky," she said, trying to keep her voice calm and gentle, as if she just happened to be in the neighborhood and had decided to drop by.

The police would arrive at any moment, and Rosemary's only goal was to see that Becky stayed put until then.

"What are you doing here?" asked Becky, turning dazed eyes to Rosemary.

"Oh, you know. Just . . . came to look at the books. It's quite a collection." She motioned toward the bookshelves, now hidden in shadow.

"Coming to take more of his things," said Becky, now looking straight ahead again, her eyes glistening with unshed tears.

"Oh, no, Becky. I would only borrow books. I wouldn't keep them. They belonged to Sam."

"*Belong* to Sam," said Becky, nodding.

"Of course," said Rosemary, taking a step forward, glancing out the window to see if any of the others were outside.

"Like me," Becky went on. "I belong to Sam."

"He loved you very much," said Rosemary.

"Loves me very much," said Becky, a spark of anger in her eyes now.

"That's what I meant," said Rosemary.

"No, you didn't," said Becky. "I know you want him too. Just like that stupid Victoria. I know you're not really here to borrow a book. *Please.* I know how all of you vultures circle around him, looking for your chance to swoop in."

Lighting flashed, revealing the outline of a man, standing behind the couch where Becky was seated. In a split second of horror, Rosemary gasped, but then realized it was Seth, who had quietly entered from the back door. She quickly looked back at Becky.

Becky began to turn to see what Rosemary had been looking at, but Rosemary, feeling safe now that she wasn't alone with a madwoman, quickly said, "You're right, Becky. I was after Sam. But he said he loved you, and so I gave up."

"Good call," said Becky, now focused again on Rosemary. "Too bad Victoria wasn't as smart as you."

"So, you visited her, at her hotel?"

"I couldn't stand the way she said that *she* was the love of Sam's life. The way she called him *my Sam*. Made me sick. I sat home alone for hours, trying to get over that. I did try, you know." Becky looked at Rosemary again, searching for understanding.

"Of course you tried." Rosemary took a quick glance at the shadows where Seth was hiding, and saw that George was there, too, now. In an instant, she knew why he was hesitating to step forward and arrest Becky. He was waiting to see if she'd make a full confession. His wide eyes caught Rosemary's for a split second as another lightening flash illuminated the room, and Rosemary knew she should try her best to keep Becky talking.

"But I just couldn't rest, knowing that somewhere in the world, that horrible woman would always believe that Sam had loved her."

"You must've been furious that morning, when you found out they were engaged," said Rosemary.

"Oh, yes," said Becky, her face filling with rage.

"So, you went to confront Sam?"

"Of course," said Becky. "Do you have any idea how long I'd waited for him? How many times he'd said, 'just a little while longer,' and that we'd be together soon. I couldn't let it end with that woman getting *my* happily ever after. That was not acceptable."

"So, you went to the meadow. You knew he'd be there."

"And when I got there, I saw him and Ben fighting."

"Ben had figured out that you were having—I mean, that Sam loved you."

"Yes. And he punched Sam right in the nose. Sam fell, hit his head, and Ben ran away."

"But Sam wasn't dead."

"From that little bump?" Becky laughed. "He was knocked out cold, though. I ran to him. He started coming around, sat up, and looked at me, except he must've been confused, because he said *her* name."

"Victoria's?"

"That tramp. I saw the rock, picked it up, and hit him in the head."

"That's how you cut your hand," said Rosemary.

"They'll find my blood on the rock, of course," said Becky. "I realized it yesterday, when that woman was talking about the lab results coming in. My blood mixed with Sam's. And they'll see the surveillance tapes and I'll be in them. The cameras weren't supposed to be working yet! That's what Ben said." She stared at Rosemary for a moment. "I didn't mean to kill him, you know. I was just so *angry*."

"Of course you were."

"I'd found out months ago that Sam was related to the Graves family—that Matthew Graves had also loved a witch, you know. Just like Sam, falling under Victoria's spell. I talked to him about it, but he wouldn't listen. Told him the curse would get him, but he wouldn't hear me. He told me not to tell anyone about any of it. He didn't want people knowing he was a Graves from way back."

"And so that morning . . . It was you who called Ingrid Clark and told her the mayor was there in the meadow. You were the one who encouraged her to confront him," said Rosemary, hoping she wasn't pushing Becky too far.

Becky paused and thought for a moment, but then nodded. "Ingrid was always opposing Sam, trying to ruin his plans for this town. I wanted her stopped. She thought she was such a sneak, lurking, trying to see what Ben and Sam were up to in the meadow that morning—never noticing that *I* was watching *her*. Then I saw her talking to you. I saw it all. But no one saw me. Good thing I'm invisible."

"Invisible? What do you mean, Becky?"

"No one notices me. I'm that girl at the side of the dance floor. The one nobody picks for their team. The quiet kid in the corner. The secretary. The wife. The good little girl in the boring clothes. I hated being invisible. But I thought Sam saw me. I thought . . . Her voice trailed off and she sighed, then continued. "I watched Benedict fight with Sam. But then when I hit Sam with that rock, I was horrified by what I'd done. But *then*," she looked at Rosemary, her eyes glazed with tears, "I remembered stupid old Ingrid. How easy it would be to kill two birds with one stone, so to speak. So, I called and pretended to be on her side. She was so easy to rile."

"So, Ingrid walked right into your trap. She found Sam, and you framed her. You knew others—like me, for example—would have seen Ingrid in the meadow, and that would seal the deal."

"I was hoping she'd actually get a little blood on her hands and clothes, but she didn't. Just checked his pulse and ran away."

"Two birds with one stone? More like three, wasn't it?" said Rosemary, knowing she was skating on thin ice, but feeling bold, knowing Seth and George were right there. "One, get Ingrid out of the way by making it look like she killed Sam, so she'd go to jail. Two was Sam. And three, Victoria."

"It didn't have to turn out that way, but yeah, I guess you're right," said Becky, a hateful look on her face. "Three stupid birds. One, two, three . . . Might as well make it an even four."

With that, she blew out the candle and lunged at Rosemary. Within a split second, her hands were around Rosemary's throat, and for one brief moment, Rosemary couldn't breathe, felt her neck being bruised. But just as quickly, Seth and George were yanking Becky away.

"You're under arrest, Mrs. Thatcher," George said, snapping handcuffs onto Becky's wrists. "For the murders of Sam Wright and Victoria Winthrop. I'm going to read you your rights now."

Rosemary was already in Seth's arms when Jack and Charlie burst into the room. And then Rosemary was in all of their arms—in one giant, soggy embrace.

"Thank heaven you're okay!" said Jack, as two other officers pushed past to help George escort Becky out. "We've been standing right outside. George told us to wait. It was the hardest thing I've ever had to do." Jack's eyes filled with joyful tears and he hugged Rosemary again.

Rosemary looked up at Seth, who was still trembling. "And why didn't *you* wait outside with the others?"

"He refused," said Jack.

"Did you?" asked Rosemary.

Seth, who had taken off his glasses and was wiping the lenses with the edge of his shirt, smiled down at her and nodded.

"Oh, Professor McGuire, I'm going to kiss you now," Rosemary said, pulling him close and encircling his neck with her arms.

"See that?" said Jack, elbowing Charlie. "I knew they'd be perfect together. Didn't I tell you?"

A moment later, Ingrid pushed her way into the room. "This has been a fun evening. How about we pile into that tiny car of yours and you take me home now?" she said in her usual dry tone.

"I think we all need to get home and change out of these wet clothes," said Charlie.

Seth kissed Rosemary one more time, took her hand, and they all ran out into the rain.

31

"I bet Benedict is in a seriously strange place emotionally," said Jack as he and Rosemary walked down the little dirt road that encircled the pond the next morning.

"He probably doesn't know which way is up," agreed Rosemary.

"I mean, it's got to be a toss-up between relief, that he didn't actually kill his friend, and horror, that his wife is an adulteress and a murderer twice over."

"And now he's lost both his best friend *and* his wife," said Rosemary, shaking her head. "*And* he's got to process the fact that they were both lying to him for years."

"He'll need a good therapist."

"Yep."

It was a glorious morning after the rain moved out. Clear and crisp. The autumn leaves lent a blaze of color to the surface of the pond. Jack and Rosemary would soon climb into Holly and head downtown to finalize the details for the festival that night, but now, Jack was as excited to show Rosemary the cottage as she was to see it.

"I'm not just going to live here as your guest, you know," said Rosemary, taking Jack's hand. "I'll be paying rent—or I can buy the place if you ever consider putting it on the market."

"You don't have to," said Jack, who was frankly just thrilled that his best friend would be living next door.

"But I will anyway," said Rosemary. "I insist."

"I'm just so glad you're staying. I never thought we'd convince you."

"But it's time," said Rosemary. "These last couple of years have been wearing me down. All the hotels and living out of a suitcase. Even when I was home, I didn't feel at home. I guess I've been . . ." Rosemary thought for a moment. "Without home. For too long. And Ingrid is right: I'm surrounded by friends and by love here. That makes Paperwick more home than anyplace else ever could be."

"Then welcome," said Jack, sweeping an arm upward as they approached the cottage.

Rosemary, who had only seen the place distantly from the pond side, almost couldn't contain her excitement. The side of the cottage that fronted the narrow dirt road was classic New England. There were chimneys on each end, cozy dormers on the second floor, and a bricked path that led up to the front door, which was painted red. The narrow wood siding was painted white, and large downstairs windows were framed by dark green shutters. There were flower boxes on the upstairs dormer windows, which were currently filled with a mix of orange and red dahlias and tiny pumpkins.

Jack handed Rosemary a keyring, complete with a Paperwick Historical Society key fob. Rosemary unlocked the door and stepped into the house. The first thing she noticed was the natural light that flooded the house from one end to the other. A wide entryway opened on either side to a study on the left and a dining room on the right. Just ahead, a simple staircase with a wooden railing led up to the second floor, and beyond that, the house opened up into a beautiful living room. The entire wall that faced the pond was windows. Even the door that went out onto the porch was glass. There was a stone fireplace on the left wall.

"Where's the second fireplace?" asked Rosemary, looking around.

"Ah. Come see your kitchen," said Jack.

The kitchen, which could be entered from either the living or dining room, was charming, with its small, red bricked fireplace and hearth. A French door led outside from here, and Rosemary already knew that the plot of land just beyond would be perfect for a kitchen garden. Everything from the warm wood cabinetry to the deep farmhouse sink communicated coziness.

"And look: We put in a double oven for when we all come over for dinner," said Jack, smiling proudly.

"Jack, I don't know how you did it. This is my dream house! Seriously, if I could design a home for myself, it would be this exactly. I've pictured it in my mind since forever."

"Well, since college at least," said Jack. "Don't you remember how we'd talk about our ideal houses when we used to get stressed before exams?"

"Of course I do, but how could you have gotten it this perfect?"

"Because great minds think alike. I knew your taste and mine always matched. So, I just made this house exactly what I would want. Wait until you see the bedrooms upstairs!"

They went upstairs to find two bedrooms—one sunny guest room, and a master suite that overlooked the pond outside. Every window looked out at the treetops or the water, and Rosemary smiled when she saw that she could look across the pond and see Jack and Charlie's farmhouse from her room.

"You'll stay at our house until you can get your things moved here," said Jack.

"Thank you. I'd love to."

There was a light thumping sound from the vicinity of the staircase.

"What was that?" asked Rosemary, looking around but seeing no one.

"We hear that now and then," said Jack. "We figure the place is haunted." When Jack saw Rosemary's wide eyes, he added, "By a friendly ghost!"

"Seriously?"

"We think the caretaker, old Theophilus Whitman, is still watching over the place."

"Well, that's comforting. I guess." Rosemary looked around the room. "Hello, Mr. Whitman."

"How's it going, Theo?" added Jack. "And don't worry: Charlie and I will just be a short walk away, if you ever need anything. This is going to be great! We can start our writing project soon, and oh, I almost forgot: You have a meeting with the dean of the history department at the university on Monday morning."

"I do?"

"I told you there's an opening."

Rosemary hugged Jack. "I don't deserve you," she said. "But I promise to be a good neighbor."

❧

"I like the changes we made to the cemetery crawl," said Rosemary as she stood back with Jack, looking over the twinkling lanterns and luminarias. "It looks *gorgeous*."

"Hey! You're looking at Seth," said Jack, laughing and waving toward Seth, who was still walking from one luminaria to the next, adding a tiny, battery-operated candle to each.

"Well, no. But he's gorgeous too," said Rosemary with a grin.

"The costumes are perfect," Jack said as the actor volunteers took their places next to their headstones.

"And the best surprise of all is waiting for folks out in the meadow," said Rosemary as she and Jack joined Seth and walked along the illuminated path, past the headstones, past the Wrights' family plot where Sam had been laid to rest, through the trees, and into the meadow. Thousands of fairy lights had been strung in the huge old maple tree that stood next to Hortence Gallow's grave. Lanterns had been spread all around it. And there, in the middle of it all, seated in a rocking chair, was Ingrid Clark, who herself looked lit from within.

"She'll tell them the true story," said Rosemary, smiling at Ingrid and giving her a little wave.

"It's about time," said Jack.

"Does she know she's being honored later tonight, as a member of one of the most celebrated founding families of Paperwick?" asked Seth.

"She has no idea," said Jack.

"She might not be crazy about the idea of all that applause," said Rosemary.

"And she'll get a lot of that," said Jack. "The whole village is in love with her after reading in this morning's paper about how she was wrongfully arrested and how she has been advocating to protect the meadow all this time."

"I'll join that fan club," said Rosemary with a laugh.

The Paperwick Founders Day Festival got underway just as the sun was setting. The whole village green was lit up and crowded with people. There were hayrides from the green out to the Potters' farm, where festival-goers enjoyed the corn maze and tasted freshly-pressed cider and donuts. There was a small carnival on Chestnut Street, complete with all sorts of food vendors, games, and local displays. People lined up and walked through the cemetery, meeting the spirits of citizens-past and especially enjoying gathering around Ingrid's feet and listening to tales of early Paperwick, when two forward-thinking young women traveled the land, delivering babies and healing the sick.

Many people left Ingrid and walked straight over to the Historical Society Museum, where both Mercy's medical records and her personal journal were now on display, along with Mayor Wright's copy of Josias King's *Paperwick: The Original Sins, A Cautionary Tale*.

Rosemary and Seth, who had lost track of Jack and Charlie in the crowd, walked hand-in-hand along the street, admiring displays of produce, jams, jellies, and pies from the locals.

"Look who's judging the pumpkins!" said Seth suddenly, pointing.

There, with an extremely proud Mrs. Potter standing by, were Jack and Charlie, who were just attaching the grand prize ribbon to a huge pumpkin. Rosemary laughed so hard that tears filled her eyes.

"What will those two do next?" she said, wiping her eyes. "Tell me this isn't all just a wonderful dream," she said, squeezing Seth's hand.

"I was going to ask you to tell me the same thing," Seth answered, pulling her into his arms. And then he was kissing her—or she was kissing him. Both, really.

"That felt very real," said Rosemary.

"It did," agreed Seth. "I'm glad you've decided to stick around Paperwick."

"Me, too."

"And I'm glad you decided to go out with me tonight."

"Me, too."

"And I'm hoping you'll go out with me again . . . say . . . tomorrow? We could go pick apples at the Potters'. Maybe get lost in the corn maze for a little while?"

"I would even go as far as level five with you," said Rosemary, raising an eyebrow.

"Would you, now?" laughed Seth. "That could take hours."

"I've got time," said Rosemary, smiling.

"So, you don't mind taking a chance on a small town boy?" He brushed a lock of hair out of her face and she looked up at him.

"Oh, I have a very good feeling about you, Dr. McGuire," she said, her grin broadening. "And you know, I have a knack about these things."

EPILOGUE

Rosemary pulled on a pair of jeans, a t-shirt, boots with thick, warm socks, and her new sweatshirt—a gift from Jack on her first day at work. It featured the official Paperwick University seal emblazoned on a sea of Niagara Blue—one of the university's colors, along with Kale Green—with an angry-looking trout in its center.

Rosemary had been thrilled to be able to start work right away after interviewing with the head of the history department, the university president, and several other deans. She'd given notice at her old job, and it was a smooth transition because she'd been on sabbatical touring Europe all semester anyway, so wasn't actively teaching any classes. She'd promised to come to New York to do a guest lecture, along with her esteemed colleague and co-author, Dr. Jack Stone, as soon as their book was published.

Paperwick University welcomed Rosemary with open arms—in part because one of their two full-time history professors had left abruptly when she'd gone into labor a month early, and they were desperate for someone to pick up her classes; and in part because the department was growing anyway, the university boasting its largest freshman class to date. Rosemary took on the absent professor's classes for the remainder of the fall semester, and would have her own slate of classes come spring.

But today was Saturday. And Rosemary and Jack had big plans this morning. They were going to explore the old barn on Jack and Charlie's farm. Their contractor, Bert Ander, was coming out after lunch to look over the project. He'd helped Charlie and Jack renovate their farmhouse and Rosemary's cottage, and was an expert at figuring out how to salvage old structures and bring them back to life.

But before Bert arrived, Jack and Rosemary went out to take a look around.

"I want to get this job done before winter hits," said Jack.

"We *have* to get it done," agreed Rosemary. "Otherwise, where will the pygmy goats and pigs live?"

"To say nothing of the chickens," said Jack. "Their coop is out in the open. I want to have Bert make a nice cozy one inside the barn. That way everyone can be safe and snug all winter long."

"This thing is huge," said Rosemary, looking up at the old, faded red structure.

"I know. Isn't it great? Look at the roof. See the cupola on top? Isn't that charming? That's where our gorgeous owl weathervane will go."

"I know it's been updated and maybe enlarged a few times over the centuries, but just imagine how it must've looked back in Mercy and Hortence's time. The Clark family were clearly quite well off."

"Oh, they were," said Jack. "They were one of the most prosperous families in the area. If only they hadn't been fooled into marrying Hortence off to Jonathan Gallow, things could've been altogether different."

"I wonder," said Rosemary. "Ingrid says we bring curses on ourselves. If Hortence had never married that awful Jonathan, and then she'd never run into the arms of the judge next door . . . How would things have been different? Would she still have made bad choices, just in different ways—and would she still have become a midwife and a blessing to this village?"

"Wouldn't it be great to sneak back in time and see?" said Jack.

"I feel like I'm about to go back in time as soon as we walk into this old barn," said Rosemary.

"Oh, it's a trip, all right. Help me with the door," said Jack.

Together, they pushed open the huge wooden door on the front of the building.

"Show me where you found the little box that Mercy hid," said Rosemary.

"Mercy's secret stash," said Jack, rubbing his hands together and ushering Rosemary into the barn. "Go around the edge, where the floor's in the best shape. Get this: There's a basement underneath part of this barn. I think it was a root cellar. We haven't even really explored it yet, because, well, we were afraid the whole thing might cave in at any moment. But now that the house is done, I can't wait to get started in here."

"Who knows what we'll find down there!" said Rosemary, stepping on a board that creaked loudly beneath her foot. "Jack, we're not going to die here in this barn today, are we?"

"Not if we stay over to the side here," said Jack. "The basement doesn't run the entire length of the barn. Right up ahead it gets a lot more stable."

They walked carefully toward the right back corner of the barn, watching each step on the old floorboards. Finally, when they'd arrived at what looked like an animal stall, Jack pushed open the old gate, which fell off with a thunk.

"Oops."

Jack knelt on the floor and pried out a small section of an old floorboard that had been cut out and then set back into place.

"Wow," said Rosemary. "It's almost invisible. Why did you ever even notice this? I never would've seen it!"

"I was in here looking for some wood to salvage for the fireplace in the living room. We wanted to create a new mantel, and thought it would be neat to use some materials from the oldest structure on the place—this barn. Anyway, we pulled out a section of this railing," Jack said, tapping the railing that went around the stall. Sure enough, Rosemary could see the gap where they'd salvaged some of the old wood. "And a bit of hay was stuck in the crack around this floorboard. It caught my eye."

Rosemary peered into the compartment, which was about the size of a glovebox in a car.

"Very good eyes, Jack," she said. "I hope you'll keep this little hiding spot intact when you renovate."

"Oh, I've already told Bert that any and all secret niches or hidden compartments stay," said Jack. "We'll probably fix up this stall for Lizzie and Jane."

Lizzie and Jane were Jack and Charlie's pot-bellied pigs. They, along with the pygmy goats, Meg, Jo, Beth, and Amy; and the Plymouth Rock chickens, Anne, Marilla, Diana, and Miss Stacy; not to mention the roosters, Gilbert, and Matthew, would be right at home. Izzy and Smudge, who rounded out the farm's menagerie, lived inside, and Rosemary and Jack had agreed that Smudge—who didn't like to leave Rosemary's side for too long—would live in the cottage with Rosemary but have frequent playdates with Izzy.

Rosemary had taken out her cellphone flashlight and was carefully examining the little compartment. She stuck her hand in and felt around.

"Jack, take another look in here," she said.

Jack looked into the compartment.

"I see . . . a lot of dust. Ew. A spider lives in here."

"Look at the side," said Rosemary. "Use the flashlight."

"Okay. Looking at the side . . ."

"On the side nearest the window?"

"What? The little knothole?"

"Stick your finger in it," said Rosemary.

Jack looked at her like she was nuts. "There could be a giant spider on the other side. Or worse."

"Just do it. Trust me."

"Spiders are to me like cats are to you," said Jack. "But okay. Here goes." He stuck his hand into the compartment, a look of disgust mixed with fear on his face. "Okay . . . I'm sticking my finger in."

"Now jiggle it."

“Jiggling . . . Hey, it moves.”

“That side of the compartment moves,” said Rosemary. “Why would it do that, unless . . .”

“Unless it opens,” said Jack, who had forgotten all about the possible giant spider and was working the side panel for all his worth. He pulled his hand back out, his index finger still in the knothole. The entire panel that formed one side of Mercy’s compartment came out, revealing another, even more hidden, compartment beyond it.

“Shine the flashlight in there!” said Jack, trying to see into the dark little hole. “I think there’s something in there, pushed back away from the opening.” He took a deep breath, gritted his teeth, and slipped his hand into the opening. But he couldn’t get very far. “Rosie, you try. Your hands are smaller.”

Jack moved out of the way, and Rosemary slid her hand awkwardly into the opening. She repositioned her body so that she was laying on the floor alongside the compartment, and tried to reach further in.

“I just touched it!” she said, moving so that she could reach just a hair further. “I have it!”

Slowly, very slowly, Rosemary pulled out an old wooden box, which was caked with dust and spiderwebs.

“Are you kidding me?” gasped Jack. “Are. You. Kidding. Me?”

"This is amazing!" said Rosemary, wiping the surface of the box off. "I can't believe it. Do you think this was Mercy's too?"

The box was beautifully crafted. Rosemary could just make out a few simple lines carved into its surface.

"Open it!" said Jack excitedly.

"You should open it," said Rosemary. "This is your barn."

"You found it. Go ahead. Do the honors," said Jack.

Rosemary looked back at the box and gently tried the lid. It didn't budge. She tried again, but no luck. "I'm afraid I'll break it," she said.

"Here, let me see," said Jack, who took the box and wiped off another layer of caked-on dust. "It's just filthy. Let's take it outside where the light is better."

As they walked back toward the house with their treasure, they talked about the day ahead.

"So, Bert is coming soon. And don't forget tonight's game night," said Jack.

"Seth said he'll be here early, so he can look around the barn too," said Rosemary, a quiet smile on her face.

"I see that smile," teased Jack.

"What smile?"

"The one you get every time you mention his name."

"Ah. *That* smile," laughed Rosemary, smiling even bigger.

"We also invited George Harris to come tonight," said Jack.

"Great! George is the best—and he's definitely the voice of reason in Paperwick law enforcement."

"And he makes a killer spiced cider," added Jack. "He's whipping up a batch for us tonight."

"Oh, that sounds so good," said Rosemary, looking at the clouds. "Perfect for a cold, gray day like this."

"Charlie says we're in for our first flurry this afternoon," said Jack.

"A little early this year. But you know he's never wrong," said Rosemary with a smile.

They took the box to the back porch. Jack went inside to the kitchen and found a soft towel. He returned to the porch and carefully wiped down the box.

"Oh, my," said Rosemary, as the cloth revealed more of the lines carved into the box. Right on the lid, plain as day: M.C. "This was Mercy's! That spot in the barn must've been her secret little place. That's why she put this there. And that's why she left the note there before she escaped with Lilly!"

“But why was this box in a different part of the hidey hole?” asked Jack.

“Who knows? Maybe she was in a hurry. Maybe there were people with torches and pitchforks coming down the lane. I bet that little compartment in the barn had been her special secret hiding place since she was a little girl.”

“Before she reached the ripe old age of nineteen and had to flee for her life, you mean?”

“Right. I bet she put things in there when she needed to be sure they’d be safe. Can you imagine? This was early America —a good Puritan family. Mercy had to keep so much bottled up. So much hidden away.”

“I’m dying to know what’s inside, but I don’t want to break it,” said Jack, wiping off the box some more. “Oh. I see what’s going on. It’s locked,” he said.

“It is?”

“Look here. A tiny keyhole.”

Rosemary and Jack looked at each other.

“The key!” they said at once.

“Did you already take the tin box with Mercy’s note to the museum?”

"Not yet. Sometimes it pays to be absent minded. Wait here!" said Jack, rushing into the house again and returning with the smaller box.

He carefully opened it, set Mercy's note aside, and took out the tiny key that lay beneath. Then, while he held the box, Rosemary inserted the key, which fit perfectly into the keyhole, and after a satisfying click, they opened the box.

"What is it?" asked Jack.

"A treasure box," said Rosemary, smiling. "Look, there's an old comb. And a broken piece of china. What's this?"

"It looks like a top. Like a child's toy."

"Maybe these were Mercy's things from when she was a little girl," said Rosemary. "Look, I think this is a handkerchief."

"What's this?" Jack carefully lifted out a brittle piece of paper.

"Oh my gosh, be careful," said Rosemary. "It looks like it'll break."

Thankfully, the paper held together, and they were able to lay it out on the wooden patio table. And sure enough, there was Mercy's beautiful, curling script.

"It's a letter," said Jack.

"But the strange thing is, it's a letter that was written by Mercy," said Rosemary. "Which means, of course, that she never sent it."

"I'm so excited I can't concentrate," said Jack. "Read it."

"Okay," said Rosemary, focusing on the writing and scanning the words.

"It's a letter to someone named Jonah. It's a love letter! 'My dearest Jonah,' Mercy writes. She says she hopes his studies at school in England are going well, that she knows he'll be a wonderful physician, and she's longing for the day when he'll return and join her in Connecticut."

"Hold on! Didn't Ingrid say Mercy married a doctor? Is this him?" asked Jack.

"Yes! That's why that name sounds familiar!" Rosemary read further down the page. "She talks about Jonathan Gallow being a hard man to live with, and that she doesn't want to abandon her sister . . . She mentions the work they were doing here, looking after the health of the village. She says she hopes that one day, as Jonah's wife, she might help him in his practice."

"This is amazing!" said Jack. "Go on."

"She says that she's hoping Elizabeth Graves from next door will take over the keeping of the records once Mercy joins Jonah in Wethersfield, where he's going to be setting up his practice . . . She says Elizabeth has a fine hand—good handwriting. She laments the fact that . . ."

"What?" asked Jack, who was now literally sitting at the edge of his seat. "What does she lament?"

"Hortence couldn't write. Mercy laments the fact that Hortence never learned to write. That's why Mercy kept all of the records."

"Seriously?" asked Jack.

"In those days," said Rosemary, "reading and writing were not taught together. They were considered to be separate subjects. So, there were many people who could read but not write. Mercy says that Hortence could read, but she didn't have the patience to take up a pen and learn to write."

"But then—" Jack's eyes grew wider.

"That's right," said Rosemary. There was a long beat of silence. "The signed confession—Hortence's confession of witchcraft. The one Judge Graves said he'd found in her hand. The one he recorded in his journal—"

"She couldn't have written it," said Jack.

"She couldn't have written it," confirmed Rosemary.

"That was the one part of the mystery that hadn't fallen into place yet," said Jack. "We knew Hortence was innocent. But that confession, back in the day, was probably the damning piece of evidence—the thing that convinced everyone that Hortence had been guilty. That was why they dug her grave right there in the meadow. That was why Mercy had to take Lilly and run away."

"That was why the shadow fell on the Clark family," said Rosemary.

"Even people right here in the 21st century still equate Hortence with witchcraft. All this time," said Jack, shaking his head. "Those lives—their lives, so hard for no reason. And now the truth is as plain as day, but it's too late."

"It's not too late," said Rosemary, laying a hand on top of Jack's. "We'll tell their story."

Suddenly, from the far side of the pond, a beautiful white swan who'd been gliding along the water's surface peacefully lifted off, it's great wings spreading as it rose into the air and flew away, over the treetops.

KEEPSAKES

WORLDWIDE TELEGRAM

LONDON, ENGLAND, UK MARCH 24, 2019

Dearest Jack and Charlie—

It's your wedding day!! If I could be anywhere in the world, I would be with you in Connecticut today. My European tour goes on for seven more months—and don't ask me why I ever agreed to spend a whole year over here. It's beautiful, but I'm missing home. Missing you! The first thing I'll be doing when I get back in the fall is to come see you two. Does November sound okay? I can't believe you bought a farm! In the photos, it looks like it has a lot of potential.

Did you get the gift I sent? I know an owl weathervane is a bit of an odd wedding present, but the photos you shared of that old barn—the one I know you guys are just dying to renovate? I thought it would look perfect with a weathervane on top, in true New England style. And since we all love anything spooky, an owl seemed the ideal creature to watch over your farm.

Anyway, isn't it cool that we can still send telegrams? I thought it was so romantic, and today of all days, I wanted you both to know that even though I'm an ocean away, I'm in Connecticut with you in spirit. Can't wait to visit and finally meet you in person, Charlie. (Did Jack tell you I'm part of the package when you marry him?) See you both soon. Sending much love and many congratulations on your wedding!

-Rosemary

TOP SECRET!

GRANDMA POTTER'S CARAMEL APPLE PIE

First, make a pie crust—consider doubling the recipe. Might as well make two, so you can save one for later.

[Note: If you're in a pinch, use a good quality store-bought crust. It won't be as good, but it does save time. Grandma usually kept a few crusts wrapped and tucked away in the freezer, to use as needed. That's what I call planning ahead. I'm talking to you, Gabby!]

Here's a good, trusty pie crust recipe:

-1 ¼ c all-purpose flour

-¼ t salt

-1/2 c. cold butter, cut up [That's one stick, Gabby.]

-1/4 c. ice water

Here's the filling:

-About 6 apples—use your favorites. I like to mix a few different ones from the orchard.

-Lemon

-Sugar—1/2 cup

-1/4 c. flour

-a couple dashes of salt [1/4 teaspoon]

-nutmeg-about 1/4 t.

-ground cloves-a pinch

-plenty of cinnamon—about 1 ½ t.

And the best part, the topping:

[Sure, you could put a second crust on top, but why do that when you can make this delicious crumble instead?]

-1 ½ sticks butter

-1/2 c flour

-1/2 c oats [use the quick oats!]

-a couple more dashes salt

-lots of chopped pecans—about ½ c

-One batch of Grandma's homemade caramel sauce [Forget it —just buy a jar of good caramel sauce that's used for topping ice cream OR you could melt a bag of caramels, add a little water, half-and-half, and vanilla, and stir. Delicious!]

Get out your big bowl. Mix in the flour and the salt for the crust. Then cut in your cold butter, and keep cutting until it looks like big crumbs. Add the ice water—but do it 1 tablespoon at a time, and stop adding water when you have a ball of dough. Wrap in plastic and chill for 4 hours or more. Then roll it out and press it into the pie pan.

Preheat your oven: 375 degrees

Peel, core, and slice the apples. Into the big bowl they go! Add the juice of about half a lemon and all the other filling ingredients. Mix it and then pile it up in your crust.

Make the crumb topping: Mix the flour and butter together first, just like you did when you made the crust. Then add the brown sugar, oats, and salt and mix it all together. Sprinkle it all over the apples.

Bake for an hour, then sprinkle on the chopped nuts, then bake for five minutes more. This will toast those nuts and bring out their goodness!

Drizzle with as much caramel as you'd like!

[Gabby: You are not to share this recipe around with your friends. This is a family secret! But feel free to share a piece of pie with them! Abbey, we already had this talk. Bubba, don't even think about selling this recipe on the internet. I mean it.]

10 JULY 1668
PAPERWICK, OLD BALLYBROOK, CONNECTICUT

Dearest Mama,

I hope this finds you well and happy. I am enjoying my stay with cousin Felicity. We are being good, and I am meeting many nice people here in the village. We visited a Mr. and Mrs. Potter yesterday, and mama, Mrs. Potter had just had two babies at once! Born the same hour! Have you ever heard of such a thing? I am helping Felicity with her chores, just as you said I should. My favorite is every evening, when she and I go outside by lantern light and check on the animals before we go to sleep. Sometimes we stay in the barn and tell the animals stories. Mama, did you know there are witches about this area? Felicity told me of them, and now, I have seen one! Last evening, we were surprised as we made our way out to the stables and saw—believe me, we saw her—a witch, dancing joyously in the moonlight! No music! No partner. It was as though she were charmed by some unseen phantom. Have you ever seen such a thing? We did not know what to make of it. But I always thought witches were hideous, frightening creatures. This one seemed quite nice and beautiful. Felicity and I ran into the house and stayed up talking of it for some time.

Reverend King came for a visit today. He has commended me on my penmanship. I am blessed that Ms. Mercy is helping me to improve.

My aunt and uncle send their love.

Your daughter,

Anne

FROM THE MEDICAL NOTES OF MERCY CLARK:

-September 1, 1668: Visited Molly Potter, who was complaining of the stomach ache. We made her a sage tea. Steeping one large bunch in a pot of boiling water. Give as needed. Also have Molly warm herself by the fire.

-John Black having trouble sleeping. Advised Anne to have him take the fresh night air and then make him a chamomile tea with honey they'd put by from the hives. He should drink this nightly before bed.

-Joseph and Patience Brown have a healthy baby girl. Hortence delivered her early this evening. All are well.

-Collect lemon balm and lavender to take to the Smiths tomorrow. Also mint. Their niece Anne who is visiting is having stomach pain. Hortence suspects too much of the new dish the

FROM THE MEDICAL NOTES OF MERCY CLARK:

Smiths have been serving, pickled oysters. Will inform Smiths to desist.

-Boiling water

Wild ginger root

Mint

Lemon balm

-Gather lavender—it grows in the meadow.

JUNE 3, 2011
MOM'S POTATOES

Hello Jacky!

So glad you and Rosemary want to make my potatoes! They really are delicious, aren't they? We loved celebrating your college graduations together and serving a big pan of these! (For that, I doubled the recipe, but only because we were serving a crowd!) They're very simple to make, as many of the best things in life are.

Here's how to make them:

-Peel 6 potatoes and put them into cold water until you're ready to slice them all. This keeps them from turning brown. Slice them as thinly as you can, but don't cut yourself!

-Melt 4 to 6 tablespoons of butter and toss the potatoes in the butter until they're all coated.

-Add salt and pepper to your taste and toss some more.

-Arrange the sliced potatoes in a single layer in a baking dish.

-Bake them at 350 degrees for about an hour. Check them a lot toward the end. You want them to start browning and crisping up a bit at the edges.

You'll never believe this, but I made these very potatoes the first time I cooked for your dad. So, if either you or Rosemary ever meet a nice young man, try this recipe on him! It works!

Love you, Jacky.

Dad says hi. We'll see you next weekend.

Mom

NOVEMBER 2019
PRIZEWINNING SNICKERDOODLES

Okay, Seth. I'm giving you the recipe for my prizewinning snickerdoodles. But guard this with your life! There are plenty of people who'd like to get their hands on this, so keep it under lock and key! I'm not even remotely comfortable writing it down. Don't forget what I told you: The key to the cookies being puffy and thick is, first, chilling the dough for a good thirty minutes after you've made it, and two, keep each cookie to no bigger than one tablespoon of dough. (I guess that's two keys.) Any bigger and they spread out and get thin. And that's not what we want! We want thick and soft!

Good luck!

Charlie

You'll need the following:

-3 cups all-purpose flour

-1 1/2 teaspoons cream of tartar

-1 teaspoon baking soda

-1 teaspoon cinnamon

-1/2 teaspoon salt

-2 sticks butter

-3/4 cup sugar

-1/2 cup brown sugar

-1 large egg plus one egg yolk

-1 tablespoon vanilla extract

Also, put 1/4 cup sugar and 1 tablespoon cinnamon in a bowl and stir them up. You'll dip the dough balls in this before baking.

Mix together all the dry ingredients, just like I showed you.

Then mix the butter and sugars until creamy, then add the egg and yolk, and the vanilla.

Add the dry ingredients to the wet and mix.

Chill that dough for 30 minutes—at least!

350 degree oven, parchment-lined baking sheets.

Make little balls of 1 tablespoon each of dough and roll in the cinnamon-sugar.

Bake 7-10 minutes.

Pour yourself a mug of hot cocoa—or George's Spiced Cider —and enjoy!

PAPERWICK FOUNDERS DAY FESTIVAL 2019

CERTIFICATE OF AWARD

Paperwick Founders Day Festival 2019
Certificate of Award
Presented to
Potters Farm
for
Grand Champion Pumpkin
on this day,
November 10, 2019

Signed,
Charlie Stewart, Judge & Jack Stone, Judge

[Dear Mr. and Mrs. P and kids: We don't know how you do it! What is your secret to growing these insanely huge pumpkins?

Congrats on winning yet again! You even beat your own record!! Can't wait to see next year's pumpkin! You amaze us. Jack & Charlie]

POLICE BEAT MAGAZINE

YOUR SOURCE FOR THE TRUE STORIES OF OUR HEROES IN BLUE

"Connecticut Cop Nabs Mayor's Murderess"

Officer George Harris, of the Paperwick, Connecticut Force, was instrumental in capturing a two-time killer in a case that had authorities baffled. The story of the village mayor being found dead in a local ancient cemetery—in the burial plot peopled by his own forebears, no less—went viral last week, most especially because the mayor's death was purportedly brought on, some locals claimed, as the result of a witch's curse from the late 1600s.

"Of course, that was never the opinion of the Paperwick PD," Officer Harris said, pointing to his fellow officers and modestly sharing the credit with all three of them.

As it turned out, the mayor's secretary, a Mrs. Rebecca Thatcher, was the actual killer in the ultimate crime of passion.

Seems the mayor had recently announced his engagement, and a jealous Mrs. Thatcher went after both him and his betrothed in a double murder that rocked the tiny town. But the story gets even stranger: the killer's husband was the mayor's friend and colleague, City Manager Benedict Thatcher. Mr. Thatcher had presumed that *he* was the killer after a fight during which he came to blows with the mayor. Mr. Thatcher had actually turned himself in with a full confession before his wife's arrest. After his release and being informed that Officer Harris had arrested his wife for the murders, Thatcher was heard saying he would be resigning his post as City Manager and moving to Maine, where his family lives.

Police Beat commends Officer Harris for his quick thinking and careful investigating. Well done, Officer Harris!

MR. AND MRS. POTTER'S PUMPKIN GROWING SECRETS

(TURN THAT 'PUMPKIN' INTO A 'PUMPKING'!)

-Here in Connecticut, we start our pumpkins off in the greenhouse. It's just too cold in March to risk putting them in the ground. We plant the seedlings out in the patch after the danger of frost has passed.

-First, pick the right seeds, for heaven's sake. Pick a variety known for growing large pumpkins.

-Think about where to plant. Look for sunny, but protected. Plant them in the sun, but do offer them shelter if it gets too hot, or if there's a bad storm.

-Light, fluffy soil is best, and pile on the manure and work it into the soil when you're getting the patch ready in early spring. You'll need a mound to plant each seedling in.

-Watch those seedlings! Keep them moist and watch for the fourth leaf to grow! That's when it's time to move them outside.

-Did you know pumpkins have both male and female flowers? The males come out first. Watch the females. They're the ones with tiny baby pumpkins attached.

-Pumpkins need a lot of water. But don't get the leaves wet unless you want to deal with fungus! And prune, prune, prune! Pick off some of the small fruits so that the potential prizewinners can have plenty of nutrients and water and space. It may seem brutal, but this is how it's done!

-Water at night—that's when pumpkins do their growing. By the light of the moon!

-The current world record holder weighs near to three thousand pounds! We've never even gotten close to that!

GEORGE'S SPICED CIDER

My mom always makes this on cold days.

Take 8 cups of apple cider or good quality apple juice. If you can get a batch of cider from the Potters, that's the best.

Put it in a saucepan and heat it up over medium heat for five minutes with a couple cinnamon sticks, some cloves, a sliced orange, and some nutmeg. I think you should decide for yourself how much cinnamon and nutmeg, and how many cloves, based on how spicy you want it and what you like. In our family, we serve each person their cider in a mug with a cinnamon stick and some whipped cream on top!

PAPERWICK CHRONICLE

NOVEMBER 15, 2019

VILLAGE LIFE:

NEW ADDITION TO PAPERWICK U—AND TO OUR VILLAGE!

by Harold T. Cutter

Paperwick. Our local university welcomed a new addition to the faculty this week. Rosemary Grey, Ph.D., who hails most recently from New York, is here to stay! Many of you met Dr. Grey during the Founders Day Festival, where she helped to put on the Historical Society's Cemetery Crawl fundraiser—an event which by all accounts was a huge success, now to become a beloved annual tradition. Dr. Grey holds a Ph.D. in History, is the author of numerous articles on early American happenings, as well as the well-received book: *What*

Happened in Salem: A New Perspective. Dr. Grey has recently wrapped up a year-long European lecture circuit, and is now glad to call Paperwick home. She and local literature professor —our own Dr. Jack Stone—have plans to co-author a book centering on our favorite local 17th century celeb, Hortence Clark Gallow, midwife and medic extraordinaire. Welcome to the village, Dr. Grey! Go get ‘em, Fighting Trout!

Made in the USA
Monee, IL
10 March 2022